KATHERINE V. FORREST

High Desert

A KATE DELAFIELD MYSTERY

Spinsters Ink

2013

Spinsters Ink
P.O. Box 242
Midway, FL 32343

Printed in the United States of America on acid-free paper.

First Spinsters Ink Edition 2013

Editor: Cath Walker and Medora MacDougall
Cover designer: Judith Fellows
ISBN: 978-1-93522-665-9

Also By Katherine V. Forrest

From Bella Books
Curious Wine
An Emergence Of Green
Daughters Of A Coral Dawn

From Spinsters Ink
The Kate Delafield Series
Amateur City
Murder At The Nightwood Bar
The Beverly Malibu
Murder By Tradition
Liberty Square
Apparation Valley
Sleeping Bones
Hancock Park

To Jo

For twenty-two amazing years
But who's counting…

Acknowledgments

Many thanks to my key advisors on this novel. Montserrat Fontes for her valued input from the earliest days of the Third Street Writers Group; and Clarice Gillis for her wisdom and friendship through the years. Michael Nava for his insights, friendship, and the always inspiring example of his own work. Jo Hercus for indispensable advice on the psychotherapy scenes. Natalie Shemonsky, MD, for checking the medical details while allowing for some poetic license: any inaccuracies are mine entirely.

I'm very grateful for the acute—indeed crucial—feedback from my wonderfully sharp-eyed editors Cath Walker and Medora MacDougall.

My profound gratitude and admiration to my publisher, Linda Hill. The continuity she has provided from the days of the legendary Naiad Press, her caring dedication to the history and permanence of our literature, are inestimable gifts to our entire worldwide community. I am proud to once more have work of mine published by the caretaker of my original home.

1

The shrill ring of the doorbell propelled Kate Delafield from her recliner. Adrenaline pouring through her, gasping, almost choking with relief, she took in her familiar surroundings. She stood shaking her head to dislodge the images.

"Get a grip, get a grip, get a grip," she ordered herself.

How could she possibly have dropped off to sleep *now*?

Checking that her shirt was tucked into her pants, sweeping a final glance over the living room, she hurried to open the door of her condo.

She knew she did not look her best, especially with her nerves awash in the aftermath of the dream. But as Captain Carolina Walcott took her in she was dismayed by the surprise that flickered briefly in her dark brown eyes.

"Captain," Kate said, amazed that her voice sounded normal. She extended a hand. "Come in, it's good to see you."

"And you, Kate." Walcott grasped her hand and held it an extra moment, her smile wide, her gaze affectionate.

"Make yourself comfortable." Kate gestured to the sofa where a tray on the coffee table held a carafe of coffee and two dark blue coffee mugs emblazoned in gold with the letters LAPD. She hung back, took two deep breaths, still dispelling adrenaline and the effects of the dream, wishing she could pour herself a stiff scotch.

Striding to the sofa, Walcott took in the combination living room, dining area and kitchen with the sweeping, acute, practiced glance of a police professional. As she sat with casual ease on the cream-colored sofa, tree-filtered late afternoon sunlight through the open balcony doors warmed the beige tones of her jacket and pants, her milk chocolate skin. She looked trim and handsome, dignified, well groomed, authoritative. Recovered from the effects of the dream, Kate now felt exposed and vulnerable to Walcott's judgment of her, of the revealing truths of her home and her own attire: pants, a shirt, sneakers. The phone call from Walcott had come in only an hour ago, and while Kate had made a wardrobe upgrade from her sweats, she could not very well don office gear, could not wear a suit jacket as she had done every day of her life at Wilshire Division.

Receiving a captain of the LAPD was an unprecedented event in her experience. Captains did not visit subordinates in their homes, they received them in their offices. Although technically Kate was no longer a subordinate, it did not matter when it came to the ingrained discipline of police hierarchy; and she felt an inferiority that had everything to do with Walcott's lofty rank.

"I don't happen to have much in the house," she said to Walcott, "but I remember you like these." She picked up the plate sitting on the tray and offered it. "Oatmeal cookies." She'd found the package in the pantry, its expiration date still a month away.

Again Walcott's smile was generous, transforming her hawk-like features. She took one. "I appreciate you remembering."

Feeling the need to sit upright, Kate chose the adjacent armchair instead of the treacherous leather recliner that had lulled her to sleep. A breeze, cool for early May, blew in through the open balcony doors, presaging evening, bringing with it a faint leafy aroma.

Picking up the carafe, Walcott poured herself and Kate a mug of coffee. There was no cream or sugar on the tray; like virtually all cops, both women drank coffee strong and black. Handing a mug to Kate, Walcott said, "Doesn't seem possible it's been four months."

"Going on five." Kate pasted a congenial smile on her face and picked up her coffee mug. Walcott obviously felt the need to perform whatever casual interrogatories and pleasantries she deemed necessary before she got to the business that had brought her here.

Walcott studied her with the hooded, expressionless eyes of a cop on the job. "How have you been doing, Kate?" Before she could answer, Walcott said, "I should know better than to ask a detective such a softball question. *What* have you been doing?"

Kate much preferred the first question, a ball she could bat around among any number of platitudes. "Oh, you know, just the usual stuff, a little travel, catching up on sleep, reading, just unwinding and taking it easy." Some of this was true. She'd been to Big Bear and had read a great many books. She gestured vaguely around the condo. "Stuff needed doing so I got that done. New carpet, painted the place."

Her changes had been in fact far more radical. Of the living room furniture, only the recliner remained from earlier days and the career memorabilia hanging on the wall. In the bedroom, only her clothes were the same. Every other item in that particular room including her clock radio had been replaced. Everything in the den, except for her computer and printer, was new. Even the barstools at the breakfast bar had been changed. She'd had to do it all; she had reached the point where she couldn't bear walking into her own home anymore, and she'd made this choice over selling the place. At bedrock she needed to live here. She needed at least that much familiarity and continuity in her life.

"Nice," Walcott commented. "This is a very nice place, Kate."

"Thanks," Kate said, and quickly sent the ball back over the net: "And yourself, Captain? How goes the war?"

"We're solving every case, being heroes to a grateful populace—"

Both women shared complicit chuckles. Pressure to clear cases was relentless and always had been, and public criticism if not outright disdain of law enforcement was an unremitting din in all of LAPD's nineteen divisions, soon to expand to twenty-one. Walcott picked up a small paper napkin, folded it around her cookie and sat back on Kate's leather sofa, coffee in one hand, cookie in the other. "So far it's only conjecture, but the west side may be losing officers to Central and South bureaus."

Kate's eyebrows rose in surprise. She was flattered that Walcott would share anything from high echelon strategy meetings, much less an unreleased major news item like this one. As Kate's lieutenant at Wilshire Division, Carolina Walcott had been blunt-spoken, sometimes profane, often confronting her detectives beyond the point of abrasiveness. But except for a few dismissive generalities she kept her own counsel about LAPD politics, and this revelation meant she was trusting her with important and confidential information. "The new chief is a brave man," Kate ventured.

Walcott grinned. "Brave? That's one word for it. How easy is it to shift troops when you've got thirty-five thousand to cover a place like New York? He'll soon find out about redeploying less than ten thousand over the five hundred square miles of LA." Walcott took a bite of her cookie and ate it with obvious relish, and drank some coffee.

What does she want? Kate's mind spun with possibilities. *Some major development in an old case of mine? No, she'd just call. An assignment? Not possible.*

Walcott added, "Wait till the people who believe they deserve greater protection find out a chunk of it's being siphoned off to people they consider far beneath their superior selves."

Even as Kate smiled at the remark, she realized that Walcott's unusual candor about LAPD's internal strategies was also a reflection of Kate's own changed status from insider to outsider, someone no longer plugged into the gossip pipeline. Nevertheless she was still pleased that Walcott had shared this with her. "Think it'll happen?"

"Without doubt. He is, as you say, a brave man. And unlike certain people we know, not interested in running for mayor."

Amused by this reference to the ambitions of a former police chief, Kate picked up her mug and sat back, appreciating the rich scent and hot bitter bite of the coffee while wishing it were laced with scotch. She made no reply to Walcott and decided not to initiate any further conversation. She wanted to be told the purpose of this visit.

Walcott too drank from her coffee. And then she asked, "Heard from Cameron lately?"

Another pleasantry. But this one happened to hit a nerve. Unwilling to let Walcott know how out of the loop she felt with Joe Cameron, how disturbed she was with her former partner, she replied off-handedly, "Not for a while." And offered, "But he's taken sick leave along with vacation." Information Walcott already knew, of course.

Walcott nodded, her gaze fixed assessingly on Kate. "Did he mention they were my orders about the leave?"

"No, he didn't mention that." He wouldn't.

"Stress to the max. We cops will never admit we're riding on the rims much less about to spin off the road. But he didn't argue. I assume you know he was lead detective on the Carter case?"

"Hell yes. It's all he talked about. It's eaten him alive."

All homicide detectives had cases that were deep and personal. She'd had several in her career. Fifteen-year-old Tamara Carter had been Cameron's first case without Kate, a rape-murder, and his first view of the brutally violated victim had ignited a rage that seemed inextinguishable. With no new leads and further progress now dependent on results from the FBI lab, Cameron had continued to re-interview Tamara Carter's friends and family and to pore obsessively over every detail in the murder book.

"How often do you usually hear from him?"

"Every week, at first," she admitted. "Sometimes more. But it's been three weeks now. We're—we were tight, you know."

Again the smile, this time sudden and disarming. "Yeah, tell me. Too tight. He was like a young colt when he transferred in and he turned my most seasoned detective into one too."

Kate too smiled. Walcott had no idea.

"I'm sure I have no idea," Walcott said.

Kate shook her head in reply. When had this woman turned into a mind reader?

"He was good for you, Kate, so I didn't step much on either one of you unless I had to. You were good for each other."

"We were. Joe was the best partner I ever had."

"From what I know, he didn't have much competition."

Kate shrugged. What was there to say? Ed Taylor had come from an earlier era and his minimalist approach to homicide investigation wouldn't see him through a single day on any detective squad in any of the Divisions today. Anyway, why speak ill of the dead? He was five years gone, an early morning heart attack, keeling over among his avocado trees on his property in Fallbrook. Marie Taylor had called her with the news, and Kate had spent an unexpectedly melancholy Saturday going to his funeral services, standing shoulder to shoulder with a few other attending police officers, nostalgic in spite of herself in an onrush of memory of the years and the cases they had shared together. As for her second partner, Torrie Holden—after her behavior in the aftermath of the arrest gone wrong when Kate had taken a bullet in her shoulder, after Torrie's concealment of a blundering violation of the terms of a search warrant that had almost let a killer walk—Lieutenant Mike Bodwin had taken her off Kate's hands before she could fasten them around Torrie's neck. Torrie had thereafter left homicide at Hollenbeck in favor of a transfer to West Valley where presumably she was doing less damage as a patrol sergeant.

"You deserved a good partner, Kate, and you taught Joe a lot, brought him to a level of professionalism and thoroughness he needed. You say it's been about three weeks? Any idea why the silence?"

She shook her head. "Truthfully, I've been very pissed with him." Especially with the burden she was carrying right now. She'd been hearing from him less and less over the past two months and had assumed their bonding as partners had been fading as her distance from their daily police life together lengthened. She was becoming ever more tense and alert over these seemingly innocuous questions from Walcott. "I left two messages and he didn't call." She sipped coffee, watching Walcott, who wouldn't know whether Cameron's behavior was normal or not.

"Is that normal?"

A sharp prickling of alarm ran up her arms into the back of her neck along her hairline. "What's this about, Captain?"

Walcott shifted on the sofa, placing one hand on the leather as if to brace herself, and Kate had a flash of memory: being called into the captain's office at Wilshire Division, standing frozen in place as she was informed that her partner of twelve years, the first woman she had ever loved, was dead in a fiery crash on the Hollywood Freeway—an oil tanker had fallen on the hood of Anne's car. She could still feel how the knife had slid into her heart, a knife that had remained lodged there every day of the twenty-five years since.

Is Cameron…Could he be…

Newer procedure had homicide detectives not making death notifications until after they'd gleaned as much information as possible, in the cold calculation that they'd lose the person they were questioning to shock and grief. Carolina Walcott had been a homicide detective and a damned good one, and all good homicide detectives were good actors. But Walcott's overall demeanor did not indicate that anything was seriously amiss, and no way could she be that good an actor. Still, Kate felt no reassurance.

"What's this about?" she demanded. "Tell me why you're here, Captain."

Walcott raised a placating hand. "Possibly—probably—nothing."

She placed the napkin-wrapped remnants of her cookie back on the tray, and leaned toward Kate, elbows on her thighs, hands together, fingers lightly interlaced. "It's about the Carter case. When I made captain in January I had SID reprint and superglue the entire crime scene—"

"Joe told me all that," Kate broke in impatiently and did a recap so Walcott would not draw this out any further. "No semen, no blood or hairs anywhere that weren't hers, but Joe said there was a palm print, a good one, behind the victim's headboard. He figured the guy had a hand behind the headboard when he was forcing himself down her throat."

Walcott nodded. "You know how they're backlogged at the
FBI lab, no case is ever moved up unless major clout comes with
it and a mere LAPD captain is hardly major clout at the FBI.
But I promised Joe I'd stay on it, follow up personally and let
him know if anything broke. I can only figure somebody back
in Quantico must have heard about the case and had a fifteen-
year-old daughter because a week ago I did hear. No way Joe
wouldn't call me back, Kate, not after I left a message that we got
a hit on his case, no matter what he was doing, no matter where
he was. He'd no more be without his cell than his right arm, we
both know that."

Kate was nodding, her mind churning. Walcott was right on
all counts. Joe would have been on this like paint.

"Any ideas?" Walcott sat back and slid an arm along the back
of the sofa, crossing her legs as if prepared to discuss this for
whatever length of time it took.

"Yeah, probably too many. Anyone checked his house?"

"Me. Last week."

Kate looked at her in astonishment.

Walcott shrugged and said, looking a bit sheepish, "I just
drove by. His car was there and another car, a Ford Escort with a
Marvell Maids sign on the door. I figured if he was in the house
and anything was wrong a housekeeper would probably notice."
Her smile was fleeting. "I rang him again from my car. Nothing."

Cameron could take care of himself, Kate reassured herself;
he was surely okay. There had to be a logical explanation.
"Anything going on with any of his cases? Any recent parole
with an interest in revenge?"

"Nothing I know of. I can't go deeper without raising flags.
No one in his professional life knows him better than you, Kate.
Anything personal you're aware of that might be...bothering
him?"

Kate shifted in her armchair and met Walcott's eyes. "Are
you asking if I know anything that might make Joe eat his gun?"

"Do you?"

"No," she said emphatically. "I mean, even if there were, he
wouldn't." Cameron was far more tough-minded than she was,
and while she had some very dark places in her, especially these

days, she'd never gone anywhere near that particular one. "He wouldn't," she repeated.

"Many killers don't look like killers." There was challenge in Walcott's tone.

Kate shook her head. "Wouldn't happen, Captain. You said it's been a week since your drive-by?" The reason Walcott was here was dispiritingly clear: to elicit what she knew. Which wasn't much. Which still didn't explain why she hadn't called her into the station or asked via phone.

"I was hoping you might take a look, Kate. A quiet look."

She hid her surprise, saying evenly, "From what you've told me I would anyway. But why a quiet look?"

"It's been a week now, but there's no justification for any official action. He's on leave. We can't act just on uncharacteristic behavior. If there's a reasonable explanation, fine. If there's a problem, let's see what it is. There's no time urgency on the FBI hit, he happens to be somebody in the jail system. I can't inform Rasmussen—you know Joe's new partner is a rookie. I don't yet trust him or his judgment. I do trust you. Anyway, Paul Rasmussen would do the same damn thing I did, call him about the hit. I did very casually ask if Joe had any plans for his time off and he said Joe didn't mention anything. What I'm saying is, until we know something I want this kept under the radar. Because I'm working on getting him into RHD. Homicide Special."

Kate nodded vigorously, glad for Cameron. "He'd be perfect." The positions in Robbery Homicide were highly prized and drew considerable competition, more so now that a new Police Administration Building was under construction downtown to replace the hopelessly antiquated Parker Center, and a restructure of LAPD's best detectives into elite specialized squads was underway.

"Career-wise he's got a clean package," Walcott said. "With all the edges he had when he first came into homicide, that miracle is due mainly to you. I don't want anything getting into the rumor mill now. I most certainly don't want anything landing in his jacket."

"I understand. When did you say the Marvell Maids were there?"

Walcott's grin conveyed that she knew what Kate was thinking. "Cameron deserves no less than the best detective he knows. Assuming he gets his place cleaned every week—"

"He does. I sometimes call him Joe Fastidious."

"Then tomorrow. When I drove by it was about eleven thirty."

Which meant that Walcott's visit today had been precisely timed. "I'll check around and let you know."

Walcott got up as if her business were completed, but instead of moving toward the living room door she headed toward the balcony.

What now? Kate followed her through the open sliding doors.

Walcott leaned both elbows on the balcony railing and gazed at the hazy Hollywood Hills in the distance, then did a slow survey of Kings Road from three stories up. "All these beautiful trees," she marveled, her face softening in pleasure. "Great street, great area, lots of historic preservation. Easy street parking, a miracle these days. You've done very well for yourself, Kate."

"I was just damn lucky, Captain. Came to West Hollywood in 'ninety-four, before the area decided to get a lot more upscale." Kate joined her at the railing, gazing in renewed appreciation at the profusion of mature trees, a mix of poplar, laurel, pine and various species of palms shading the other three- and four-story apartment buildings lining her block of Kings Road.

"I wish I'd had the brains to move in from Simi Valley," Walcott said. "Before the city went to hell with all the traffic." She was watching two young men strolling along pushing a baby carriage. "And before LAPD got taken straight to hell by those fucking bastards at Rampart."

Kate nodded and remained silent. Walcott glanced at her and then said quietly, "I did everything I could for you, Kate. I hope you know that."

"I do know that, Captain," Kate answered just as quietly. "I was glad to have the five years. Even if they happened for all the wrong reasons. I consider myself lucky on a number of counts."

"You and me both. Bad enough you had supervisory involvement as the D-Three, but for the grace of God you and Torrie could have been the catching detectives on that clusterfuck of a case. I could have been transferred in sooner rather than later and been the lieutenant of record."

Walcott fell silent, seemingly absorbed in the activity on the street, and Kate took up her own thoughts. Not even a fiction writer could have imagined that the drive-by shooting of a rap star in March of 1997, however sensational it seemed at the time, would explode into a decade-long roiling turmoil for Wilshire Division and the entire LAPD. The homicide of Notorious B.I.G., gunned down in his SUV on Wilshire Boulevard in rumored payback for the killing of rap star Tupac Shakur in Las Vegas, had erupted into a crossfire of accusations that had implicated two of the renegade cops in the anti-gang CRASH Unit at Rampart Division as suspects in the murder. Their infamous, lawless behavior at Rampart in fabricating and planting evidence had resulted in scores of overturned convictions and brought the morale-destroying humiliation of a federal receivership down on LAPD, along with it endless lawsuits and accusations of a cover-up of the Notorious B.I.G. murder by Wilshire Division. The path of destruction had smashed a number of police careers and reputations, and hers could so easily have been one of them.

While she had shared the anger and embarrassment of her fellow officers over all the events and revelations, she had not shared their despondency; out of the disaster had come additional time beyond the normal thirty-year expiration date on her police career. With Wilshire homicide detectives inundated by the demands of the murder case and its lawsuits, Kate's continuing service had become essential, and her tenure had been extended an additional five years under DROP, LAPD's Deferred Retirement Option Program, her application signed off on by the chief of police himself. But no additional extension beyond those five years had been possible, and Kate's retirement had become official as of December.

Watching Walcott's grim face, Kate called upon the one ray of optimism she could offer. "It feels like things are changing, Captain. Like the world's finally turning on its axis into a better place. How good is it that we have an African American candidate for president and he actually stands a chance?"

Walcott's smile chased the grimness from her face. "I'll believe it when I see it. But you can feel the hope in the city, Kate. And the country." She turned away from the railing and walked back inside.

Kate accompanied her while she strolled around the living room looking at the framed memorabilia on the wall. Walcott never wasted time; she had other business she had yet to get to. But she took in slowly and without comment the photos from Kate's police career, of her in uniform at official functions, in informal photos in the Detectives Squad Room, *Los Angeles Times* photos of her with other officers at crime scenes, promotion certificates, awards and citations, the shadow box containing an exact replica of Kate's gold detective shield with her badge number that Aimee had had made for her years ago.

Not looking at her, Walcott inquired, "How long have you been drinking again, Kate?"

Totally ambushed by the question, Kate felt an intense burning in her face and an equally hot surge of anger. *Cameron. He's told her.*

"Why?" she snapped. "I'm retired. What's it to you?"

Walcott turned to her, arms crossed. "Some of us actually care about you. Plus, you look like hell."

"However I look, whatever I do, it's my business."

"Where's Aimee?"

"My business."

"Has she left?"

In welling rage, struggling to not order this woman out of her house, Kate did not reply.

"You're right of course. It's your business."

Walcott uncrossed her arms and for a moment Kate thought she would reach for her. Instead she dropped her arms to her sides. "Just know this, Kate. You're highly respected. You're very much missed. You're still in the police family. You're as important to me—to us—as Joe Cameron. Lots of us care about you. One more thing." She reached into her jacket pocket. "Someone else left our confines a few months after you did, she's a free agent too. She helped you once—she might be willing to help you again."

Walcott withdrew a business card from the pocket and laid it on the coffee table. "Thanks for the hospitality. I'll let myself out."

As the door closed on Walcott, Kate was already stalking to the kitchen. She yanked the bottle of Cutty Sark out of the cupboard, slammed a glass onto the counter and glugged a large quantity of scotch into it and took two deep swallows.

She directed a poisonous look at the closed door. *You don't know one fucking thing about me or the kind of hell I live in.*

Feeling easier, calmer from just the burn of the alcohol in her mouth and down her throat, she carried the glass to the den that used to be Aimee's office and opened the door.

Vehemently meowing her displeasure, Miss Marple marched from the room and down the hallway into the living room. Kate followed her, and picked up the business card from the coffee table. Placing the glass of scotch and the card on the end table, she dropped heavily into her recliner and rubbed her face with both hands. Miss Marple leaped into her lap and began purring, her head butting Kate's elbows.

Scratching her delicate ears, Kate whispered, "Miss Marple, you're still the only female who understands me."

She picked up the business card and held the plain white side of it between her thumb and index finger for long moments before she finally flipped it over to read its simple black print:

Calla Dearborn, Ph.D.
Licensed Psychologist
Lic. # PSY 705536
Ph: 323-555-1954

2

The next morning, after the worst of peak rush hour traffic, Kate drove unseeingly, her head throbbing, through misty gray overcast to Sunset Boulevard and along Fountain Avenue, then up the graceful arc of Hyperion Avenue in Silverlake. She parked the Focus under an oak tree, one of several that sheltered a secluded house tucked amid a wooded enclave of modest frame and stucco homes. Eclectic Silverlake, with its conglomeration of ethnicities and its proximity to downtown, had become a hip place to live during the last decade or so, and the value of the unpretentious dwellings around her had inflated with their newly acquired cachet. Kate quashed the automatic impulse of disapproval, reminding herself of her vow not to lose the flexibility for accepting inevitable change. Along with the relentless congested traffic and roiling politics of a diverse city, Silverlake was part of an ever-evolving LA, whether or not she happened to like any particular aspect of it, and as Maggie had often told her, "Everything changes, Kate. Nothing stays the same."

She let Stevie Nicks finish singing "Rhiannon," turned off the radio and sat for some moments sipping from a tall container of strong Starbucks coffee, listening to the birds and the ticking of the cooling engine, waiting for the caffeine hit to lessen the lightning strikes of pain in her head. She finally gave up, opened the glove compartment and poked around till she found the bottle of Tylenol, tossed three more tablets in her mouth and washed them down with the remainder of the coffee.

"Get yourself moving," she muttered. But still she sat, in a kind of torpor, waiting for the willpower to kick in that would get her out of the car. Summoning willpower seemed to take longer each time she came here.

After all those years she had arrived at homicide scenes and performed her job with authority and confidence, viewing up close beaten, mutilated, sometimes dismembered corpses in the most visceral, nightmarish displays of bloody mayhem—why was it so hard to do this now? Because, she answered herself, those bodies had been drained of life, they were husks, and her task, her mission in work and in life, had been to determine responsibility for that ultimate robbery, the taking of life and all the promise of that life to everyone around a murder victim. Grueling as it had been at times to spend hours gathering evidence and information amid the worst of human savagery, none of it seemed so difficult as bringing herself now into the presence of imminent death, keeping company with someone on death's threshold, someone she could not bear to lose.

She pushed herself out of the car, taking a Starbucks bag with her.

The latched wrought iron gate opened onto a smooth concrete path bisecting leaf-strewn grounds and leading to a boxy, unadorned, yet architecturally pleasing white frame house that filled a considerable portion of its quarter acre of land. An expanse of attractive mullioned windows on all sides of the house faced an urban forest of jacaranda, ficus, fan palms, bird of paradise, thickets of scarlet bougainvillea and lantana in full May bloom.

Kate opened a tall oak door and entered a light-filled room. The immediate impression was of a living room with a blond hardwood floor decorated with bright geometric-patterned area rugs, and sofas and chairs and armchairs in cheerful sherbet-colored fabrics arranged into three conversation groupings. Only a light cherry wood reception desk, angled out from the wall nearest the door, and a faint odor, indefinable but distinctly, astringently medicinal, gave any immediate indication that this was anything but a large private home. One of the conversation groupings, arranged around a fireplace of dark blue tiles, was occupied by three people, two heavyset women with graying hair seated on either side of a white-haired, round-shouldered old man in a wheelchair whose head shook with tremors. The women were each grasping one of his hands and did not look up as the pneumatic door hissed closed behind Kate.

No one was at the desk, and Kate made her way quietly through the reception room and down the rear corridor, nodding to a white-clad male attendant who was carrying a tray. She stopped at the fourth room on the left.

In a narrow bed closest to the window, Maggie Schaeffer lay gazing out into the lush greenery, a light blanket over her emaciated body, a translucent hand resting on the cover of a book lying beside her. Her roommate, new to Kate, an ancient, wizened woman with yellowish skin and gray hair so thin her scalp showed through, was asleep in the bed along the wall near the door, her exhaled breaths blubbery snores. A television mounted on the wall was on, emitting muted sounds of movie conversation into the room.

Kate paused in the doorway looking at Maggie, pierced by memory of when she had first met her at the Nightwood Bar. A robust, supremely confident Maggie Schaeffer, wearing a lavender T-shirt and shorts festooned with zippers. In later years a Maggie Schaeffer with weathered skin always tanned by San Fernando Valley sun, her handsome face framed by a shock of pure white hair, flirting with her lesbian customers as she served drinks amid the noisy conviviality of the Nightwood Bar. The wraith-thin woman in the bed, her head covered with a fine dandelion fuzz growing back after chemotherapy, oxygen prongs leading from her nose to a canister at the head of the bed, seemed the cruelest of impersonations. The one unchanging element that connected this person to that other vibrant woman was the glazed ceramic coffee mug on Maggie's bedside table, a fixture in her tiny Pacoima house—and in Maggie's hand—throughout the twenty-three years Kate had known her. It was one of the very few items she had taken with her to this final stop.

"I see you over there," Maggie said in a wispy voice, not turning her head.

Kate, used to her preternatural awareness these days, moved into the room and over to her bed, rattling the Starbucks bag. "I brought your good friend Frappuccino."

Maggie turned her head toward her then, and the taut skin on her gaunt face stretched whitely over her cheekbones with her smile. She indicated the other bed with a slight movement of her head. "That's Alice. She arrived on death row yesterday afternoon."

The hospice held ten people at any one time, two in each bedroom, and beds in this attractive, well-staffed hospice were only briefly empty. Maggie had no family; they had disowned their unabashedly butch lesbian daughter decades ago. Shortly after the diagnosis of terminal cancer Kate had taken it upon herself to discover and evaluate Silverlake Haven—welcoming LGBT people being a major criterion—and had gotten Maggie on the waiting list. By the time it became clear that twenty-four-hour palliative care was all that remained to be done for her, her name had reached the top of the list and Kate had had her transported here by private ambulance.

Kate poured the Frappuccino into the ceramic mug and inserted the flexible straw from Maggie's water glass and served it to her. Maggie raised her head and took an appreciative sip. "Good. This too," she said, picking up the KG MacGregor paperback from the bed. "Patton finished reading it to me yesterday."

Kate nodded. "I'll bring you one of your favorites tomorrow, a new Kallmaker." She pulled a blueberry muffin out of the bag. "How are you?" she dutifully inquired, and sat beside the bed.

"Never better. You eat that muffin," she instructed Kate. "I don't want it unless it's baked around those pills I asked you for."

Glancing at the new roommate, who seemed to be stirring, Kate shook her head. "Let's not go there again today, Maggie."

"Why not? I have a new idea that'll satisfy all your qualms of conscience. How about next time you bring two guns, give me one, and you shoot me in self-defense?"

Kate let out a bark of laughter in spite of herself and heard a snort from Alice in the other bed that did not seem to be a snore.

Maggie was speaking with a faint wheeze and pushing out words with some effort but without coughing, thanks to the new concoction of aerated medication delivered via her oxygen tube that today seemed to be holding open airways. Kate understood that it was possibly not her lungs that would kill her. The stage four squamous cell carcinoma had metastasized to the liver, Maggie was being given palliatives on demand, and the medical staff had told Kate it was only a matter of weeks if not days before one or more vital functions shut down.

"Kate, when Audie took sleeping pills, you were okay with that, you agreed she had a right to do what she did about her cancer—"

Kate scowled. *But she did it to herself. And finding Audie's body almost killed Raney too.*

"Kate, how can you wish these last few weeks of dying like this on your very best friend?"

Because I can't bear even the thought of losing you. "We've talked about this," she said.

"Be grateful you gave up smoking so long ago, Kate."

"If it weren't for Anne..." She didn't finish because she would not have said she was grateful. Undoubtedly, had Anne not made her stop she would have been stupid enough to still be smoking. "I think this happened from the secondhand smoke you breathed in all those years at the Nightwood Bar."

"So you're telling me my lesbian sisters killed me?"

Kate smiled at her. "Maybe just the ones you seduced and dumped."

"Are you the police detective?" called the woman in the other bed, her voice shaky and querulous. "I need you to help me."

Kate raised her eyebrows at Maggie, who shrugged. "So I told her about you. I told her you're retired."

"Miss Police Detective, can I talk to you?"

Kate rolled her eyes at Maggie, then got up and walked over to the other bed. "Hello Alice, my name is Kate. I can't help you with anything. I'm retired from the police."

Alice surveyed Kate's khakis and yellow polo shirt with something like approval in her watery blue eyes, then she fixed her gaze on Kate's face. "I need you to find somebody. Jonathan Philip Souza. Like John Philip Sousa except it's Jonathan and the Souza's spelled with a zee."

"Don't you have family—"

"My family won't have a thing to do with him. I need to see him. I need to tell him..." Tears formed and overflowed down her shrunken cheeks. "I love that boy. Please find him. Tell him his Aunt Alice wants to see him."

"Alice, I'm sorry," Kate said gently. "I just can't do that."

Alice dismissed this with a contemptuous wave of a claw-like hand. "What kind of detective are you?" The tone suggested she'd asked Kate what kind of human she was. She rolled away, turning her back to Kate, facing the wall.

"Kate..." Maggie beckoned to her.

Kate returned to her bed, and obeying Maggie's signal, bent down to her. "Pancreatic cancer," Maggie whispered in her ear. "Cut her some slack, she's on God knows what medication." A hand on Kate's shoulder, Maggie held her in place and continued, "This boy, he's no boy, he's thirty-five years old and gay. He was a throwaway like me. Years ago."

"I don't know what I can—"

"Don't give me that crap," she rasped. She weakly pushed Kate away. "Just figure it out and do it."

Kate sighed.

"You look pretty rough," Maggie remarked, inspecting her. "Hung over?"

"A little," Kate admitted. She was feeling better with the Tylenol.

"Aimee was in last night."

Kate nodded. Aimee was visiting when Kate was not. A few days ago, coming out of the hospice, Kate had seen her drive off after seeing Kate's Focus parked in front of Silverlake Haven.

"If you don't get off the sauce…"

Kate held up both hands in peremptory command. No need for Maggie to deliver this message yet again. "I have to go," she said. "There's somewhere I need to be by eleven thirty." She patted Maggie's hand.

Maggie grasped hers. "Please, Kate, I want this to end. Just bring me pills. That's all I ask."

"Maggie, I can't."

"You can."

Kate withdrew her hand and turned away from Maggie and moved sadly, dispiritedly toward the door. "I'll be back later today."

"Miss Police Detective, you find Jonathan Philip Souza," Alice called to her. "That's Souza with a zee."

3

Still strategizing how she would go about her next actions of the day, Kate stopped at her condo to pick up some necessities before proceeding to Cameron's house.

In the living room she took from the wall the shadow box that displayed the replica of her badge and pried open the back of the box, telling herself all the while that this was about Cameron and only in the most extreme circumstances would she ever make use of the badge. Also wryly thinking that in similar circumstances Cameron wouldn't have a single qualm, he'd be laughing at her: "What, you have a problem with impersonating the officer you used to be?" Unhooking it from its blue velvet backdrop, hefting it in her hand—she had never before touched it—she noted that the replica felt slightly heavier than the real one.

In the bedroom she changed out of her khakis and into roomy cargo pants. She slipped her wallet and phone into one of the pockets along with a pad and pen and a few other items, still glad these four plus months later that she never again had to carry the shoulder bag she had always thought of as "that goddamn saddlebag" the entire time she was a cop. Carefully, she buttoned the badge into the remaining empty cargo pocket so that she could not inadvertently display it while pulling out something else. Or worse, lose it. Losing a fake badge with her number on it would potentially be a greater calamity than being caught using it.

"You have a nice day, Miss M," she whispered, stroking Miss Marple who was curled up on the bed, a white paw under her head, jade eyes fixed on Kate.

Striding down to her car, she felt an exhilarating sense of purpose. The sun had evaporated the shroud over the city, and her mood remained elevated as she drove through West Hollywood traffic and the busy commerce on Santa Monica Boulevard without her usual snarling impatience. Then took even heavier trafficked Highland Avenue up to Franklin where half a block later she turned off and gunned the Focus up steep, winding, but traffic-free Hillcrest, arriving at Cameron's house well before eleven thirty.

Few of the mostly fenced-in houses along this woodsy street had garages, and Cameron's black RAV4 was parked perpendicular to the street in one of the two spots along the fence to his property, a Marvell Maids car beside it.

Kate found a slot to park in further up the road and made her way down to the house, planting her sneakers with care on the road, feeling as though a slip would send her in a skidding, uncontrolled roll to the bottom of the hill. She liked Cameron's house and this area, but she couldn't imagine living on so steep a slant that it constantly challenged her sense of gravity. The area felt surreal. Up here amid trees and a density of foliage filled with chittering insects and twittering birds was a quiet neighborhood only a stone's throw downhill to teeming Hollywood Boulevard and Grauman's Chinese Theater with its masses of tourists and sightseeing buses and street merchants hawking their souvenirs and maps guaranteed to lead to the homes of the stars.

Intentionally skirting close to the RAV4 as she approached the house, she noted the uniform coat of dust and that nothing unusual appeared to be inside the car; the interior was as immaculate as Cameron always kept it. She unlatched the gate.

She couldn't look around, not while Marvell Maids was here; she could not risk raising alarm or drawing attention to herself. Entering the property as if she belonged there, she casually swept a glance over the low-maintenance front yard, the cocoa brown frame house with darker brown shutters, and saw nothing out of the ordinary. The large ceramic pots of white and yellow daisies on either side of the door appeared well tended but were undoubtedly watered by an automatic drip system—Joe Cameron was no gardener.

She made her way down a series of asymmetrical flagstones laid in mossy turf to a tree-shaded patio area with a few lawn chairs scattered over clay-colored tiles. On the raised brick entryway to the house were a mop, a broom, and a plastic pail holding some rags. The front door stood slightly ajar—fortuitous. She walked up the two steps and rapped briskly on the door, then pushed it open.

To her left, behind a breakfast bar that separated the kitchen from the living room and dining nook, a middle-aged Latina in a blue work smock was rubbing a cloth over the granite counters. She looked up in alarm.

Kate waved a hand in an enthusiastically friendly manner. "Hi, I'm a friend of Joe Cameron's." She hoped the woman spoke English.

"Not here."

"Yes I know. I need to check the water in the backyard. I'm a friend," she repeated, edging in the door just enough to point to the fireplace mantel in the living room and the framed photo she knew would be there. "See the photo? Go look. That's me and Joe."

Looking Kate up and down without evident hostility, the housekeeper came out of the kitchen and went into the living room, pushing up her glasses to inspect a photo of Cameron and Kate in uniform taken at a ceremony honoring police heroes at the academy.

Kate explained, "I need to check the sprinklers in his backyard."

The housekeeper turned and smiled at her. "You police like him. You go ahead."

"Thank you."

If the woman wondered why Kate was going through the house when the backyard was accessible from outside, she said nothing, and Kate had an excuse prepared about needing a wrench from the toolkit in the utility room if she did. Passing the kitchen and moving down the hallway, she went into the utility room with its washer and dryer and out the deadbolted door leading into the backyard. She pulled back the deadbolt, took a roll of Scotch tape from her pocket, tore off a small piece, taped back the lower locking system, and carefully shut the door behind her. With a brief wry smile she remembered a homicide committed during the robbery of a liquor store and a store employee she'd arrested for using this exact method to facilitate entry. A single clear print of his index finger had been found on the Scotch tape. As Cameron had often contended, "If it weren't for stupidity, we'd never catch anybody."

In case she was being watched she did spend some moments checking the tap for the watering system, turning it off and on. A drip system fed a patch of bright green lawn and the jasmine and bougainvillea vines with their scarlet blooms clinging to the back fence. Built into the yard was Joe's barbecue, large and seriously elaborate in its base of used brick, its long silver hood gleaming in the sun. The gray plastic cover for the hood lay folded on the brick expanse beside it as if Joe were about to use the barbecue or had just used it and hadn't yet cleaned it. She'd check later.

She came around the side of the house to the open front door. "Thank you," she called. "All set."

"Yes, goodbye," the housekeeper answered from somewhere in the reaches of the house.

Kate walked back up the hill.

While she waited in her car for the Marvell Maids vehicle to leave, she sat quietly and thought about Joe Cameron, trying to impartially apply to her ex-partner her training and experience to methodically arrange the facts she knew about him. And how any of them might have relevance to this present context.

August it had been, seven years ago, when they became partners on the homicide table at Wilshire. Cameron a transfer out of Devonshire, boyish looking, a left-hander who for the first two years of their partnership had worn a wedding band on that hand. Good dresser, voluble, thirty-six years old, light in the experience department and young for homicide by her standards. Squeamish at autopsies, a reaction they shared, but she was much better at concealing it from the pathologists. Wore aviator glasses, pretentious by her standards. Blushed easily, a serious defect in a detective by her standards. Interrupted her during interviews of witnesses and suspects and blurted facts before Kate could elicit the witness's version of them—deeply unacceptable behavior by any standard, which she had not minced words pointing out and he had worked hard to correct. A very quick study, he'd made steady impressive progress, becoming in the space of a year skilled and intuitive at crime scenes and a complementary partner. She couldn't remember the last time Joe Cameron had made a mistake in an interview— or had blushed.

In the beginning, when she asked the traditional question about why he'd wanted to become a cop, his answer had been pedestrian to the core: job security. During that first year, from what she learned about his zeal for apprehending the takers of lives, she came to understand that it had been a glib deflection away from much more subterranean and angrier motives.

Two of their cases remained standouts. Only three weeks into the new partnership they had caught the Herman Layton murder, a stabbing committed in broad daylight as the victim sat on a tar-spattered bench beside the ancient sleeping bones of the La Brea Tar Pits. Three years later had come the sensational investigation of the death of Victoria Talbot in upscale Hancock Park and the resulting trial. During those two cases and in the intervening period they had learned each other's styles and strengths. Her support during his bitter unhappiness over his divorce had brought them closer. After he rescued her the first time Aimee had walked out, they became friends and confidantes, spending time together, sometimes significant time outside of their work hours, and she had come to his house any number of times for barbecue dinners. Times when he got bombed on wine and she on scotch and when they weren't endlessly talking shop, he learned her family history and much about her lesbian life, and she heard more than she ever wanted to know about the women who'd done him wrong and all the girlfriends parading through his house and his life.

But there was a gulf between them. Some of it could be ascribed to Cameron's overall cool style and diffident persona, but she took more than partial blame for what had taken root in that very first major case together. For her, the Herman Layton murder had, for good or ill, been resolved. For Cameron, his first case remained a maddeningly ambiguous mystery. Over the next few months afterward he'd parsed through the process of the investigation and begun to express suspicions about Kate's separation from him during key moments, concluding that he had been intentionally shut out of crucial developments. The topic still came up, although rarely in more recent years, and he continued to dismiss her consistent and dogged denials that she had concealed from him any knowledge or evidence. She'd had no choice but to stonewall, as she euphemistically told herself, preferring that word to "lie." She could not break her solemn oath to keep secret the international implications that had brought a CIA officer out of retirement and covertly but deeply into the case.

Compounding the situation, during the investigation of the Layton murder Cameron had placed trust in her by offering to help with a stalker-husband whose escalating threats to Aimee's close friend Marcie had exposed the inadequacies of law enforcement to protect women like Marcie Grissom. Kate well remembered his visceral account of a gruesome double murder and suicide in Victorville, a battering husband who had taken hedge clippers to the wife who had pleaded for police intervention numerous times. He'd used a shotgun on his son and himself. Investigating that case may have provided justification for Cameron to act in what potentially could be similar circumstances, but his solution for Marcie Grissom and her part in it had been such a violation of her bedrock standards as a police officer that guilt had darkened her conscience for many months, indeed years afterward. Today, she was willing to admit, she was not all that certain she would take the same inflexible stance of moral rectitude, but it no longer mattered.

Her morose mood in the aftermath of his intervention was perfectly readable, and had cost her his unconditional trust.

Cameron did not remotely compare himself or his unorthodox methods—which he described as "pragmatic"—to the dirty renegade cops at Rampart, whose actions he contemptuously dismissed as "thugs on thugs with drugs." And she was absolutely certain that he had continued to run, with one or more other cops, similar off-the-books "pragmatic" solutions to problems that seemed beyond the effective reach of law enforcement.

She glanced up at Cameron's RAV4. Wherever he was, why had he not taken his car? One strong possibility for his non-response to Walcott's and her own messages was that he was on a "pragmatic" mission right now and had not wanted to use an identifiable car. And something had gone awry.

Also possible, she reassured herself, was something having to do with his family. His police career had begun in his home town of Victorville, and he had still had a buddy from VPD he sometimes camped with, a lean, deeply tanned, taciturn fellow she vaguely remembered meeting at a barbecue at Joe's house, someone he simply called Dutch. Dutch seemed to be the extent of any Victorville friends, and Joe had alluded to having reasons to get out of that desert city. But he would never be more specific, not even when she applied her skills at interrogation, his responses always monotone utterings of "boring" or "nothing for me there" or just an impatient shrugging away of the topic.

If he had family beyond a brother with whom he seemed to have a distant relationship, and a sister who had returned to Victorville from Phoenix after a divorce, she didn't know about them. She remembered his siblings' names only because they were the simplest of names, all one syllable beginning with J: Jack, Jean and Joe. Jean was the only relative he mentioned with any regularity, usually to shake his head over the penchant for bad relationships his younger sister shared with him. He rarely spoke about his parents beyond acknowledging commonality with Kate of having lost parents too early in life. Lined up along the mantel where the housekeeper had gone to view the photo of Cameron and herself were a formal portrait of those parents, taken perhaps in their forties, another photo of the parents with pre-teen Joe, Jack and Jean, one of all three siblings climbing a rock formation, and one of twelve-year-old Joe with his father kneeling beside him, an arm around him, in front of a rust-colored cabin against a desert backdrop. Cameron's boyhood dream, she remembered, had been to be a geologist or paleontologist.

She had never confronted him, as a friend, about his reticence and evasions over his family and his Victorville origins, and now she wondered if she even fit the definition of "friend," much less "close friend." Now that it might really matter, she had that much less to go on.

There was his ex-wife, Janine, still an instructor at the police academy but five years gone from Cameron's life. She'd met Janine several times in the early days, found her friendly in a polite and distant way, and thought anyone meeting the Camerons could easily take Janine for Joe's sister. She admired Janine's cool Nicole Kidman demeanor, her tall, willowy, small-breasted body, the heavy textured dark gold hair she wound into a simple French twist. The Camerons were childless, by choice Kate had always assumed; she had never heard him voice any desire to be a father. And she had never forgotten a remarkably bleak response of his when she expressed concern about children at the La Brea Tar Pits having in their view the corpse of the murdered Herman Layton: "A dead stranger's a painless way for kids to know the reality of death." Another of the many ambiguities about him that in retrospect she wished she'd pursued.

The Camerons had been married fourteen years before he discovered that for the last six Janine had been conducting an affair with another officer at the police academy. His fury had been apoplectic, less about Janine's infidelity—he'd had a fling or two himself, he drunkenly confessed to Kate—than at being so thoroughly duped by her for so many years. "I'm a *detective*, a fucking *detective*," he fumed at the bar where she accompanied him to get plastered with him in sisterly solidarity. So sloppily intoxicated, so falling down drunk had they gotten that night that the bartender had called Aimee to come collect the two of them.

She also knew Cameron had been in LAPD's Threats Management Unit for, as he termed it, "a minute or two" because, he said, he felt like a guidance counselor, not a cop. And because the victims were the ones who spent their lives in jail while the harassers ran free, the victims' lives and dreams torn to tatters while the men who believed they owned these women found every justification for terrorizing them.

Looking up she was surprised to discover the Marvell Maids car had departed without her noticing, so immersed had she been in her woolgathering about Cameron.

She started her car and drifted it down to park it next to the RAV4. Better she appear a visitor than a burglar.

Once again inside Cameron's property, she first checked the mailbox—empty—and then let herself in the back door. Released the lock and peeled the tape from the lock, balled it up and tucked it in her pocket. Squaring her shoulders, taking a deep breath, she walked into the house.

She and Cameron had served and executed many search warrants together, but this felt odd, too odd, too deeply unsettling. She was about to invade her own partner's house and his private life without his knowledge or anything resembling probable cause. "Get on with it," she muttered. "For Joe."

She pulled her notebook and pen from a cargo pocket and decided she would do no more than a noninvasive walkthrough to assess whether anything seemed amiss compared to any of the times she had been in this house. Regrettable, however, that Marvell Maids had been here and perhaps had cleaned or tidied away something important. "It's not a fucking crime scene," she rebuked herself.

But what if it is? came the unbidden thought.

The house was small, probably less than nine hundred square feet, and Cameron, she knew, had stretched himself financially to afford it. The small, shag-carpeted living room held a tan suede sofa, matching armchair, a two-shelf coffee table with stacks of magazines on its lower shelf, and a floor lamp. Low bookcases of mostly paperbacks lined one wall, paintings and photos of desert scenes above them. The fireplace with the photos on the mantel dominated the room. She had never seen a fire in the grate and the arrangement of abstract sculpture on the hearth declared it was for ornamental use only.

Thinking of all the times she had ordered this done for her by Scientific Investigation Division photographers and videographers, she got out her cell phone and took photos of the room from various angles. She pulled out each stack of magazines from under the coffee table, examined each cover of *Sports Illustrated, GQ, Esquire, Maxim* and *Newsweek* and replaced them exactly as she found them, making notes on her pad.

She spent no time in the dining nook beyond taking a photo. It held only a maple table with a removable leaf and six dining chairs. A few pieces of art, more desert scenes, hung on the walls.

The kitchen, separated from the dining nook by the breakfast bar with its three stools, was a U shape, a smart-looking compact design, but two people would crowd it. Not that Cameron would ever want two people in his precious kitchen. After he moved in here, he had spent what little money he had for renovations in it. The cabinets were high gloss white, the appliances chrome, the counters pearl gray granite. Everything gleamed from the housekeeper's ministrations.

She opened the refrigerator. The shelves and door held an array of condiments and preserves—peanut butter and jam, margarine and mayo and mustard, olives and soy sauce and tapenade and salad dressing—along with a canister of ground coffee, two bottles of white wine, cans of Rolling Rock and club soda. The deli drawer was neatly stacked with packaged turkey, ham and cheeses, a pound of bacon. On the freezer shelves were a half dozen packages of frozen vegetables and soups, hamburger buns, shellfish, ground turkey and chicken, raspberry sherbet, a bottle of Kamchatka vodka.

Kate took a photo, made a note on her pad and moved to the cupboards to quickly check dishware, pots and pans. Then she opened the pantry door and did a slow, careful survey. Cereal, canned goods, packaged rice and pastas, boxes of crackers, jars of pistachio nuts and almonds. She took a photo, made a note.

On the cork floor of the second bedroom, converted into a den, were scattered pieces of exercise equipment including weights and a treadmill. Cameron's ancient desktop Dell sat on the tiny leather-top desk he had picked up from Steve Henderson in Burglary when he moved to Dallas. On top of a file cabinet behind the desk rested Cameron's bootlegged copy of the Tamara Carter murder book. She photographed the room, made a note.

She moved to the bathroom. All the surfaces gleamed from cleaning, the immaculate room smelled of cleanser. She opened drawers and the cupboard under the basin, then the medicine cabinet. She inspected its contents, took a photo, made another note.

She had left Cameron's bedroom, the most personal of all rooms in his or anyone's house, intentionally for last. She had seen it only once, the first time she visited, when he'd proudly shown her what he'd bought after the financial settlement of his divorce.

On most searches she had performed during her career, significant evidence emerged from bedrooms where people expressed their most personal and often malevolent selves. But never before had she felt so morally compromised over performing such a search. This was more than an invasion of a friend's privacy. It was a violation. Another assault on Cameron's trust.

Again squaring her shoulders, she surveyed the room from the doorway. Nothing appeared different from what she'd seen three years ago: the king-sized bed, the dresser facing it, the old Panasonic TV on the dresser. She immediately went to one of the pine nightstands flanking the bed. Easy to tell which one he used: the clock radio sat on this one, and a reading lamp was clipped to the side of headboard next to it.

She opened the drawer, gave it a few moments of scrutiny, touching nothing, then photographed and closed it. She checked the other nightstand and did a cursory look through the drawers in his dresser. They held nothing she didn't expect to see, boxers and socks and sweatshirts and T-shirts and sweaters, a few laundered dress shirts still in their wrappings.

Returning to the bed, she pulled up the quilted maroon bedspread, crouched down, lifted and peered under the mattress, doing so on her knees around the entire perimeter of the bed. She restored and smoothed the bedspread to its previous neatness.

Then she moved to the walk-in closet, looked in. Stopped and took a deep breath, balling her hands into fists. She was so familiar with some of these suits and jackets hanging on the racks, Joe Cameron could have been in the room. There was even a lingering scent of the sandalwood scent he sometimes used.

"Joe, you better be all right, you bastard," she muttered.

She entered the closet and began to inspect all his clothes, careful not to move anything, making notes as she looked over dress shirts and casual shirts and polo shirts, dress pants and track pants, suit jackets and bomber jackets, the double rack of shoes. There were no noticeable gaps between the clothes on hangars, nor between pairs of shoes on his shoe rack. From the doorway she took several photos.

She had only one item she needed to look at in the backyard. She went out and lifted the hood of the barbecue. The grate had not been cleaned; charred bits of what appeared to be ground meat adhered to the surface. No mold. She replaced the hood, returned to the house.

Seating herself on one of the barstools at the breakfast bar, Kate placed her notebook on the bar, pulled out her phone and called the number she'd programmed in.

The phone was answered on the first ring. "Are you inside?"

Kate smiled. "I am, Captain."

"Start with the bottom line."

"He's gone somewhere but has taken great pains to make it appear that he hasn't."

A faint sigh was followed by silence. Then Walcott said, "Tell me how you know."

Kate looked at her notes. "There's no mail. He has five magazine subscriptions and the latest issues of the two weekly ones are two weeks ago. So his mail is being held at the post office. His fridge has a lot of food, but everything not in plastic or glass containers is packaged or nonperishable or frozen. Joe eats salad with every meal but breakfast. There's not so much as a lettuce leaf, nothing that could spoil. His pantry has nothing but nonperishables. His barbecue hasn't been cleaned, that must have been the hardest for Joe Fastidious to leave it like that. He takes a cholesterol drug, Lipitor I think, his prescription bottle is missing from his medicine cabinet. His computer is here, but not his Acer netbook—"

"This is why I had you do this, Kate," Walcott interrupted. "I miss you, Detective Delafield."

She smiled. "Likewise, Captain. He went to the most trouble in his closet to make it appear he didn't take any clothes or shoes and anyone who didn't know him well would believe it. His suitcases are here but not his backpack. He likes jeans with distinctive back pockets, and the pair with buttoned flaps on the pockets is here, but the one with zippered back pockets is missing—"

"Couldn't he be wearing them?"

"He could be. But then he wouldn't be wearing a pair of black track pants. Or his Dockers. Or three pairs of shorts. He might be wearing his Nikes, but his boots and sandals are missing."

"His sandals?"

"His sandals."

"Has Joe perchance joined your team?" There was a smile in Walcott's voice.

Kate chuckled. "Never happen. They don't come any straighter."

"Kate, what about his service weapon?"

"Not here." She did not mention that his second gun was not in his nightstand where most cops, including her, kept their personal weapons. Interesting that Walcott said weapon and not weapons.

"Captain, I need you to do a few things to help with the next step."

"Which are?"

"I did a review last night of the cases we worked and didn't come up with anything, but if you could do just a casual check with Rasmussen whether Joe mentioned somebody surfacing from a previous case or paroled out—"

"No problem."

She was covering a base; she did not believe there would be much of anything there. If someone had surfaced to come after Cameron, more likely it was one of his escapades off the books.

"His ex-wife we can't ask. He has absolutely nothing to do with her and she's LAPD and might not keep her mouth shut."

"What about non-cop friends? Family?"

"Joe's family is in Victorville. A brother, Jack. Sister's name is Jean. I checked online this morning for phone numbers or anything else I could find out. Nothing. There may be something more in Joe's personnel file."

"Can't you find more—"

"Captain, I've searched through Joe's house as much as I'm comfortable with, at least for now. I'll arrange it so I can get back in if I need to. But if there's some reasonable explanation for all this, I'm Joe's friend and he will never—"

"I understand," Walcott said crisply. "Jack, Jean," she repeated. "I'll run them through DMV and AutoTrack. Common names like that, we may get more than a few hits. But Victorville is a smallish place."

"Fine. Jean returned there from Phoenix, that may help narrow her down."

"Friends?"

"A lot of relationships dropped away with his marriage ending. There's a couple of guys he camps with—"

"*Camps*? Our Joe?"

Kate smiled. "First class, I'm sure. He loves the desert. It's the only place he goes. Death Valley, Joshua Tree."

"Probably not at this time of year."

She shrugged. "May is a little late but maybe not for somebody who really loves it out there. Otherwise he pretty much hangs out with other cops, like most of us do. I don't know of any close friends."

"Besides yourself."

"Right." She was not about to go beyond this, to so much as hint at his off-the-books version of police work that she was certain he pursued with cops from other divisions, perhaps Devonshire.

Kate had also been thinking about Walcott's mention of AutoTrack, thinking about this method of tracking individuals' addresses via telephone and utility databases along with or instead of DMV files. She said to Walcott, "While you're on AutoTrack, could you run another name?"

"And what would that be?"

"Jonathan Philip Souza. Like John Philip Sousa except the Souza is spelled with a zee."

"Jonathan Philip Souza," Walcott repeated as if the name were Donald or Daffy Duck. "And what the hell does this have to do with anything at all?"

She grinned. "It's not related to this. Call it a favor for a favor."

"Fair enough. I'll trust you have no ulterior motives."

"The opposite. I appreciate it, Captain."

"Kate, I don't like the damn feel of this thing with Joe. What vibrations are you picking up over there?"

"I'm not sure," Kate said honestly. "There may be a reason for this, it may be perfectly okay. But let me see what else I can find out and let's do it as quickly as we can."

"I'll call you." Walcott clicked off.

4

Kate returned to her condo. Refilled Miss Marple's food dishes, flicked on the TV, sat in the recliner and grabbed a book from the shelves she'd placed next to her, stocked with new books like unopened boxes of chocolates, their awaiting pleasures always in view. She put aside the novel she'd promised Maggie.

Unable to muster interest in the latest fulminations over the election from the talking heads on MSNBC, bouncing her fingertips on the book in her lap, she could no longer ignore the unwelcome thrumming and rawness at the edges of her nerves.

She clicked off the TV, jumped up and paced, and soon went into the kitchen and drew ice water from the refrigerator dispenser, gulping it as she strode from the kitchen to the balcony and through the living room down the hallway to the bedroom and back.

She could not drink anything alcoholic. She had no choice but to wait to hear from Walcott. Depending on what she learned from the captain and how soon, she might be taking more action today, including possibly a trip to Victorville. She had to see

Maggie again today. No matter how hard it was to go there. Nothing mattered beyond the fact that Maggie was dying—time with her friend was ticking toward midnight. Time. She glanced at the clock beside the patio door. Two o'clock. Aimee would be back from her lunch hour…

She congratulated herself. Only the second time today her mind had gone there.

She diverted her thoughts to Cameron. But there was nowhere left to go with him, only to some paranoid place that would make her want a drink all that much more. Maggie. Maggie. She should go to her now. No matter what, she had to go and sit with Maggie—

The phone rang. Not her cell phone, which would be Walcott. She glanced at the caller ID on the phone on the breakfast bar and picked up.

"Aunt Kate, a heads-up."

Glad to engage with her nephew, she asked, "Is the sky falling, Dylan?" She was fairly certain of the reason for this call. "If that's so, the worst thing I could do is put my head up."

"Then you should definitely consider this a heads down. It's my dad."

She nodded at this confirmation of her guess. Two nights ago she had taken a call from her brother, the first one in over four years, and she had answered this time only because he had no reason whatever to call unless perhaps, just perhaps, his Neanderthal view of his son had taken a few evolutionary baby steps.

His first words to her had been, "Nan told me what's going to happen with Dylan."

Her astonishment at this news left her bereft of a reply. Had the woman lost her mind? Why in the name of every inhabitant of hell had she revealed anything at all about Dylan to her husband? To the man whose rock-solid bigotry had overcome his every parental instinct and emotion and driven his only offspring into the streets?

"Something like this," Dale informed her, "she thought I had a right to know."

She really didn't have a good argument for that. She countered with, "So?"

"You have to stop it. You have no *right* to let this happen," he stated, his tone resonant with certainty, with accusation.

"Dale, as long as it's legal, I have a *right* to do any goddamn thing I want."

"She's not your daughter. She's *our* daughter—"

"Son. *Son*. Dylan is your *son*, Dale. And he's my nephew."

"Son? Nephew? You *agree* with this craziness? It's *unnatural*! Dylan is a *girl*. You're letting her mutilate herself. Turn herself into a *freak*. For *what*?"

"Because it's what he wants, Dale. He's turning twenty-one. Dylan can do anything he wants."

"*She!* She doesn't know any better! She's too young! She doesn't know what she's doing! She can't undo this, she'll regret this for the rest of—"

"You know *nothing*," she spat. "All this time and you still know *nothing* about Dylan and everything he's gone through his entire life. You haven't even *tried* to educate yourself—"

"*Educate?* The Bible tells me it's *wrong*! What more—"

"Dale, listen. Just listen. You've chosen your Bible over your son. Leave Dylan alone. You and your Bible, you go and be happy together."

And she'd hung up.

"Dylan," she said now, "did you actually talk to your dad?"

"No way. My mom called. I think she's scared spitless to call you. She said to tell you he's coming to LA to kick your ass."

She couldn't help herself, she laughed. Her sixtyish, paunchy brother couldn't kick anything larger than a rodent without falling over. "Is he really."

"I don't think this is all that funny, Aunt Kate."

But much of the alarm had gone from Dylan's voice. She could imagine him holding his cell phone, probably slouched against the wall of his room in the house he shared with other transitioning youngsters, wearing his habitual uniform of baggy shirt tucked into low-cut jeans cinched with a belt with a huge belt buckle. Kate said in an easy, affectionate tone, "Maybe not. Better he try and kick my ass than yours. He takes you on, I know whose ass would end up on the floor."

Dylan said, a smile in his voice, "He doesn't know where I am. Mom told him she didn't know, said I'd called just to let her know what was going on. So you're the one he's coming after."

"Don't worry about it, okay? Everything all set?"

"Yeah!" he said buoyantly, and she could imagine his fist pumping the air. "I check into the hospital two weeks from now at six in the morning. Best twenty-first birthday present in the history of birthdays!"

"I'm glad I could make it such a big day for you. Heard from your Aunt Aimee?"

"Yeah. She's managed to get the time off, she'll be there too. Gotta go, Aunt Kate."

"Okay. Don't worry, Dylan. I'll keep my head down."

She hung up smiling.

Glancing at the card beside the answering machine on the breakfast bar she obeyed an impulse before it dissipated, seizing on the elevation in her mood to punch the number on the card into her cell phone.

Fully expecting to reach an answering machine she was thrown off balance when the phone was answered with a simple "Hello." Kate recognized the voice from just the one word; she would know that chesty tone anywhere, anytime.

"It's Kate Delafield," she said tentatively. "I don't know if you remember me—"

"I do," Calla Dearborn replied. "Of course. How are you?"

"I…" She regrouped. "I understand you've retired."

"From Behavioral Science Services, yes."

Kate cleared her throat, trying to keep her prickling anxiety out of her voice. "Then I take it you're done with seeing cops."

"Depends on the cop. You're always welcome, Kate. What's going on?"

Needing to avoid this direct question, she replied, "I…well, I thought a session at your convenience might…"

"What about this afternoon?"

"*Today?*"

"Yes, I could do four o'clock."

Again she cleared her throat, tried to regroup. She needed this, yet she was not ready for this. Not right now. Going on five months she had spent in suspended animation and suddenly she had been transformed into a pinball rocketing from Carolina Walcott to Maggie Schaeffer to Joe Cameron to her resurfacing brother to Dylan to Aimee. And now to Calla Dearborn. "I have stuff going on," she temporized. "I'll probably get to wherever you are and have to leave."

"I understand. Let's take our chances. Come on over and let's at least get started. Where are you?"

"West Hollywood near La Cienega." Okay, she would go. She could always make an excuse and leave.

"Very close. Come straight down La Cienega. I'm below Pico. It will take you maybe twenty minutes depending on—"

"Traffic," Kate chorused with her.

Kate went to her closet and looked over her clothes. Should she wear jeans to give the impression she was approaching this whole thing casually and it wasn't that much of a big deal? No, Dearborn wouldn't think much of her if she couldn't be bothered dressing in anything better than jeans. Maybe jeans with a jacket would be the right touch. Or maybe dress pants with a shirt. She sighed. She'd just try on various combinations till something felt right.

About an hour later, wearing navy pants and a blue polo shirt, Kate parked her Focus in front of Calla Dearborn's home.

Third house from the corner, it was one of a series of small, handsome stucco homes with attached garages, Spanish tile roofs, and neatly landscaped front lawns separated by waist-high hedges. Their distinguishing features were individual window designs—some arched, others large picture windows—and flower gardens, in Calla Dearborn's case, blooming rose bushes.

Dearborn, clad in tan pants and a lighter tan scoop-neck jersey top, emerged from her front door, closing it behind her, and came down the sidewalk adjacent to the driveway. Kate walked up to meet her. Except for a full-scale invasion of gray into what had previously been dark hair with hints of frost, she looked much the same to Kate as she had twelve years earlier. If her hair was grayer, her hairstyle was unchanged, a corona evenly encircling her head and emphasizing a high forehead made even higher by virtually invisible eyebrows. The fashionable rimless eyeglasses were a new addition. The solid body on its six-foot frame had picked up a bit more padding. But her polished, wrinkle-free almond skin and pink-brown cheeks were the same as Kate remembered. As was the dimple now emerging with her smile.

"Kate, how good to see you again."

In Calla Dearborn's sable brown eyes Kate saw nothing more than welcome, nothing like the flash of disconcerted surprise she had seen in Walcott's eyes. Kate gladly took her extended hand, Dearborn's palm cool, the long fingers firmly curling around her hand. "Thank you, Calla. Thank you for seeing me."

"Come on back."

Walking behind the sturdy, high-hipped figure, she followed Dearborn down a pathway that led around the side of the house, through a gate into the backyard and to a tree-shaded white frame cottage separate from the house.

"My office," Dearborn said, opening the door to a room with a pine floor, a two-seater leather sofa, bookshelves with two vases of freshly cut white and yellow roses on top and two armchairs facing each other. A small desk abutted the wall. Sunlight dappled the floor in a lovely rippling pattern. "It's why we bought this particular house two years ago."

Kate took one of the armchairs, noting it had wheels, the same as the one she'd sat in in Dearborn's office at BSS. She'd liked the wheels; they allowed her to feel not quite so trapped in the chair. She commented, "If you have this office setup, then you're not retired."

Dearborn sat down in the other armchair. Her dimple showed again as she smiled. "Ever the detective."

Right now the defective detective. "Plus, you're too young to be retired."

"Certainly true." The smile widened. "I'm taking a year or so to do some writing. Among other things a study on police officers nationally and the psychological needs that aren't remotely being met so you can perform your jobs and take better care of your mental health. And I'll be seeing a few private clients. Speaking of health, how's that shoulder, Kate?"

"Still stiffens up a bit during cold or rain," she admitted, flexing it. "But I'm grateful every day to have full range of motion." The bullet she'd taken in her shoulder during the bad arrest on Gramercy was what had precipitated her into the presence of Calla Dearborn for the psychological counseling mandated following an officer-involved shooting. Fear of Dearborn's power to put her career on hold had led, on her part, to three tense, mistrustful and often adversarial sessions.

Dearborn nodded. "So, Kate, what brings you here?"

I don't have a career anymore. You don't have power over me anymore. "Dreams," she said.

"Dreams. Undoubtedly far less than pleasant ones. Before we go there, Kate, would you tell me what's going on with your life right now? How are you dealing with retirement?"

"What has Captain Walcott told you?"

"Captain Walcott?" Dearborn sounded and appeared astonished. "What does Carolina Walcott have to do with anything?"

"She didn't call you? She gave me your card."

"We know each other. We're in African American organizations together."

"She knows I saw you twelve years ago," Kate said doggedly, needing to connect the dots that had somehow led her back to this particular woman after all this time.

"Maybe she saw the notation in your personnel file. It's not a black mark in anyone's file." Dearborn added acerbically, "It's not the mark of Cain anymore, even for the most macho of you cops. Maybe it was the LAPD rumor mill. Cops are worse gossips than Joan Rivers."

Kate smiled. "True. It's been a long time, Calla. What do you remember about me?"

"Ah, Detective Delafield," Dearborn sighed. "The master at deflecting questions with her own questions. Let me remind you, this is my interview room, not yours." She shook her head at Kate. "I always considered you one of the more interesting of my clients. Elusive as a gopher."

"I'll take that as a compliment and not a judgment on gophers."

"Indeed. Let's go first to the biggest issue we had between us, the issue of trust. You wouldn't allow me to make any notes during our final two sessions together. Does that still apply?"

Kate hesitated. Dearborn no longer would be reporting to anyone. Professional ethics guarded what was said in this room. Still, she did not like anything personal about her residing in someone's file cabinet. *You need her*, she told herself. *If she wants to do this…*She conceded, "I guess not."

Dearborn got up and opened a drawer in the small desk and took out a lined pad and a pen that Kate recognized. "That's the same pen you had twelve years ago," she marveled.

Dearborn turned the slender malachite rollerball in her fingers. "I don't know how I've held onto it. I've lost every other pen I've ever had."

"It's beautiful. A nice touch of continuity."

"Continuity is important to you." It was a quasi-question.

"I don't have all that much of it."

Dearborn sat down again, placed the pen on the pad in her lap, propped her elbows on the arms of her chair and steepled her fingers. "Let me tell you what I remember, you correct me if I'm wrong. You came to me because you'd been shot in the process of trying to arrest a young man—"

"Darian Crockett. Seventeen years old," Kate said, melancholy all these many years later over the stupid, unnecessary waste of his young life. "You didn't know at the time but my bullet was friendly fire. From my own partner, most likely," she added.

Dearborn raised her vestiges of eyebrows. "How did that work out?"

"I didn't shoot her back," Kate joked. She shrugged. "Shit happens."

"Sometimes a lot of it." Dearborn inspected Kate for a moment, then said, "You told me you lost your first lover of more than a decade in a horrific accident—"

"A flaming wreck on the Hollywood Freeway. Her name was Anne. We had twelve years."

"Yes. Terrible. So awful. And you lost your parents at quite a young age. Especially your mother."

"I was seventeen."

"The same age as Darian Crockett."

She was startled. She had never made that connection.

"And you were in your thirties when your father died. The parent you were closest to."

Kate nodded and offered nothing more. Surprised and touched that Dearborn remembered this much so many years later, she was fighting down a welling of tearful emotion over this tallying up of loss. Grief over Anne and her parents seemed to easily ambush her these days, despite all the intervening years.

"You're a college grad. Military service in Vietnam. Back then you had been more than a decade in homicide—"

"Fourteen years, when I saw you."

"So twenty-six years all told in homicide when you retired. With most of that service at the detective-three level and no interest in promotion to lieutenant or any other higher position."

Her hackles began to rise. Dearborn had once sharply challenged her on this. "A wise choice as it turned out."

"Or not. Perhaps your integrity at a higher command level would have made some difference in all the shit that happened."

Kate did not reply. *Water under the bridge.*

Dearborn said after a moment, "At that time you were not out as a lesbian on the job—"

"Not true. People knew. I did not make an announcement."

"In these years since, did you ever make one?"

"Everyone knew," she insisted and gestured expansively. "The rumor mill you mentioned."

Dearborn picked up her pen, made a note so quickly it had to be shorthand and put the pen down. "I remember clearing you for duty. I remember giving you several warnings. One was that you were a textbook candidate for alcoholism—"

"You were right."

"—And you were running grave risks with your female partner—"

"You were right."

"—And it was imperative you continue therapy."

Kate smiled. "And here I am."

"And here you are." Dearborn returned her smile. "Your dreams, Kate. Would you tell me about one of them, whatever you can remember?"

She shifted on her chair and rolled it a few inches away, crossing her arms. "There's two. Well, more than two. But these two...I get them all the time."

She spoke slowly, groping for exact words. "I'm sitting in an empty house, I don't think it's my condo but it could be. If it is, there's no furniture except the plain wood chair I'm sitting in and a gray carpet like nothing I have in my place. I notice the carpet around my feet feels squishy, it's saturated with wet. I walk through this squishiness, leaving wet footprints, and the patio door is open—rain's coming through. I'm angry because I've been stupid enough to leave the door open in all this rain and there's wind besides…"

Calla Dearborn was both watching her and making notes. Kate continued, "I do have a patio door in my place but it's not like this one. This one's old and rickety and hard to close, I have to jerk on it to get it closed. I go back to my chair. But on the way I feel warm wetness like a mist with a big few drops that hit my neck and arms."

Kate swallowed, took a breath, crossed her arms tighter. "I look up and the ceiling is dripping, fine drops coming through, but not from all over the ceiling. Only about half, the part toward the windows. But that part of the plaster's gray and looks like…it's got these little holes, they're in a regular pattern, like the water's coming through a precise pattern in the plaster like a sieve…"

Again Kate swallowed and finished in a rush of words: "I notice my arms feel oily and warm and then I look down and what's falling on them is red, it's blood, the wet on the floor is blood, all of what's falling all over me is blood, I'm getting wet with blood." She took a deep, shuddering breath.

"Oh my heavens, Kate." Dearborn's pen had frozen over the page.

Kate rolled further back and crossed her legs. She took a deep, deliberate, effortful breath. "The other one is worse. I'm riding in a car—"

The phone in her pocket vibrated. She all but sobbed with frustration. But she had no choice but to pull it out and look at the caller ID.

"I need to take this, Calla. Believe me when I say I need to take this call."

Dearborn nodded, but her eyes held an amalgam of anguish and exasperation, and her full lips were tightened into a straight line.

Kate opened the phone and got up and walked toward the door, saying abruptly, "You have something for me?"

"I do," Carolina Walcott said. "More than you want, but it's what came up and you'll have to sift through it. Do you have a fax?"

"Sure. It's in the same place as my airplane hangar," she snapped. "Why would I have a fax?" Aimee had taken hers with her.

"Of course you don't." Walcott's tone was apologetic if a bit taken aback. "I didn't think beyond hoping not to leave too many electronic traces. I'll have this stuff scanned right now and sent it to your email address. You do have a computer?"

"Sure. Of course. Sorry I snapped at you." She added for the benefit of the woman sitting in the armchair hearing every word as well as the woman on the phone, "I'm a little on edge. My closest friend is in hospice care and my mood is all over the place these days."

"I'm very sorry to hear that, Kate," Walcott said softly, and from behind her Kate heard a murmur from Dearborn.

"Thank you." She gave Walcott her email address, said, "I'll get back to you," and clicked off.

"I do need to go, Calla," she said over her shoulder. "Now. Can I send you a check for—"

"Give me just thirty seconds. Thirty seconds." She pointed at the chair. "Sit. Thirty seconds, not an instant more."

Kate sat down again.

"Trust. We began this with my telling you the biggest issue between us twelve years ago was trust. I know enough about you to understand that you asking to see me means one thing: you're in trouble and it's serious trouble."

Dearborn leaned toward her, held Kate's eyes in her intense gaze. "I can help you, Kate. I can. Trust that I can. I want you back in here the moment you can get here."

"I feel better from just getting out what I said," Kate admitted. But she needed to assess what had happened for her here. "I'm grateful." Whether she could actually go through any more of this was another matter.

"That's fine but not what I want to hear. What I want to hear is your voice on the phone telling me when you can come here again. We'll talk about payment and I'll have you do the paperwork my profession requires next time."

Calla Dearborn pointed to the door. "Now go do something good."

5

Back at the condo, Kate went into the den, booted up the Dell and located her reading glasses. In her Yahoo account the column of messages with attachments, lengthier than she expected—after all, the search was only Victorville, not LA—daunted her with all the scans she might have to download and sort through on this older computer, perhaps print out on an even older printer. Techno-savvy Aimee had taken with her not only her own top-of-the-line lightning-fast Mac but also her expertise. Kate hadn't wanted to deal with the learning curve that went with buying new technology, had figured the old PC would meet her simple requirements for Internet access to email and newspapers and casual research.

Miss Marple trotted in, leaped up on the desk and settled down beside the computer. "I could use your detective smarts, Miss M," Kate whispered, stroking her as she studied her computer screen.

Two messages drew her immediate attention. One topic line stated: SOUZA. She opened the two attachments. While they were printing she clicked on the second message, its topic line an exclamation mark to draw her eye. The body of the message merely said, "Nothing useful from PR."

Meaning Paul Rasmussen. So Cameron's new partner had no knowledge of any jeopardy from existing cases or recent parolees. If Cameron's vanishing act turned out to be protracted she would need to go to Records and Identification and do a closer review of cases old and new…

Get a grip, you fool. You're no longer LAPD.

Even if she were, she wouldn't be allowed anywhere near the disappearance of someone as close as a partner, especially a partner who was an LAPD homicide detective. Any investigation of one of their own would be turned over to the elite detective squads at Parker Center.

She pulled the Souza DMV printout toward her and studied the thirtyish man in the blurry driver's license photo, his liquid gaze, the delicate lips. "Hello, gay brother," she said softly, looking for the number shown as current for him on AutoTrack. She picked up the extension phone.

"This is Jon," said the tenor voice on the answering machine message, "I'll call you when I can."

She liked that he didn't say he wasn't available or to leave a number or wait for the beep. "My name is Kate Delafield," she said for the recording. "I'm calling on behalf of your Aunt Alice. She's in Silverlake Haven, a hospice. I'm sorry to tell you she has terminal pancreatic cancer. She's expressed a wish to see you, she's very anxious to see you before she passes on, she asked me to find you. Let me give you the information where she is…" Kate left the address and phone number for the hospice and her own number and hung up.

"Alice," she murmured, "let's hope the two of you aren't too late for each other."

She turned to the other incoming messages. Brother Jack should be immediately obvious. If Cameron's sister had picked up her original name after her divorce, if she had applied for utilities and credit cards under her birth name…These days it was virtually impossible to cover up the myriad electronic tracks people left just by living their daily lives. Confident she would find both of them, she just hoped it wouldn't take long.

Half an hour later Kate had downloaded all the DMV and AutoTrack records for all twenty-six Camerons in Victorville and environs, which included Apple Valley and Hesperia, had done a cursory search through the photos and tracking data, and was shaking her head. Given the commonality of the name, the paucity of current Jacks or Johns—save for a nineteen-year-old boy and a man in his eighties—was most surprising. And most disappointing was no evidence of a Jean. The DMV photos were of limited use beyond grouping the collection of Camerons geographically and then into the youngest, oldest and those in between. She had not seen anyone who bore an identifiable sibling resemblance to Joe Cameron, and she had been too stupid to take a close-up of that early photo of the preteen siblings on Cameron's mantel, which might have been of some use. None of what she was looking at was all that helpful.

Jean could be explained. She must be driving with an Arizona or a California license under her married name. But how could there be no tracking of any kind for Jack Cameron? Cameron's references to his brother had been vague and dismissive, but always in connection with Victorville. He had to be there. He didn't drive a car? Have a land or cell phone? Pay for utilities? It was all so unlikely that there had to be an explanation. Was he perhaps a half brother with a different name? Undoubtedly Joe would have mentioned such a fact to distance himself that much further from a brother he seemed to want little to do with. Maybe Jack was too mentally deficient to drive or conduct a normal life? Not possible. No way the Joe Cameron she knew would ever disdain such a brother. Maybe he was in prison. But for so much of his life? Possible but improbable, short of a conviction for first degree murder. There would be relatives of the Camerons in town who would know, she mused. Unlikely there wouldn't be. They must be among these records…

Then a memory surfaced from a case she had investigated long ago in an apartment building near Beverly Hills, a suspect who went by a middle name, and she went through the records again. A license had been issued in 1989 to Magnolia J. Cameron, born in 1971. "If someone named you Magnolia," she said to the yawning Miss Marple, "I bet you'd use any other name, even Fluffy. I bet you'd scratch their eyes out." The license had not been renewed. Possibly because Jean had married and moved to Arizona—the timing looked exactly right. Kate printed out the license with its photo and put it aside.

An hour or so later, her eyes fatigued from sifting through pages of AutoTrack records, she tossed her glasses aside and sat back from the computer. She would need to dust off the practice dating from the dawn of police work, door-knocking. Fine with her. Investigative phone work was distinctly different and inferior in this age of caller ID when people ignored calls from people or numbers they did not know or, worse, were given forewarning that you'd found them. She had the added complication of needing to be careful not to raise any alarms in ferreting out information about Joe Cameron. By phone it was always a delicate dance, and trying to gain cooperation and then glean information regarding someone who'd been gone from the city for fifteen years was that much more daunting. Someone answering a door, she could play it situationally, come up with an explanation that fit. An in-person look-see would give her that many more pieces to fit together about the Joe Cameron she didn't know.

She rested her elbows on the desk and rubbed her eyes. In the early stages of a case she and Cameron always used to ask each other: What's your instinct here?

Her answer now: caution. Her objective was simple. To find out why Joe Cameron had needed to vanish beyond the reach of communication and whether he was in trouble. And if so how much trouble. Wherever he was, he had gone to great pains to not have anyone know or find out he was gone. Including her. However slighted she felt by his lack of trust in her, she wanted to think that Cameron's hurtful withdrawal from her over the past two months had been part of a plan. That he had so methodically plotted and obscured his absence to buy time suggested he wasn't in imminent danger. So, proceed with caution. But the fact that he had needed to disappear without leaving obvious traces more than likely meant something serious was happening with him. Use caution yes, but proceed with all due speed.

In truth, if Cameron was running one of his "pragmatic" interventions and had to disappear for more than a few days to accomplish it, maybe he had let his sister, at least, know. If not, her options looked vanishingly small.

She would get on the road early, she decided, turning off the computer and rotating her stiffened shoulder.

Time for a drink. She could use a drink. To help the shoulder.

But instead she took two more Tylenol and left the condo, taking with her the book she had promised Maggie.

* * *

After stopping at Wendy's for a hamburger, she drove back to Silverlake Haven. This time the front desk was occupied by its usual inhabitant at this hour, Marla, a very pretty Latina in white nursing scrubs who sat typing on a computer at a table beside the desk. "Hello, Kate," she greeted her. She stopped working and turned to her and smiled.

"Marla," Kate said, nodding to her. "How is she?"

"The same, which is good. Ate a few bites of dinner. Go on back, she'll be glad to see you."

Not without a pocketful of sleeping pills, Kate thought, walking on.

At the doorway to the room, she stopped short, almost dropping the book she carried, her heart lurching. *Aimee.* How had she not seen her car?

Aimee got up from Maggie's bedside and came toward her. She was still wearing office attire, a blue patterned silk shirt and midnight-blue pants that heightened the violet of her eyes, and silver earrings visible through her silver-threaded hair. She smiled, and she looked more beautiful than Kate could ever remember. Aimee reached her and wordlessly pinched between her fingers some fabric on the sleeve of Kate's polo shirt to draw her back into the hallway.

"I'm sorry," she said quietly, "I've been trying to give you space, as much time alone with Maggie…and to not have Maggie concerning herself with the two of us. The Outback's in the shop, Marcie had to drop me off. She'll be back for me in a few minutes."

"I thought you were avoiding me," Kate said bluntly.

"Oh God." Aimee closed her eyes briefly. "It never occurred to me you'd interpret it that way. I just thought…It was so very good of you to get her into this place, I was just trying to give you…"

"I understand. Thank you. I'm glad to know."

"This, and Dylan too." Her smile was sudden, luminous. "You're racking up lots of points for good deeds."

Kate shrugged and returned her smile. A faint aroma of perfume reached her, and she inhaled a musky fragrance that seemed to coat her very bones with its essence of Aimee. She was happy she hadn't had a drink before she left the house, had no liquor on her breath. "If Aunt Agnes knew what I'd be doing with her money…"

"She'd have left it to her dog."

Aimee was chuckling, but Kate said suddenly, heatedly, "I didn't want one damn dime of her conscience money for what she did to me when I was a kid. What I don't spend on Maggie and Dylan is going to the Obama campaign."

"Wow. She'll be clawing her way out of her grave." She asked, studying Kate's face, "How are you doing, Kate?"

"Doing. How does Maggie seem to you?"

Aimee shrugged. "She's still pretty feisty, good to see. I managed to coax her into eating a few bites of pasta before they gave her medication."

"Please come here as often as you can. Maggie needs all the support—"

"I know. Is the old gang turning up?"

"From the Nightwood Bar? Patton, Tora, Kendall, Ash, Roz—they've been really good since Maggie got her diagnosis. Patton comes in and reads to her. Raney hasn't been in lately, it's just too much for her, too much like when Audie died."

Aimee shook her head. "I understand that. Maggie probably does too."

She looked at her watch. "I have to go. Marcie will be here. Take care of yourself."

And she was gone, striding down the hallway and out of sight.

Kate took a deep breath and entered Maggie's room. Again she felt a lurching when she saw the other bed: empty.

"Alice," she uttered.

"Still with us." From her bed Maggie waved a languid hand. "Out in the yard. Wheelchair. She's spryer than me, can even walk a little." The words sounded slurred.

Relieved, Kate placed the book she had brought on Maggie's bedside table and told her, "I found her nephew. Left a message on his answering machine over an hour ago. I don't know if it's a good idea or not to tell her. In case he doesn't show."

Maggie nodded. "Aimee," she said, "you need to get her back."

And the Cubs need to win the World Series. "I know." Kate took her hand. "You look a little tired." In truth, Maggie looked gray and ill; her jaw was sagging.

"They gave me...coupla pills."

"I'll be back tomorrow," Kate said, smoothing the covers around her bony chest. "But late in the day. I have to go to Victorville."

"What the hell for," Maggie said, her eyes drooping.

"I have to see a sister about a brother. Or two."

Maggie was asleep.

As Kate went back down the hallway she heard, "How stupid do you think I am!" in a loud, querulous old voice, and she veered casually into the doorway of Room 3. She peered in to see two old women in their beds watching television, an episode of *Law and Order* so ancient it featured Jerry Orbach playing Detective Lenny Briscoe. One of the women had been talking back to Briscoe. It struck Kate that the two rooms she had been in in this hospice proved the demographic of women outliving men.

Pointing at Kate, the woman by the window demanded in the same querulous voice, but in an even more truculent tone, "So what religion are you?"

"Agnostic," she replied, grinning.

"Thank God," she said and muted the TV with her remote control. "I am so sick of television, I am so sick of people coming in here and trying to save my worthless soul at the very last minute. Come in and visit."

It occurred to Kate to wonder how many of these residents of the hospice actually received visitors during their final days.

She had a few minutes, why not? "My name is Kate," she said, coming into the room. She detected a faint iodine odor and the more acidic smell of urine, familiar to her from death scenes.

"Welcome. I'm Ida, that's Mary."

An aged woman with orangish hair and alligator-leathery skin and deeply sunk eyes glanced at Kate without interest. "Visit Ida," she said, waving her over to the other bed. "I had visitors today and I'm a little tired." She rolled over on her side, away from them.

Kate went over to Ida's bed and pulled up a chair alongside it, smiling down at the old woman. Tendrils of Ida's pure white hair were spread over her pillow like antennae. Her thick-rimmed glasses did not diminish the brightness of her blue eyes. Her cotton gown, covered with yellow and white daisies, was buttoned up to her neck, and her liver-spotted hands constantly worked the folds of her blanket.

Kate soon learned that Ida was from Wyoming, had been in LA for fifty years, had outlived most of her contemporaries, and her two children and their families were living in San Diego and Santa Barbara.

"Tell me something about yourself," she said to Kate in a soft, rattly voice. "What do you do besides visit dying old women?"

"Not much. I'm retired," Kate said. "From law enforcement." She let this hang.

"I would have guessed," Ida said sagely, looking at her with her bright blue eyes. "It's the way you carry yourself. It was so very different in my generation. I'm glad I lived long enough to see women like you."

"Thank you, Ida. I'm glad you did too. I was a police detective for many years. Since your family's away, do you get many visitors?"

"My son and daughter do what they can, but they've got their own children and grandchildren. My fault, they wanted me to come to San Diego or Santa Barbara, but this city is home and where I want to be when I go. I've been very unreliable about this dying business. It's my second time in hospice with heart failure. You can only stay so long before they decide you're not dying and kick you out, and I keep on living."

Kate was laughing. "Good for you, Ida." She liked this old woman. "Who else visits you?"

"Carlos and Josephina. I think they come only because they want something. But I'm happy to see them."

Kate looked at her acutely. "Did you promise them something?"

She shrugged and grinned at Kate. "Yes. I'm trying to remember if there was something else besides. I still have my marbles but not every single one of them. I paid them well when they looked after me, an extra something at Christmas and their birthdays, that I do remember."

"They're trying to rip you off," called Mary from the other bed.

"She doesn't even know them," Ida whispered to Kate. "They're wonderful and they were always good to me."

"Tell me more about your children," Kate suggested, changing the subject but filing away this information.

Ida said querulously, "They're just so upset about me dying and I love to see them, but it's hard for them to deal with me being here and hard for me because I've accepted that I'm dying and they haven't. That's the wonderful thing about you hospice workers."

Kate smiled and chose not to correct her.

"No offense intended," Ida continued, "I don't know you from a fence post, Kate, and you don't know me and we can have a decent conversation and it's a pleasure and we don't have to avoid my dying because I know I can talk about it with you if I want to. Besides, I like you. Will you tell me something about the police work you did? Why you wanted to be in the police back when you did?"

"Sure, Ida, I'd be glad to." Kate sat back, making herself comfortable.

* * *

More than an hour later Kate emerged from Ida Appleby's room and went back to the front desk.

"You're quite the impromptu volunteer," Marla told her with a warm smile. "You and Ida really hit it off. I saw you in there and Miguel told me he heard her laughing. For the first time in days."

Kate grinned. She had enjoyed herself too. "I got to dust off some old police stories about dumb crooks and what they did to get caught. She told me some stories about early LA. She asked me to come back and I will." She said casually, "Ida said a Latino couple visit?"

Marla nodded. "Every Thursday in the month Ida's been here. Always just before seven. I think they come after work."

"I think I'll be visiting Ida again if that's okay."

"It is, Kate." She smiled charmingly. "She doesn't get many visitors."

6

The next morning Kate was on the road by eight o'clock for a trip that would take about two hours if traffic allowed, driving the 10 Freeway toward Highway 15 and Victorville. She had taken this route to Las Vegas a few times with Aimee but not for many years. As she drove alongside, around or through such places as Alhambra, Rosemead, El Monte, West Covina, Claremont, Upland, she reflected that after four decades of living in the Los Angeles sprawl there were entire cities she had not set foot in, never even driven through.

The jagged peaks of the San Bernardino Mountains, with crowns of snow and traceries of white remaining on their flanks even into May, materialized from the low morning mist as she merged onto the 15. With pickup trucks, SUVs, delivery trucks and commercial trucks swarming around her, she sped along a five-lane strip of road snaking through hills iridescent with the soft green stubble of spring and inhabited only by steel skeletons clutching electrical wires.

With twenty-seven miles left to go to Victorville, the car's exterior temperature gauge read ninety degrees. Desert landscape began to encroach on the greenness, ancient rock configurations of bleached beige reminding her of the dramatic stone compositions she had first seen with Anne in Joshua Tree National Park. The distant hills held an almost Aztec aspect with their pattern of triangular tops. She found the landscape newly absorbing as she tried to imagine the thoroughly LA-transplanted Cameron growing up in these surroundings, his refined tastes and fastidious manner and dapper dress seeming improbably, utterly at odds with so majestic and elemental a landscape. Except, of course, for humankind infesting it with utility poles and the crawling, endless, antlike streams of cars visible well into the distant vista of foothills.

A Highway Patrol car passed her at high speed, bringing back echoes of one of her dreams, but this one was not flashing its lights or sounding its siren. It was a Crown Victoria, the car she had driven or ridden in much of her professional life. She tossed a mock, dismissive salute its way. No other occupation she could imagine, outside of soldiering on a battlefield or battling fire, held the adrenaline rush of police work, but there was something to be said for driving free and easy in her own car on a highway into an open horizon instead of heading pell-mell into unpredictable jeopardy.

Sandy desert raced past, scrub brush pockmarked with green bushes, and the beige hills were now striated with trails and paths made by ATVs. She hadn't been aware the car had been climbing, but here she was at 4190 feet, Cajon Summit, and her temperature gauge had dropped from ninety to eighty-three degrees. Fifteen miles to Victorville. She was in the high desert.

Then she was at Victorville's city limits: population 107,000, elevation 2700 feet. Its mere six exits seemed to cover all the blessings of Los Angeles, she thought as she passed a Red Lobster, Marie Callender's, Comfort Suites, Macy's, Staples, Olive Garden. A Red Roof Inn too, if need be—she could always call Ramon in the condo adjacent to hers, have him look in on Miss Marple.

A few highlights told her she wasn't in LA anymore: a fairgrounds, a Boot Barn, two Harley-Davidson dealers, a Rotary Club; and Highway 18 feeding off to the east, to mountains the color and shape of crumpled paper bags. But then she was back in

Hollywood with Roy Rogers Drive: Roy Rogers, Dale Evans and Roy's horse Trigger, film figures much beloved to her parents. A balloon of Godzilla bowed in the wind on the roof of an auto dealer. Auto garages, light manufacturing, fenced-in areas of trailer parking—where were the grace notes in this town? Why would anyone stop for anything beyond a quick necessary meal before driving on through?

A sign announced Historic Route 66 and she took it. What if she vanished like Cameron, she thought. Just fled from the pain of Maggie, the pain of Aimee, the torment of her dreams, the aimless direction of her life. Just kept on driving Route 66 clear across these more or less United States of America...

A sign captured her attention: Victorville Federal Correctional Complex. She'd forgotten the Feds had prisons out here. Correctional prisons. *What is it you correct?* she sneered. Exacting vengeance didn't balance any scales, didn't make anything whole, didn't rectify what people perpetrated on one another...

She should know. Bringing someone "to justice," offering the declaration of "justice was done" to survivors when sentences were handed down in the courts did not remotely remedy the devastation wrought by murderers whether they were impulse killings, drunk driver killings, stone-cold killings. If she'd ever believed she brought "justice" to anyone, she'd long since lost the illusion. With all her dedicated effort over the years what was it that she'd accomplished? She'd taken stupid or damaged or defective or monstrous human beings off the streets. And that, she supposed, she guessed, was something good. That they served their sentences in feral, overcrowded hellholes like San Quentin and Corcoran and Pelican Bay instead of in a well-maintained complex like this one in the California desert did not bother her a whit. Vengeance might be inadequate, but it was better than nothing. Not that this facility was any picnic—its three prisons, low, medium and high security, were all essentially high security considering the escape route was the Mojave Desert.

With a Union Pacific train pulling a serpentine trail of railcars coming into and out of view between piles of pale, granitic rock, Kate stopped at a light on Seventh Street, surveyed shack-like housing she could not recall from her vague memories of having driven through here, and wondered if the town had changed or if she had. If her life circumstances had imploded roseate memories from a more optimistic time.

Pulling over to consult the Google map she had printed off the Internet to chart out the logical driving order of the addresses she needed to visit, she rolled down her window. Hot dry air poured in, carrying a faint smell of petroleum. She glanced at her watch. Just after ten. She would grab some coffee and a muffin, then get the lay of the land, drive the route before she rang any doorbells.

* * *

The Golden Sunset Trailer Park, the fifth address on her list, looked to have been in existence a good many years. The main road was asphalt, wide and well maintained, the lot sizes generous, unlike the more modern trailer parks she'd seen over the years where residents lived within a few feet of each other. The complex held many mature trees shading an assortment of trailers in various stages of life, most of them older vintage, single- and double-wides, others much larger with elaborate awnings and covered carports. Landscaping was haphazard, some yards decorated with mature cactus plants and pathways of ornamental rock, others with a few skimpy plants left to fend for themselves in stony sand, others with sparkling white rock dumped over the entire area. The chesty barks and high-pitched yips of dogs provided a continuous soundtrack.

She parked in front of a trailer on a corner lot overhung with drooping queen palms with many dead fronds, its yard so defended by prickly pear and other bristling cactus varieties that protection by a dog seemed superfluous. The trailer was dingy white with a slanted brown roof, its front window covered with opaque reflective plastic, its other windows shrouded in dirt. The entrance was on the side, off a small rickety-looking porch.

She took out her cell phone and called Carolina Walcott, who picked up immediately. Kate heard papers rattling; apparently she was at her desk in her office.

After an exchange of the briefest of pleasantries, Kate told her, "I'm in Victorville. It turns out Jack and Jean aren't that easy to find either." She succinctly brought Walcott up to date on her work with the DMV and AutoTrack records and why she was here, concluding, "I think I may have tracked down Jean—"

"Just so you know," Walcott interjected, "I had some contacts run a check on Joe's credit cards and cell phone. No charges in the last thirteen days." She added in a solemn tone, "Not only no calls on his cell phone, but no signal. Either something's happened to him, Kate, or he's going to great lengths to keep his location hidden."

"I'm going with hidden, Captain. He went to too much trouble to cover up a deliberate plan to leave." But everything she was learning made her uneasy. That he was in some kind of trouble had become an increasing certainty. Still, if something had happened to Joe Cameron, she was somehow certain she would feel it in her bones.

"I'll go with that, Kate. But we haven't much time before I have no choice but to act on the FBI hit and blow the whistle on him."

"I hear you, Captain. I need an ID on a late nineties Toyota Corolla. I believe it may be Jean's car." She read off the numbers on the license plate of the car she was staring at. "Arizona plates."

"Arizona," Walcott muttered. "Crap. Give me a few," she said and clicked off.

* * *

Fifteen minutes later, Kate got out of her car and made her way through the cactus to the trailer. After several insistent raps on a door with fading scuff marks along the bottom as if someone had once tried to kick it in, Kate heard someone within tromping so heavily toward her that the trailer vibrated on its foundation. The door was flung open by a beefy, barefoot man with a scraggly beard and greasy blond hair to his shoulders. He wore a maroon Harley-Davidson T-shirt with the sleeves cut off, exposing snake tattoos on his muscled arms. Threads dripped over his thighs from the ragged hems of shorts hacked from jeans.

"Yeah?" Looming above her in the doorway, he looked immense.

"I'm looking for Jean."

"Yeah?" he repeated.

"Jean Velez. Is she here?"

Inspecting her from head to foot, he crossed his arms and spread his feet, further blocking the door.

"I'm a friend of her brother."

Staring at her as if she were an impenetrable puzzle he'd given up on, he stepped back to shut the door.

"I'm calling the police," she told him.

He stopped in mid-shut. "What the fuck? Are you crazy?"

Pulling her shoulders back, Kate took a step toward him, staring into his hostile blue eyes. "You're trespassing. Or squatting. Or holding her against her will." She pointed behind her. "Her car's right there."

"Who the motherfuck *are* you?"

They held each other's stare for seconds longer, then Kate said, "Like I said, a friend of Joe's. Tell her that."

"Joe," he said incredulously. "A friend of Joe's!" He flung back his head laughing, and slammed the door so hard the trailer shook.

"Christ on a crutch," Kate muttered. "Have I driven to Mars?"

She picked her way through the cactus and back to her car, and drove off.

She turned on the air-conditioning, then grabbed her can of Coke from the cup holder. Her hand shook from a backwash of adrenaline and hot anger at herself. In confronting the man at the door she had acted with the reflexes of old. She should have either flashed her fake badge or had the brains to realize she no longer had the authority a badge gave her with the resources of LAPD protecting her and backing up every move she made. She was damn lucky that bozo hadn't smashed her face in. Cooling off, calming down as she drank her very warm Coke and drove around the trailer park, she focused on the surrounding trailers and the road, the cars and trucks parked outside the trailers. She already knew that two city blocks lay between the place she had targeted and the entrance to the trailer park.

She drove all around the complex, studying its layout, then up and down the main road, confirming there was only one way out, the way she had driven in. She parked one block from the entrance, down the road from the car with the Arizona license plate registered to Magnolia J. Velez, finding a place of partial concealment under a clump of fan palms on the intersecting block and just back from the main road.

How on earth did police conduct stakeouts in this town in this heat, she wondered. Knowing that a running engine would draw attention, she sat with all the windows down, perspiring into her short-sleeved cotton mesh shirt, gusty desert breezes whipping her hair around her face and providing intermittent relief. One consolation, she felt no urge whatever for a bathroom. Her body was apparently absorbing liquid as fast as she could drink it.

Two hours later, her eyes sore from dryness and from watching a parade of vehicles go past her, she saw a dusty gray Ford F-150 roar through the intersection on its way to the main gate. She recognized the truck as one of the vehicles parked near the trailer and the driver as the hulking man from the trailer. He was alone.

She sat for another ten minutes in case the F-150 immediately came back, then returned to the trailer.

She pounded on the door half a dozen times. Then called out, "Jean, answer the door. I'm a friend. I'm not going anywhere till I talk to you."

Kate heard the side door of the trailer next to her, a single-wide with a front picture window, pop open. A deeply tanned older woman wearing red shorts and a matching halter top, her platinum hair in rollers, called out to her from the threshold, "She's in there. Jean's in there." She nodded vigorously at Kate and disappeared back into her trailer.

The door in front of Kate was yanked open and a woman leaped out, pushing Kate aside to shriek at the adjacent trailer, "Dora you fucking bitch why don't you mind your own goddamn fucking business!"

She turned on Kate. "What the hell do you *want*?"

Kate looked into the eyes of a buxom woman with a freckled face and sandy hair. She appeared to be an older version of the

1989 DMV photo Kate had looked at the previous night. She wore a white tank top, red shorts and flip-flops. Her brown eyes looked angry—and perhaps scared. The main resemblance she could see between this woman and Joe Cameron was skin and hair coloration.

"Are you Jean Velez?"

"Can't exactly say no, can I?" She raised her middle finger and jabbed it at the trailer next to her and screamed, "*Fuck you, Dora! You fucking bitch!*" She glared at Kate. "So what the hell do you want?"

"To come in," Kate said calmly, "so we don't conduct our business by loudspeaker in front of all your neighbors. I'm no threat—I'm your brother's police partner."

Jean Velez flicked her startled gaze away from Kate. Then, her shoulders heaving with an exaggerated sigh, she turned and stalked back into her trailer, flip-flops flapping, leaving the door ajar. Kate entered the trailer and closed the door behind her.

The side door opened into a living room carpeted in thin shag. Jean Velez had seated herself in a tweedy ocher recliner, feet up, arms crossed. She did not look at Kate. Visible was a kitchen with yellow appliances and brown cabinetry, separated by a railing from the living room. A small round kitchen table with three chairs sat adjacent to a side window. A corridor led, presumably, to a rear bathroom and bedroom. The place was pungent with the sickly sweet smell of marijuana.

The only other seating in the living room was a sofa, apparently foldout, also yellowish in hue, and Kate sat on it. There was no coffee table, only TV trays at either end of the sofa. A cheap walnut-colored cabinet occupied the wall under the side window across from Kate, and an old Sony 26-inch TV, tuned to Oprah Winfrey, rested on a TV stand across from Jean Velez, who picked up the remote control and muted the sound instead of turning it off, the latest in clear messages to Kate that she wasn't welcome. A circumstance with which she was amply familiar from many homicide investigations and which did not remotely faze her now that she was inside the trailer. She would conduct her business and get out of here, but not before.

She began, "Mrs. Velez…"

"Don't call me that."

"Jean?"

She lifted a hand off the arm of the recliner. "Whatever."

"When did you last hear from your brother?"

"Which brother?"

"Joe." Not that she wasn't curious about Jack.

Jean's eyes were fixed on Oprah Winfrey's earnest face mouthing soundless words on the TV screen. "When did *you* last hear from him?" she flung back at Kate.

I'm asking the questions here, she wanted to say. Again she struggled with her frustration at having no power, no implicit authority. Though even if she were still a cop she had no jurisdiction here. Maybe there was a possibility of thawing some frost and establishing a kind of rapport.

She glanced around. A small bookcase held a carelessly stacked array of paperbacks with cracked spines and curling covers, romance novels judging by those she could see. Nothing in common there. She looked at the walls and the few flat surfaces in this room for clues. Several strings of colorful papier-maché cutouts of various species of butterflies trailed down a wall, but nothing else was on any wall except for a calendar tacked up near the door. Her darting glances found a framed photo on the cabinet next to Jean of her with brother Joe, both of them wearing jeans and denim shirts, arms around each other's shoulders.

"How old was Joe when that was taken?" She recognized the rust-colored cabin in the background, the same one as in the photo on Cameron's mantel.

Jean flicked her eyes at the photo to which Kate was pointing. "Twenty."

"And you?"

"Eighteen."

"There's quite a resemblance. Hair color, your features."

Jean shrugged. She kicked off her flip-flops and curled her legs up under her, scowling at the TV screen.

Kate's glance settled on another photograph, this one near Jean's elbow. The three figures, seeming posed as if for a professional photographer against a red curtain backdrop, were of Jean in perhaps her thirties, wearing a lacy white dress; a handsome Latino man in jeans and a fancy western shirt; and a child of perhaps six, a quite beautiful dark-haired boy in a white suit. Cameron had never mentioned that Jean had any children.

"That photo next to you, is that your family, Jean? Your husband?"

"Ex-husband."

"And your son? What's his name?"

There was the barest hesitation. "Jason."

Another J name. "He's beautiful."

Jean reached for the photo and turned it facedown on the cabinet. "He's dead."

"I'm so sorry," Kate uttered, shocked by the news and the flat, emotionless tone.

Jean stonily watched Oprah interviewing a group of people sitting in chairs lined up on a stage and did not reply.

She wanted to ask how the boy had died but knew the question would be neither welcomed nor answered. "I'm close to Joe," Kate told her earnestly. "We worked together every day for seven years."

"He mentioned you." It was the most grudging of acknowledgments.

"Jean, believe me, Joe's a friend." She forced a chuckle. "Maybe you'll tell me—he never would explain why your parents named you Jack, Joe and Jean. That must have been a pain for all of you."

"My parents…" A wince passed nakedly over Jean's face. "They gave me a different first name but it was so awful…Look, what the hell do you want here? What do you want with me? Or Joe?"

Kate was still processing the expression of pain at her mention of the parents, but not at the death of her child. "I haven't heard from Joe. I'm worried about him. That's all. Nothing more."

"And you drove all the way to Victorville to tell me this."

Kate spread her hands. "Look. He means a great deal to me. We're *friends*."

"How the hell did you even find me?" She was staring fixedly at Kate; it was not a friendly question nor was it an idle question.

Two could play at the withholding game. "I'm a detective. Like Joe. I care enough about him to drive here from Los Angeles and find you. Isn't that good enough? Why is this such a big deal? Why on earth did that friend of yours slam the door in my face?"

She shrugged. "Yeah, well, that's just Brandon. He's harmless. He thinks he needs to look after me. He probably thought you were a bill collector."

The explanation had been given with such easy casualness in contrast to the clipped and hostile manner of her other responses that Kate knew it was a lie.

"Where is Joe?"

"I don't know."

"Would Jack know?"

"*Jack?*" Jean Velez's body jerked as if she'd received an electrical shock. "Shit no."

"Jack is here in Victorville, right?"

Jean did not answer.

"Where might I find him?"

"You're the detective. You found me. Try the garbage dump. That piece of shit, we have nothing to do with him."

"Why is that?"

"Family business," she spat. "None of yours." She sat back again, arms crossed, and stared at the TV screen. "You've stated your business. Now go. I can't help you."

"Meaning you *won't* help me."

"Meaning I only have your word for who you are and what you say and what you mean to Joe. If he really wanted to see or talk to you, he'd be doing it. So I'm not about to tell you anything."

"Can you tell me if he's all right?"

Jean's mouth twisted down sharply with anger. "Why the hell wouldn't he be all right?"

"He's been gone for days. How he's acting," Kate said doggedly, "it's not like him."

"How the hell he's *acting*—" she made double quotes with two fingers of each hand, "—means nothing to me. I have nothing more to say, we're done. I want you to leave my house."

Jean Velez was not a suspect asking for a lawyer, but for Kate her words held the same force and finality. She got up and walked out of the trailer, closing the door firmly behind her. She thought she glimpsed Dora watching from the corner of a window in her trailer.

She returned to her car and drove out of the complex, air-conditioning at full blast.

She soon pulled over and parked, engine running, to think. There wasn't much to think about; she didn't have many moves left. Driving here had been a bust. She had come up with zero.

Not exactly zero. Jean knew something—of that she was convinced. And Jack, what was the deal about Jack? He was a puzzle wrapped inside a fortress of family reticence, if not secrecy. She was not about to give up on either Jean or Jack.

Looking at her watch, she picked up her cell phone from the console and called the lead number in her preset list, Silverlake Haven. It was not the phone in Maggie's room, which she rarely called, not wanting to chance disrupting any sleep of Maggie or her roommate. Head back against the headrest, eyes closed, she listened to the phone ring six times.

"Silverlake Haven, this is Marla." Her voice sounded breathless.

"Marla, it's Kate Delafield. How is Maggie today?"

"Kate, I'm glad you called. Not good. I did call your house. We had to get the medical team in. She seems to be resting more comfortably now, but she seized up with panic—"

So much for further moves in Victorville. "I'm about two hours away, Marla. I'll be in as soon as I can get there."

"She'll be glad to see you."

Her heart pounding, she folded her phone. Speaking of panic. Breathing hard, trying to fight down her fear, she understood, conceded that she needed help. Of some kind. Any kind.

She pulled Calla Dearborn's card out of her shirt pocket and punched in the numbers. This time she did reach an answering machine.

"It's Kate," she said, feeling calmed just by the low tones of Calla Dearborn on her answering machine message. "Thank you for seeing me yesterday. I'd like to come in again whenever you can see me." She glanced at the dashboard clock. "I'm two hours out of LA and have to be at the hospice for my friend as soon as I get in. I won't answer my phone while I'm driving or while I'm there. Would you leave a message and tell me when you have an opening?"

She left calling details and shut down her phone. Then gunned the Focus toward the 15 and LA.

7

Kate arrived at Silverlake Haven just after three, exchanged grim nods with Marla at the front desk and made her way quickly back to Room 4. Maggie sat propped up, hands moving spasmodically on her chest. A plastic cup covered her nose and mouth, a cylinder of oxygen, larger than the usual one, hulking beside the bed. Focused only on the chest that rapidly rose and fell under Maggie's hands, Kate came directly over to her. Maggie pulled the cup away from her face and reached for Kate. Her eyes were glassy, vulnerable, the pupils huge.

Gripping her hand, leaning over her, Kate said quietly, "You should leave that mask on. How are you feeling?" The area around Maggie's bed smelled acrid, medicinal.

"Better. Better than I was." Her voice was a rasp. She raised a hand that was bandaged across the back. "They ran an IV." She grinned faintly. "Good stuff."

Kate touched her cheek, brushed her forehead. She looked feverish. Her skin felt dry and hot. Kate wanted to cry. She said, "Maybe you should put that oxygen mask back on."

"Maybe I should die. I wish I had a hollow tooth with poison like those old spy movies…I can't stand this, Kate. Are you hearing me?" The expenditure of words cost her; she sucked in breath, then coughed, a heaving, sobbing, choking cough that moved up her body in a wave. She clapped the mask back over her face.

"Miss Police Detective," a voice called from behind her.

"In a minute," Kate snapped in sharp annoyance, staring down at Maggie, gauging whether she should call for help. But after several deep, gasping breaths Maggie seemed to gain control, and she gestured toward Alice, the other hand holding the mask to her face.

Understanding that Maggie wanted a few minutes without her staring, she turned around. She had not noticed Alice when she came in, so intent had she been on getting to Maggie's bed. Wearing a nightgown festooned with smiley yellow faces, Alice was sitting on the side of her bed. A slight young man, the tips of his close-cropped hair bleached blond, stood beside her, holding her hand. He wore a pale yellow banded-collar shirt open at the throat, khaki pants and sandals.

"Guess who this is," Alice crowed. Her skin looked sallow and the flesh of her withered cheeks sagged as she spoke, but her eyes, glistening with tears, were radiant.

"Jonathan Philip Souza, I presume," Kate said, walking toward him and managing to dredge up a smile.

"I can't thank you enough," he said, extending both hands to her. His blue eyes were also liquid with tears, his smoothly shaven cheeks wet. She grasped his hands and he pulled her in for a hug. "This means so much to me."

"Glad I could help," she murmured, thinking that this was the one good thing to happen today.

He released her, only to have Alice reach for her, pull her in and give her a feathery kiss on the cheek. She whispered, "I owe you, Miss Police Detective."

"Please call me Kate. I'm happy it worked out, Alice."

"Our whole family should look into their hearts, what we did was wrong. It was cruel and awful. Jon's managed to find it in himself to forgive me. After all these years." Her voice was quavering and Jon swiped the back of a hand across his eyes.

Dylan, she thought, this was like Dylan having only her for family. He knew that somewhere inside themselves his mother and his father loved him too, but they loved their image of a different person and the only acceptance of the real him came from Kate. And Aimee too of course…

"Can I buy you a drink sometime?" Jon asked Kate.

"Why don't we do that," Kate said, smiling at him.

"I've got your number from your phone message. I'll call you."

Again Alice bussed her cheek, then shooed her toward Maggie. "She's had a bad day," she whispered. "And just remember, Miss Police Detective, I owe you."

Kate went back and sat with Maggie. While Alice and her great-nephew chattered nonstop in the background, Kate, not wanting Maggie to have to talk and confident that she would not be overheard, related the events of the past two days, about Joe Cameron and Walcott's visit and everything else leading up to her own visit to Victorville. Maggie listened raptly, eyes fixed on Kate, her breathing easier under the mask. She even chuckled when Kate described Jean Velez's confrontation with "Dora you bitch," the woman in the trailer who blew the whistle on Jean. She pulled away her mask to tell Kate, "Talk to this Dora. Bitch neighbors know things."

Kate nodded. "I plan to." She would have already, had her call to Marla not drawn her immediately back here.

"Tomorrow," Maggie slurred, eyelids drooping. "You'll go tomorrow?"

"Yes, but I'll be back here with you as soon as I can. I have some other ideas too."

Kate kissed her on the forehead and made her way to the door, tossing a wave at Alice and Jonathan Philip Souza.

In the hallway she thought to power up her cell phone. There was a single message: "Kate, it's Calla. Ring me as soon as you get this message."

But Kate instead stopped at Room 3.

Spotting her in the doorway, Ida Appleby clicked off the television, propped herself up on an elbow and called over to her roommate, "Guess who's here. Kate the agnostic. Come to try and convert us again."

Kate laughed, and marveled at how good it felt. A few minutes with Ida might be something positive, along with Souza, that she could accomplish today. "Are you up for a brief visit?"

"Are we ever. We've got more questions. Come in, sit down. We've been talking all about you and we want to know, are you anything like that Brenda Leigh Johnson on *The Closer* when you interview your murderers?"

Kate laughed again. "I'm even better," she joked, walking into the room and pulling up a chair between the two beds.

* * *

Half an hour later, sitting in her car, she returned Calla Dearborn's call.

Dearborn picked up on the first ring. "How is your friend?" she asked.

The visit with Ida and Mary had so shored up her spirits that the question from Dearborn was like a bullet from an assassin. Kate found herself suddenly and utterly unable to answer. She gasped, swallowed, swallowed again. "Sorry," she finally managed to whisper. "It's been a long bad day."

"Is your friend still with us?"

"Yeah. She is."

"And you're there now? At the hospice?"

"Outside, in my car," Kate said with difficulty. "She's asleep, she seems okay again."

"Come here now. Right now. I'll be waiting in my office." And she clicked off.

* * *

Again Kate parked in front of Dearborn's house. As she made her way along the side of the property to the cottage/office in the rear she peered at the front windows of the house, wondering whether the "we" who had bought this house was Dearborn and a husband, or Dearborn and a partner, and if there were children, pets. Wondering about Dearborn's friends, what they might be like, whether Dearborn and Carolina Walcott might be more than "professional" acquaintances. In their previous interactions Dearborn had deflected Kate's probes, telling her that their time together was for Kate. So presumably, probably, she would never learn much of anything. Beyond what was printed on the business card in her shirt pocket, this woman who felt suddenly, urgently, indispensably important to her, was a blank.

Closed miniblinds on the windows of the cottage concealed its interior and deflected the citrus rays of late afternoon sun. Kate rapped gently on the door. Calla Dearborn promptly opened it. She nodded gravely at Kate.

"Welcome. Excuse my appearance, I've been out here all day writing." She wore a black long-sleeve jersey T-shirt and white drawstring cotton pants.

"I'm grateful you can see me, I wouldn't care if you were—" *Naked*, she was about to say, and amended it to "—wearing a bathing suit." The cottage, darkened by the blinds but illuminated by a few track lights, was redolent with the smell of coffee. She sank gratefully into an armchair, the rich aroma, the walls of the cottage, the enclosing sides of the chair somehow feeling like a refuge from the day's fundamental frustrations and disappointments.

Dearborn went over to a sideboard holding a tray with a carafe and several coffee mugs. "I figured you could use some coffee."

"What I could really use is a drink," Kate confessed.

"I know you could," Dearborn replied gently, pouring coffee into a mug. "But I wouldn't offer you that if I could. It's called enabling."

"Yeah, I'm familiar with the term," Kate muttered.

"Rehab? AA?"

"Both."

"This'll help. Drink up. There's plenty more." Dearborn handed her the steaming mug and sat down across from her. She did not bring any coffee for herself.

Dearborn leaned toward Kate, dark eyes fixed on her, her hair an illuminated gray halo in the cottage's track lights. "We were interrupted last time while you were telling me something really important. About your dreams. And I want to go back to that. But first, will you tell me about your friend in hospice? How long have you known her?"

"Twenty-three years." Kate gulped down coffee, heedless of its heat, before she could continue. "Her name is Maggie Schaeffer. We met during a murder investigation. It was particularly horrific—a nineteen-year-old lesbian named Dory Quillin, killed with a baseball bat."

Dearborn sighed, shook her head.

Kate added, "It happened in the parking lot of the bar Maggie owned. The Nightwood Bar."

"She named her bar after the Djuna Barnes novel?"

Kate nodded, impressed that she knew. "Actually, Maggie dumped the book after only a page or two. But she thought the title made a good name for a lesbian bar. Especially in the eighties."

"Definitely atmospheric," Dearborn commented, "and somehow sadly appropriate for so tragic a murder. Did you get the killer?"

"Yes," said Kate, not wanting to elaborate. Not now.

"Tell me about Maggie. Why does she mean so much to you?"

Gathering her thoughts, Kate finally answered, "She's always, always, been there for me. But she's never let me hide anywhere. She's always told me the truth no matter what. The blunt, unfiltered truth."

"From what I'm hearing, some of that truth was hard to hear."

"In retrospect," said Kate ruefully, "not just some of it, all of it."

"What was the hardest truth for you?"

Kate shifted in her chair, gripping the arms, its cradling sides no longer feeling like a refuge. She sighed. "This is going to be the same drill as before, isn't it, Calla. You asking me questions I don't want to answer."

Dearborn said easily, "That's how it works, Kate. I do the torturing, you do the suffering."

Kate managed a grin, picked up her coffee and took a couple of sips. "The hardest truth Maggie told me? I can at least tell you why that one's so hard to answer. It's because I've done so goddamn many stupid things it's hard to pick one out. To this very day I can't imagine why she was ever my friend, much less such a loyal friend every day of these last twenty-three years."

"Without doubt she thought you were worth it. And you are." Dearborn picked up her malachite pen and made a brief note on her pad, put the pen down again. "What kind of stupid things did you do, Kate?" Her dimple appeared with her smile. "Pick out a few from all the thousands."

"I can tell you the great big ones. Aimee. Booze. The job. Booze. Being out. Booze. They're all related, I can actually see that now. Maggie could always see it, clear as the sun. Me?" She shrugged. "It's like…it's like if I were a car, I'd be a car equipped with only a rearview mirror."

Dearborn smiled again. "That's actually remarkable insight, coming from a rearview mirror."

Kate shrugged and finished her coffee. "Hit somebody with a crowbar enough times, insight may eventually penetrate about where the pain might be coming from."

"My, aren't we being hard on ourselves. Get yourself more coffee," Dearborn said. "And bring me some too."

Kate obeyed, and when she was settled back in, Dearborn asked, "What's her diagnosis, Kate?"

"Lung cancer. Advanced. She has a few weeks, at most."

Dearborn put down her coffee mug with a thump. "Oh, dear God, how awful. That's just the worst…" She did not finish.

Kate said thickly, looking down, "She's asked me…she wants me to help her die."

Receiving silence in reply she looked up. To her shock, Dearborn's eyes were glittering with tears that now spilled over. Her own throat closed up and it was as if Dearborn's unguarded emotion broke through a dam in herself. She lost control, knew there was no way she could control anything any longer. "I'm going to cry," she gasped.

"Permission granted," Dearborn snuffled. She plucked a couple of tissues out of the box on the small table beside her and took off her glasses and dabbed at her own eyes before passing the box over to Kate.

Sometime later Dearborn blotted her tears, put on her glasses and said, "I'm so sorry, Kate." She asked, "How are you dealing with this? With what she wants?"

"I'm not. I want to help her. I just can't." Kate bent over again in her chair, her body heaving with her emotion.

"Of course you can't."

"It's crazy. It's totally fucked up. I carried a gun for years and years, I had a license to kill—" She jabbed at her eyes with her tissues. "My best friend, she can hardly breathe, she wants to die, she's begging me to help her and I owe her and I can't—I just *can't*."

"You don't owe her this, and of course you can't do it, Kate." Dearborn's voice had firmed. "You shouldn't and you can't and she shouldn't be asking you."

Kate's head jerked up. "Who else would she ask?"

"No one. No one should ever ask anyone to kill anyone, including themselves."

"You're blaming *her*? If she were *your* closest—"

"I'm not blaming her," Dearborn said heatedly, flinging her tissues aside, her hands flattening on her thighs. "This is not her fault. This is not your fault. It's the fault of terrible laws that give us no access to humane assisted suicide, almost no agency over our own death."

"It's wrong, it's wrong…"

"Of course it's wrong, it couldn't be more wrong. Tell me, Kate, and this is another difficult question I know—what is it you fear most about losing her?"

"Everything." Kate sat up, clasped her hot wet face between her hands and uttered, "Her strength…counsel…humor… wisdom…sanity…everything. She's always *always* been there, she's…my North Star."

"Is there anyone else in your life who gives you any of those things?"

"I suppose…Aimee mostly. Although she's not exactly in my life."

"Your partner, yes? For how long now?"

"It would have been nineteen years in February. We've been off and on for about the last five years."

"Off and on…" Dearborn contemplated her, waiting.

"On when I wasn't drinking," Kate admitted. "Off when I was."

"And it's been off again since…"

"Going on five months."

"Is that the longest stretch?"

"By far."

"And what happened five months ago?"

"Maggie's diagnosis. And," she added reluctantly, "I had to give up my badge. My career." *My life.*

Dearborn wrote on her pad. She looked up at Kate, forklike lines between her vestiges of eyebrows. "Either one of those— Maggie or your career—would have been exceedingly hard. Much less both. Where is Aimee now?"

"She rents the guest house of a friend of hers in West LA."

Dearborn nodded. "And how is she doing with all of this?"

"I'm not sure." Kate sighed. "Better than me, I'm sure. She visits Maggie a lot—Maggie always tells me when she's been in. Maggie's been a great friend to us both. Beyond that, I don't know what Aimee's been doing these past months and I don't ask."

"Because?"

"To tell you the truth—"

"The truth is always what I want in this room."

"—I don't want to know," Kate finished, annoyed by the scolding.

"You're afraid to find out?" Dearborn suggested.

"You could say that," Kate admitted. "You could definitely say that." She sagged in her chair, feeling exhausted from all her spent emotion. "Look, it's been a long, bad day."

Dearborn was regarding her closely. "You do look really beat. You had a long drive today from what I gather."

"Four hours, actually. I have to go back to Victorville tomorrow."

"What's in Victorville?"

"Another problem." Kate tried to come up with a short version but gave it up. "It's a long story," she offered lamely.

Dearborn nodded. "I'm good at long stories. But later, for that. We need to go back to your dreams because those are very, very important. But we should stop here, Kate, I don't intend to push you."

Again Dearborn leaned toward her. "You need to be seeing me often. For a while. How does at least once a week sound—more if possible?"

Cringing, Kate looked at the floor. "This is hard, Calla. Really hard for me."

"I know. But you do need to be here."

"I get that."

"Let's say twice a week, for the time being."

"I guess…I'm sure that would actually be good." She looked up at her, into her calm, kind face. "Thank you, Calla."

"One other thing. It's my opinion that you need some additional help besides talking to me to get you through this—"

"Meaning pills."

"Yes. You show every indication of severe stress and anxiety. For now you should be taking an antidepressant."

Kate shook her head. "I really don't want to be taking any stuff like that."

"You're already taking 'stuff like that.' You've been self-medicating for years, Kate."

She felt as if she were five years old. This was the kind of humiliation she hadn't experienced since she was a child. She managed a shrug. "It's the kind of medication and dosage I know," she muttered.

"And how has that worked out for you?"

Kate looked at her wryly. "However badly it works, it works. It's the devil I know."

"Devil is the right word for it. Alcohol is a depressant. It makes things infinitely worse."

How could they be any worse? "Yeah, well…I remember one time I warned a friend of Aimee's about how often he was going to tanning parlors. And he told me, 'I know I'll get skin cancer. But not today.' Having a drink really helps me today."

"If you've been to rehab and AA you don't need me to tell you what a load of crap that is, what a complete rationalization."

The dismissive words had been spoken while she wasn't looking at Kate; she had gotten up and was rummaging in a desk drawer.

Feeling even more humiliated, Kate sank back into her chair and didn't answer.

Finally Dearborn produced a card and a form, placed them on the table beside Kate. "Therapists can't prescribe medication as you probably know. This is the psychiatrist I work with. I'll call her tomorrow and explain the situation, and my recommendation. She'll want to see you, of course, and you'll want to answer all the questions on this form before you get there. It's up to you whether you do this, but I very strongly advise you to do it."

Kate looked at the card, did not pick it up.

"Listen to me, Kate," Dearborn said. "Everybody on this earth needs major help from time to time. Including you. And there's no shame in it. One of the most frustrating problems I remember from before—and it wasn't just you, it was virtually every police officer I worked with—was that all of you needed help because of the job and none of you sought it because you've all been trained to be tough guys and to think—to believe—you shouldn't need to."

Kate thought of Joe Cameron. This partner of seven years—and, she had thought, a close friend—had excluded her from whatever situation he was in, had not asked for help he might really need, had not trusted her…"That's very true," she conceded. She picked up the card and the form.

"Good," Dearborn said. She opened the desk drawer again, pulled out some forms of her own. "I've got a bit of paperwork for you to do, nothing onerous. You happened to pick a good time, in my life at least, because I'm able to see you pretty much when you can work it in with everything else that's going on in your own life right now."

Kate said, without a trace of irony, "I consider myself lucky, Calla."

8

The next morning, after consuming several slices of toast and imbibing doses of Tylenol and caffeine out on her deck for her aching, hung-over head, after immersing herself in the process of watching misty fog lifting itself from the street and the trees as well as her own mind and body, Kate felt enough in command of herself to check in by phone to the hospice.

"Maggie had a reasonably good night," Marla told her. "The doctor will be in around eleven." She added quietly, "She seems comfortable, Kate. We're doing our best to keep her that way."

"I know. I'm grateful," Kate said. She provided Marla with her cell phone number for any critical updates.

She then called Walcott. "I'm sorry I didn't check in yesterday, I had to leave Victorville to get back to the hospice and the day just—"

"Don't apologize, Kate," Walcott interrupted. "I know you have a lot going on. How is your friend?"

Kate sifted through several possible responses and settled on Marla's latest report. "She seems to be comfortable."

"I guess that's the best we can wish for," Walcott offered.

"Yes. Thank you, Captain," Kate said, touched by the "we." She proceeded to summarize her reception in Victorville—the door-slamming friend of Joe's sister, Dora-the-bitch in the next-door trailer—and the paucity of information gleaned from the brief, hostile interview with Jean Velez.

"That desert sun must bake people's brains," Walcott remarked. "What do you make of it?"

"Pretty much the same as you do."

"So, bottom line, we've yet to make an inch of progress in finding Joe."

"That'll happen today," Kate said. Knowing Walcott would see through her confident statement as the bluff it was, she continued, "My plan is to be on my way back to Victorville as soon as we finish this call, and work a few other angles."

"Fine. But we haven't much leeway," Walcott warned, her tone low and somber. "The palm print hit we got on the Carter case, the fact he's on ice in the prison system is fortunate, Kate, but in good conscience we owe it to the Carter family to let them know we may have found Tamara's killer."

"I know that, Captain. I agree. I hear you."

"Speaking of prison," Walcott said, amid a crackling of either static or a scattering of papers, "let me run this mysterious brother of Joe's through the prison system, see if there might be an incarcerated Jack Cameron from Victorville. That'll either eliminate the possibility or explain him."

"Good idea. I'll be in touch," Kate promised.

"Likewise," Walcott said, and clicked off.

Kate made one additional phone call—to the Dr. Sherman listed on the card Dearborn had given her. Then she gave Miss Marple fresh food, a final few pats, and went down to the garage to her car.

* * *

Occupied by circular thoughts about Cameron, about Maggie, about Aimee and Dylan and Calla Dearborn, Kate drove though the LA basin and into high desert country with the landscape flying by unseen until she reached the outskirts of Victorville. The day was again bright and hot, which she supposed most days here would be from now until late fall. At just after eleven in the morning the temperature was eighty-nine degrees. She made her way back to Golden Sunset Trailer Park.

Dry palm fronds fluttered and clattered in gusty breezes over the trailer belonging to Jean Velez. Neither the Toyota Corolla nor the Ford F-150 was parked outside the trailer or anywhere along the street. But Jean's trailer was not the immediate focal point of her attention today.

In contrast to Jean's haphazard cactus landscaping, the front yard of Dora's next-door trailer had Zen-like circular patterns of sparkling white rock with a few rows of prickly pear and other species of cactus interspersed. Kate walked along a narrow concrete pathway lined with a half dozen knee-high pink plastic flamingoes, up the four steps of the small porch, and rapped on the flimsy screen door. The door was opened immediately.

The constant desert sun and Dora's deep tan seemed to have inflicted minimal skin damage on her face, but from the wrinkles imbedded in her neck and throat Kate gauged her to be in her sixties. The pink rollers of yesterday had given way to wings of bouffant platinum hair, and today's outfit was knee-length yellow shorts with a stripe of yellow sequins down the sides and a leopard print scoop-neck top stretching over ample breasts. Arms crossed, she surveyed Kate, her bright blue eyes glinting with curiosity.

"Dora," Kate said, smiling at her. "That's your name, right?"

She grinned. "How did you guess?" She gestured to the other trailer, ivory bracelets clattering on her wrist. "Jean's gone," she said succinctly. "The both of them," she added. The nails on her gesturing hand were painted yellow and red and looked like flames were coming out of her fingers.

"Gone," Kate repeated.

"Yeah, like, with suitcases and lots of other crap."

Kate shook her head. This was as inexplicable as any of the rest of Jean Velez's previous behavior. "My name is Kate. Kate Delafield. Would it trouble you if I came in and asked a few questions?"

"Come on in. You might brace yourself first." The flame-tipped fingers rose again, this time beckoning welcome.

Kate entered, expecting, from Dora's warning, considerable clutter. She stood rooted in thick shag carpet, blinking in amazement. The carpet was white and black zebra stripes, the wallpaper a leopard skin pattern that included the ceiling. The same carpet and wallpaper extended throughout the trailer including the kitchen and its floor. In the living room a gold sofa and love seat were decorated with pillows embroidered with animal images or shaped like lion and tiger heads, Scottie dogs and Persian cats. A TV on a cabinet was partly obscured by various sizes of bird, animal and reptile glass sculptures. Accent tables and a coffee table were also festooned with figurines that ran the gamut, Kate was certain, of every creature that sought refuge on the Ark. A bookcase held not books but ceramic animal and bird statuary crowding all its shelves. Next to the picture window, spread before a faux fireplace in a corner of the living room, was a pure white bearskin rug on top of the zebra carpet. Small fabric-covered giraffes stood in gangly formation along the hearth.

Kate had been in many strange homes throughout her police career; this one ranked with the strangest. An image flitted through her mind of an art exhibit she and Aimee had wandered into years ago in New York: this could be the animal kingdom as envisioned by Picasso. The trailer's fantastical interior was so out of place in this prosaic desert town it was as if some conveyance had accidentally deposited Dora and her trailer here instead of in outlandish Las Vegas where eccentricity like hers was the norm.

For lack of any other response, she stated the obvious: "You really love animals."

Dora had been watching her, arms crossed, grinning. "How did you guess?" she repeated in what was apparently a standard phrase. "What can I get you to drink? I've got everything."

Kate suspected she did, imagining liqueurs she'd never even heard of. "Nothing, Dora, I'm fine."

"Of course you're not. This is the desert. Don't you know you need to stay hydrated? I'll get us some water."

Dora padded toward the kitchen, waves of flowery scent wafting behind her. Kate could hear the whirr of an air conditioner somewhere in back, but the place was warmish and smelled cloyingly of perfume and hairspray. Although brilliant light flooded through the picture window and the windows on the sides of the trailer, Kate felt as enclosed by the animal skin floor and walls and ceiling as if she were in a submarine. Faintly repelled, she walked to the leopard wallpaper, shoes sinking deeply into the carpet, and focused on a large grouping of photos occupying much of the wall. They showed Dora with a variety of men clad in a range of attire—from bathing trunks and Hawaiian shirts, shorts and safari shirts, to formal suits—against different backgrounds at various times in Dora's life, at parties and formal events, quite a number of the photos appearing to have been taken in Africa. In all of them, Dora, with her bouffant white-gold hair, her busty chest, wore her splashy dresses like the plumage of a flamboyant bird. She had been, Kate decided, quite a looker in her younger years.

Dora returned bearing ice water in two huge tankards shaped like elephants, their trunks forming the handle, and plunked them down on the coffee table, bracelets jangling, not bothering with coasters. As she bent down her brackets of hair did not move at all. "My rogues' gallery," she said to Kate, nodding toward the photos. "I've had plenty of fun in my time."

I'll bet you have, Kate thought, making a place for herself amid the animal pillows on the sofa.

Dora settled herself on the love seat and pointed to several of the photos. "I've survived three husbands. And all the boyfriends in between. Now I live exactly the way I want." She swept an arm in a circle. "With my friends all around me."

"Good for you, Dora, I'm glad for you," Kate said, content to establish some rapport.

"Animals—the best creatures on earth. Absolutely dependable, you know exactly what you get. A lion, depend on it, it wants to kill and eat you. A vulture, it'll pick at what's left on your bones. A dog, you feed it, it's gonna love you to death. Cats…" She shrugged. "Cats, whoever knows about cats, so I guess they deep-six the whole theory."

Chuckling, Kate said, "I have one, I know exactly what you mean." She picked up her elephant glass, took a sip. The icy cold water was refreshing, head-clearing.

"This place," Dora said, suddenly serious. "My animal friends all around me all day, all night, they bring me peace."

Peace. Kate envied her. When was the last time she'd felt any peace? She said, "Very different from the kingdom of humans. You seem to have a pretty bad relationship with Jean next door."

Dora's solemnity dissolved in a harsh, cackling laugh. "How did you guess? 'Bitch' is the least of the things she calls me."

"You say she's gone. When was this?"

"Yesterday. Right after you left. What the hell did you say to her?"

"Nothing." Kate held up a hand. "I swear. Nothing I know of to cause what you're telling me."

"Well, you'd think you threatened to kill her the way Brandon came busting down the street a million miles an hour and piled out of that truck like he had bees up his pants." One fiery fingernail pointed out the picture window.

Confounded by what she was hearing, Kate could see that Dora had a perfect view of the street and a partial view of the front of the trailer next door.

"Jean must've called him on his cell phone. Soon as he got in the door I could hear them going at each other, him yelling he had other stuff to take care of besides her and her screaming how dumb it was for him to go right after you were here the first time with a mouthy bitch like me next door and he'd left her alone to deal with this mess."

"This mess?"

"Mess. That's what she said." Dora cackled again. "Are you a mess? Did you know you're a mess?"

Kate grinned. "Jean Velez has no idea how big a mess I actually am. How long have you two been neighbors?"

Dora lifted both feet simultaneously and propped her jeweled sandals on the blond coffee table, stretching her arms out along the back of the love seat. "Since she came back from Phoenix. At least two years ago." She languidly raised one hand from the sofa back and aimed a finger toward the neighboring trailer. "She's a renter. Been driving that car on those Arizona plates this whole time. Some people..." She sniffed disapproval.

"What do you know about her, Dora?"

Dora held her relaxed posture on the sofa and said easily, "I guess I should first maybe ask why you want to know. And what you came here for yesterday."

Suspecting Dora would tell everything she knew regardless of any motive she gave her, Kate reflected yet again that only the willingness of people to talk made any success in police work possible. Not that this was actually police work—if it were she'd be asking the questions and providing precious few answers to any that were asked of her.

"I'm a close friend of her brother Joe," she told Dora. "I'm looking for him. That's it. That all I came here for, that's all I asked her, I promise you."

Dora shrugged and muttered, "Then none of this makes much sense."

"Have you seen Joe around?"

"Not in a while. Not for ages."

At least she knew him. "Would you happen to remember when that was?"

"Yeah. Because it was odd." Dora pulled her arms from the back of the sofa, removed her feet from the coffee table. She sat forward and picked up her elephantine container of water and sipped from it. "It was a coolish day here. He was wearing a khaki jacket. I'm thinking maybe February."

Kate nodded. She knew the jacket. Dora was an ideal witness, nosy and highly observant. "Did he stay long? I mean, like, the day, the weekend?"

"Actually he didn't. Maybe an hour. It was strange, like I said." Dora's eyes narrowed as she extracted more memory of that day. "I remember thinking he'd driven here through all that LA traffic and why would he do that for just an hour? Maybe he had someplace else to go but the way he looked, I don't think so. He looked grim as death going into Jean's place, his shoulders all hunched over like someone might fly down from the sky and hit him, and when he came out Jean was with him and they hugged and patted each other like one of them was going to the moon for a year."

Prickling with apprehension, Kate used this information to total a few thoughts into a hypothesis. He had driven here to deliver news he couldn't or wouldn't say over the phone. She asked, "Would you tell me what happened to bring on the bad feeling between you and Jean?"

"Noise," Dora retorted. "Just noise. But noise, noise, noise till I couldn't take it anymore." She flicked a hand, bracelets clacking, toward the adjacent trailer. "The place was way too small for all those people."

"What people? Besides the two of them?"

"It was *supposed* to be just the two of them, that's the thing. Bad enough with him carrying on like he does and the television and his video games, but then that bozo boyfriend Brandon was there, and it got so much worse I couldn't sleep nights. They wouldn't pay attention to one thing I said so I called Mack who owns the trailer, to have him talk to her. Mack and I go way back," she said meaningfully. "And when Mack came over and yelled it was supposed to be just the two of them in the trailer, that's when she went bonkers and I've been Dora the bitch ever since."

Kate just nodded while she tried to sort through the welter of information. In a park like this with people living in close quarters, friction if not open belligerence was inevitable. It happened all the time in her own condo building, squabbling over everything from parking to parties to hogging the common areas. She ignored it all; she couldn't be bothered, she would not be drawn into the building's quarrels. "The noise, Dora—was it fights too? Parties?"

"No," Dora said emphatically, "no parties. Fights, I really don't have a problem with fights if it's just yelling and no hitting. Everybody fights sometimes. I had enough of them myself with some of the losers I married. Mostly it was that kid."

"What kid?"

Dora frowned and looked at Kate with a first glimmer of suspicion. "*Her* kid. You *sure* you're a friend of Joe's?"

Even more confused, Kate managed a smile. "Very sure, Dora. He was my partner for seven years. I could show you a shoebox full of photos of the two of us."

"Then how come you don't know his sister has a kid?"

Has a kid. Kate looked away to conceal her surprise. So that explained Jean's odd lack of emotion when she said her son was dead. Everybody lied, everybody—she'd learned that reality probably her first day as a sworn police officer—but why had Jean laid claim to something so bizarre as a dead child? What the hell was going on with this family?

Kate answered Dora honestly, "We were close, but Joe always seemed reluctant to talk about his family, about his years in Victorville. Whenever I asked him anything, it was like he didn't want to remember. So I don't know much about his family or anything to do with here."

"Guess I can understand that," Dora said with a dark glare toward the adjacent trailer. "His sister calls me a bitch, she could give lessons in being a bitch."

Kate asked cautiously, carefully phrasing her question, "What can you tell me about her...kid?"

Dora nodded, her eyes softening. "A good boy. I like Jason in spite of everything. He's a beautiful kid. Hardly ever see a smile on him but when he does it about breaks your heart. I blame his father. It's the father's sperm that makes a mess of the genes, you know." She took a drink of water.

Kate reached for her own tankard, wondering what whacko radio show Dora might have picked up that particular belief from. "How old is he? she asked, wondering why Cameron had never ever mentioned this apparently mentally challenged son of his sister's.

"Hard to say, a boy like him. Maybe nine, ten? You see what happens," Dora went on earnestly, "you get a kid like Jason from the father. Autistic, you know. Maybe it's his daddy's genes, but how he behaves, that's the mother. And he's bright enough, you can't tell me she couldn't have better control over him, you can't tell me he doesn't know better than to scream and yell and play his video games loud enough to drown out the voice of God."

"He wasn't there yesterday."

"No, of course not. He's gone."

"Gone? Gone where?"

"Dunno." Dora shrugged and waved a hand. "Jean's not about to tell me." She added, "I could kill the bitch. I like that boy."

"When was this? The last time you saw Jason?"

Dora sat back and thought for some moments. "Two, maybe three weeks ago."

Around the time Cameron was organizing his disappearing act. "Did someone pick him up, take him?"

Even the vigorous shake of Dora's head did not budge her platinum bouffant. "Last I knew, he was climbing into that truck of Brandon's. Brandon came back that night by himself."

"So he dropped him off somewhere."

"Had to be." Again she shrugged. "Maybe with his father. Whoever that might be. I went over there and told Jean I hoped she didn't send him away on my account. I never meant for that to happen, I just wanted the kid to behave and all of them to be less noisy. She told me to go do you-know-what to myself and slammed the door in my face."

Kate smothered a smile. "Dora, have you ever seen Jack Cameron?"

"Who's that?"

"Another brother."

"No kidding. Where does this one live?"

"I'm not sure," Kate said. "But I thought here."

"I guess if I did see him, I wouldn't know it."

"Maybe not."

"They sure as hell are one funny family."

She couldn't argue with that. "Dora, you said when they left they had other stuff besides suitcases. What do you mean?"

"It looked like they packed up clothes and took things out of the kitchen, food and some plates and pots and stuff. Wherever they're going, they're gonna be awhile."

Kate shook her head. Still, this new development hardly mattered when Jean had made it more than clear she was not a source for further information. "Dora, did you know Joe is a police officer?"

"Well, sure. And that makes you one too, right? You being his partner?"

Deciding not to correct her, she said, "He started here. Years ago he was a cop here in town."

"I knew that too. Jean told me all that before we got on the outs with each other."

Kate asked, with very little expectation, "Joe has a friend here from his days as a cop. A guy named Dutch."

"Dutch Hollander. I know Dutch. He does all kinds of stuff for animal rights, I see him at our meetings. He's about as Dutch as I am. It's a nickname because of his last name."

Kate was elated. *Let's hear it for small worlds and animal rights and animal lovers.* She had already planned an approach to the Victorville Police Department but now that she had Dutch's last name, it would be much, much easier. She pulled a notebook out of her pocket and wrote the name down. Turned to another page and wrote out her contact details, tore the page out and placed it on the coffee table. "If you see anything, hear anything, if Jean or any of her family come back, would you be willing to call me right away?"

"Sure." Dora looked at her in grave concern. "All this peculiar behavior, something bad's going on over there, that right?"

"I don't know yet. I hope not. I'm trying to find out. One last question, Dora. As much as you love animals, how come you don't have pets yourself? I hear dogs barking all around the place."

Dora sighed deeply. "One good reason. I always adopted old dogs—them's the ones that need it, everybody else wants puppies or kittens. Those older ones, that short life span they have, I've mourned so many of my little friends. That on top of so much in my life I've lost, I've had too much loss, Kate, I can't do it anymore."

When Kate didn't answer, Dora peered at her and then said softly, "Hit you where you live, did I?"

"You did," Kate managed through a thick throat. *What the hell is wrong with me?* She was losing emotional control even in public.

She got up. "Dora, thanks for your time, for talking to me."

"Anytime." Dora also got up. "Gimme a piece of that paper, I'll give you my phone number, you call too if you need anything."

She went to the TV cabinet, pushed a few sculptures aside and scribbled quickly. Kate hoped she'd included her last name.

Dora handed her the paper, touched Kate's hand with her fire-tipped nails. Then threw her arms around her and hugged her. "You come back anytime. I like people with good hearts."

9

Sitting in her car, the air conditioner fan at full blast against the stifling interior, Kate called the Victorville Sheriff's Station. She'd already noted on her city map the location on Amargosa Road and the phone number. The phone rang once.

"Police department."

She adopted her most official, most authoritative tone. "Detective Kate Delafield, LAPD, for Deputy Hollander. My badge number..." She closed her eyes, gritted her teeth and recited the number.

"He's on patrol," said the crisp but courteous female voice. "I'll patch you through, Detective."

Moments later, amid crackling, she heard a resonant baritone announce, "Hollander."

She sagged in relief. "This is Kate Delafield, a friend and former partner of Joe Cameron's. I met you—"

"At Joe's house. Yeah, sure, I remember you. Joe's always talking about you. What can I do for you?"

"I wonder if we could meet. Today. I'm in town. Near the station."

"What's this about?" The tone was friendly, cautious.

"I'd rather discuss it when we meet."

"Business? Personal?"

"I'd rather discuss it when we meet."

"Okay, I hear you." His tone had changed, had picked up concern. "Is it urgent? Can it wait till I break for lunch at one thirty?"

"It can."

"How about we meet at Rusty's Café? It's right next to the station."

"I'll be there."

"If you get there before I do, tell them Dutch asks that you be seated at the rear of the place where we can best talk."

"I appreciate this, Dutch."

"No worries, Kate. Gotta eat. See you there."

* * *

Kate cruised slowly past the station. Under the jurisdiction of the San Bernardino County Sheriff's Department, its operations were housed in a modest, rectangular, newer one-story yellowish beige stucco building situated on a street corner across from an Avis car rental. Large generic block lettering along the roofline across the narrower side of the rectangle facing onto Amargosa Road announced POLICE DEPARTMENT, and repeated on the longer side fronting a short side street. White police vehicles, their sides emblazoned with gold police insignia, were parked in a gated lot behind the station; only civilian cars were visible along Amargosa and the intersecting street.

She gazed at the building and its apparent lack of security with a twinge of nostalgia. In this era of bomb threats and access by virtually anyone to every kind of weapon—thanks, she believed, in full measure to the gutless politicians who went along with the witless, inflexible belief in the right to bear arms of any lethality—all big city police stations had enhanced security systems these days; none were immune from potential catastrophe. But trust still existed in small town America, places like this one.

Rusty's Café fronted the street on Amargosa, in a U-shaped sand-colored mall with two stripes of dark green and reddish brown running along the low roofline of all the small businesses within. Under the Rusty's Café sign was the slogan, "Where Good Friends Meet." It was across an alley and, as advertised by Dutch Hollander, right next to the station.

Already liking the feel of the place, she pulled into the ample parking lot. She was a half hour early and on her way in she stopped at a newspaper vending machine, dropped in some coins and took out the *Victorville Daily Press*.

As she pushed open the door she looked at the place with some dismay. It was smaller than she'd imagined, with perhaps fifteen tables and no booths. Most of the tables were full.

"Deputy Dutch Hollander told me to ask that you seat me in the rear where it's quiet," she told an attractive waitress in her fifties. "He'll be here at one thirty."

She looked Kate up and down as if gauging her as a rival, then shrugged as if dismissing the notion. She grinned and grabbed two menus. "Follow me."

Kate sat down at a rear table for two near the restrooms, which were around the corner of the long narrow room and cordoned off by a low barrier. The table was beside a window looking out on the driveway separating the café from the police station. She put her menu aside, ordered coffee, and glanced around. The place appeared to have been here for many decades. The tables were woodgrain blond Formica, the chairs with chrome frames and leatherette seats and backs, the windows covered by venetian blinds. All available wall space was covered by long black frames holding photographs of happy looking customers. Families, not a celebrity in the bunch, she was sure. The rise and fall of conversation, a soundtrack that was currently playing "Who'll Stop the Rain" eased her concern about having a private conversation in this place. Anyway, she had no choice. His turf, his terms.

While she mulled over what and how much she would say to Dutch Hollander, she glanced idly through the paper, the headlines over articles on the presidential primary featuring clashes between Hillary Clinton and Barack Obama, reports of truck rollovers causing traffic headaches on the I-15, reports of residential burglaries, civic happenings. She turned to the classifieds and marveled at the low cost of real estate compared to Los Angeles.

Dutch Hollander came in promptly at one thirty, unmistakable in his sharply pressed tan deputy sheriff's uniform. Kate waved at the same time the waitress turned and pointed to her. Kate got up and waited to shake hands with him.

He grinned at her as he slid into his seat, adjusting his gun belt. She only vaguely remembered meeting him at Joe's house, and as he settled himself on the small chair she examined him with keen interest. A handsome man, mid-forties, tall and rangy, square-jawed, with a lean bronzed face adorned by a tidy mustache, he wore his prematurely graying hair close-cropped. His uniform shirt, open at the throat over a spotless white T-shirt, was fitted closely over his pecs. His badge was perfectly placed over his heart, the top point on the badge at the same height as the patch on his left sleeve, his nameplate at the exact same level on the adjacent side of the shirt. He was hatless, had apparently left it in his patrol car. She had always found deputy sheriff hats with their indented high crowns faintly ridiculous—they seemed like scoutmaster hats, and she would have felt ridiculous wearing one of them. Most LAPD patrol cops, though, would envy the weather-friendly color of Hollander's police uniform compared to their own heat absorbing dark blue. Not her. She would never have traded her uniform, back when she wore one every day, for Hollander's. In her view LAPD officers, the thinnest of thin blue lines protecting a vast and chaotically diverse city, looked imposing, intimidating, and best of all, starkly authoritative in their dark uniforms, their flat, visored hats, their Sam Browne belts bristling with weaponry.

"Thank you for seeing me," she began.

He too had been surveying her, searching her face. "Retirement looks pretty good on you. Lost weight, maybe?"

"Maybe," she said and let it go.

He grabbed the menu—Kate noted he was left-handed, like Joe, and wore a wedding ring—then he looked up at her and held her gaze steadily with alert, intelligent hazel eyes. "Let's order first, get that out of the way. They've got great sandwiches and they serve breakfast all day."

"Sounds good," Kate said, but she had little appetite these days.

An older waitress—they all seemed to be "of an age" as Maggie would have put it—marched up to the table, coffeepot in hand. She dosed Kate's and Hollander's cups with coffee, then left the carafe on the table. She pulled an order pad out of her apron pocket. "Your usual, Dutch?"

"How you doing, Sally? Yup, my usual."

"Good thing, already got it written down. And you, young lady?" she said, her blue eyes twinkling at Kate.

"This desert air must be more rejuvenating than I thought," Kate said, grinning back at her. "Scrambled eggs and bacon, hash browns, please."

"Biscuit with that, hon?"

"Why not."

As Sally strode off, Dutch Hollander took a deep swallow of coffee and then sat forward, arms on the table, and looked at her. "So what's this about, Kate?"

"Joe."

"Figured that much." His gaze unwavering, he again picked up his coffee cup.

She asked baldly, "Where is he?"

He peered at her over his coffee cup. "If he's not at Wilshire, if he's not at his place in Hollywood, I don't know anything more than you do."

"When did you last see him, Dutch?"

"See him?" He drank more coffee, thinking. "Guess it was February. We went to Joshua Tree. Yeah, it was early February, second week, maybe. What's this about?" he repeated.

She ignored the question. "Do you do that a lot?"

"Two, three times a year." He smiled, revealing large teeth preternaturally white in his tanned face. "Whenever the little woman lets me. Not in summer, for sure. It's a bake oven."

"Do you talk to him much between times? Email him?"

"Not much." He shrugged. "We don't go in for that stuff. We've been friends since we were kids. That doesn't go away no matter how long we go between seeing each other. Kate, tell me what's going on."

"I'm not really sure. But I have to trust your friendship with him. I have to trust what's said here will go no further."

"You have my word." He braced an elbow on the table, held up a hand and bent his arm toward her as if to arm wrestle; as she clasped his hand it strengthened powerfully around hers. "You have my word," he repeated, and released her hand.

She believed him not because of his iron grip but the integrity she sensed in him. She began with Joe's mysterious withdrawal from contact with her over the recent weeks, her hurt and disappointment. "He never returned my calls, never responded to any of my messages—"

"He must have a goddamn good reason," Hollander interrupted, twin lines deepening between his eyes. "He would never do that, Kate. I think you're the closest friend he has."

She gaped at him.

He looked startled by her reaction. "What, you don't think so? Or didn't you know that?"

She shook her head. "We have a ton of history together on and off the job but..." She trailed off, still digesting the words. *His closest friend?*

"Joe's got strong beliefs, strong feelings. I guess we both know how buttoned up he is, pretty much crap shit at letting anybody in."

She nodded. Joe had always presented an aloof persona to the world.

"As long as we're talking about stuff that won't go beyond the two us," he said, "I don't think that ex-wife of his would've hooked up with the dude at the Police Academy if he'd offered a little more of himself, know what I mean? Janine could've been his business partner."

"Well, I always thought Janine was a pretty cool customer herself," Kate offered.

Hollander muttered, his lips thinning, "You got that right. Ice cubes wouldn't fucking melt in her mouth."

Kate did not mind Hollander's profanity in the least; it was affirmation that even in retirement she was still encircled in the fraternity of cops where latitude in language was accorded to one another freely and without regard to gender.

"Christ knows why he married her. Well, I guess I do know. She looks like a million bucks. But he thinks the sun rises and sets on you, Kate. He hates, I mean *hates* that you've retired and he has a new partner. He thinks you're the finest cop—" he made air quotes, "—'the most thorough, honest, best fucking detective I'll ever work with.' He thinks you have more backbone and integrity than anybody he's ever known in his life."

Seared, scalded by the praise, utterly astounded, she felt her cheeks, her neck burning.

"More news to you, I see." Hollander was looking at her in high amusement, his eyes glinting, his big teeth exposed in a wide grin. "Good old Joe, telling everybody about the people he loves except the people themselves."

She was rescued by their food arriving, served with a flourish and with more repartee between Sally the waitress and Hollander. Hollander's "usual" turned out to be chicken fried steak covered with gravy, scrambled eggs and hash browns, which he proceeded to liberally douse with hot sauce from the bottle on the table.

"Why is Joe like that?" she asked when Sally left, glad to occupy herself with her food. "You know him probably as well as anybody. Why does he keep his feelings for people so much to himself?"

Hollander shrugged, and dug into his potatoes. "Without doubt, because of his totally fucked-up family."

"What—"

"Finish what you were telling me, first. I need to know what's going on."

"Sure. Sure you do." She told him about the phone contact from Captain Walcott, her visit to the condo.

"Wait," he said, looking up from his food. "An LAPD captain? Actually came to your house to see you?"

"Yeah," Kate said and did not elaborate. She speared a piece of bacon.

"The sun really does rise and set on you," he marveled.

She chuckled wryly. "On Joe, not me," she countered, thinking about the confrontational aspects of her meeting with Walcott.

"So what did she tell you?"

"That Joe had taken vacation time, which I knew, along with ordered sick leave for stress, which I didn't know. And she'd been trying to get hold of him because the FBI lab got a palm print hit on a case he was obsessed with and he didn't respond to her message."

His head jerked up from his food. "The Tamara Carter case?"

"That's the one."

The fork Hollander tossed hit his plate with a clatter. "You gotta be shittin' me."

"So you know about the case."

"*Know* about it? I must know every goddamn word in the murder book. It's all he talked about at Joshua Tree. Went over and over it, absolutely convinced he'd missed something. Drove me fucking nuts—"

"Me too," she interjected.

"His captain couldn't reach him with news like *that*? Christ, Kate."

She watched the thinning of his lips, the narrowing of his eyes conveying apprehension, and knew she needed to do no more work to convince him of the seriousness of Joe's disappearance. "Now you know why I'm here."

"So LAPD's looking into this—I assume they checked out his house?"

"Right now, for the time being, this ex-LAPD—" she pointed to herself, "is all there is. The captain's asked me to do some quiet checking. We don't have probable cause to consider or report him missing, Dutch, plus he's in line for a move up and she doesn't want anything in Joe's package that could hurt him."

He nodded approvingly. "This captain, she seems like good people."

"She is. Loyal to her people, wants the best for LAPD. My very first stop was his house. Everything normal—it took someone who really knows Joe to figure out he'd be gone for a while and he'd done what he could to not make it look that way. He's completely off the grid, Dutch, I mean completely. Cell phone silent, credit cards too, nothing."

"Fuck," Hollander muttered. "What weird shit is Joe into? What can I do? Tell me how I can help."

"With information. You were boyhood friends, you were cops together."

"Yeah, but never partners. I came on the department two years after Joe." He pointed to her plate. "You might eat some of that food. I'm not going anywhere till we're totally done here." He picked up his fork and ate a big piece of his steak.

She smiled. "Thank you, Dutch." She consumed some egg and three strips of bacon without tasting them while she considered her next question. "Joe didn't talk much about his time here in law enforcement. I got the strong impression he didn't have...a good experience."

"He did for a while. Early days, you couldn't ask for more gung ho. Till the day it all went south. Funny how the world can change in an instant—"

"Tell me," she murmured, pushing around her hash browns and thinking of Anne and the fiery wreck on the Hollywood Freeway, thinking of her last case, unsolved, the wailing mother prostrate over her dead six-year-old son, collateral damage in a drive-by on Normandie.

He put down his fork. "One call out...and it was like Joe was a grenade and his pin got pulled."

He had her rapt attention. "What happened?"

"Not what, who. Sam Raddich," he spat. He downed the rest of his coffee as if pronouncing the name had burned his mouth.

For Kate the name somehow, somewhere, pinged ominously. The look on Hollander's face, the way he was pushing his plate away, was further warning, and she put her own fork down.

"Joe was first responder," Hollander told her. "My partner and I were backup by seven minutes. A domestic, he'd been called out there before, hell, we all had. Only this time it was the abuser that called it in, told dispatch we needed to come out there and see what we'd find. Joe pulls up to the place, hears the final shotgun blast, Raddich offing himself. So Joe busts into the house and Raddich has blown his own head off, and his eight-year-old, he'd put four shots into him. Raddich just blew his little body apart, Kate. He did it in front of his wife from what forensics pieced together. Then his wife, he…"

As he groped to put words to memory Hollander's eyes held a glassy vacancy Kate still recognized, even decades after the year she had served in the Marine Corps in Vietnam: the thousand-yard stare. Then a vein in her own memory opened up. This was the case Cameron had told her about, only once, seven years ago, but once had been more than enough. "Christ," she whispered. "This was the guy who used hedge clippers. He took hedge clippers to her."

Hollander's eyes cleared. In not having to explain himself to her he looked like a man reprieved. But he said, "Pieces of her, body parts everywhere. Worst thing I ever saw. Bar none. The scene was so bloody, so hellish…It was ten years ago, I've still never told my wife, my friends…"

"I understand," Kate said. "I never shared the really bad stuff I saw either." *But maybe I should have. Maybe we all should have…*

"Joe went nuts and stayed nuts till he got out of here." His lips firmed into a tight thin line, and Kate saw he would say no more about Sam Raddich.

"So Joe left and you stayed…" she offered mildly, to open the way to the next channel she needed to explore.

"Yeah, and I actually do some good around here." He dredged up a faint smile, patted the gold badge on his shirt. "Shit happens, Kate. Sometimes really bad shit." He shrugged. "I think Joe just didn't belong here, so close to home, everything so personal. He'd already warned everybody the bastard was going to hurt his family, and everybody told him the same damn thing, Kate. Told him there was nothing more we could do, the wife needed to get the hell out of there." His voice picked up anger. "He kept saying she had no place to go where the asshole wouldn't find her, she had zero options against a crazy piece of shit like him. He was right." He spread his hands, his face drawn and grim. "Okay, he was right. I mean, what could we do? Bad guys don't have rules, we do. But in Joe's book we had to do something and it was our fault what happened…happened."

She nodded. She was finally penetrating a few previously murky aspects of Joe Cameron, piecing together some of what drove him during the years they were partners. She was beginning to understand his obsession with the Tamara Carter case. "How long after that did he leave?"

He shifted his body on the bench, poured more coffee into both their cups, then sat back and rubbed two fingers over his mustache as he thought. "Maybe three, four months. Before, he used to call LA a hellhole. But he got a line on this LAPD job in Threats Management in the West San Fernando Valley and he was gone just like that—" he snapped his fingers, "—didn't even let a friend like me know till he was there. He'd laid such a shitload of guilt on all of us, more than a few people here weren't sorry to see him go."

"Dutch," she said, leaning across the table and choosing her words with care, "what you tell me explains why Joe got me to run a scenario together. Off the books. We scared a stalker off a friend of a friend, it was a total scam—"

"The planting drugs one?" He was grinning widely.

Relaxing, easing back into the booth, she grinned back at him. "The very one. You too?" She picked up her coffee mug and inhaled the scent of coffee as strong as any found in a cop shop. This café definitely catered to its cops.

He nodded. "After the Raddich murders. First time was some punks running an extortion racket on illegals. We stashed two kilos of baking soda in the fuckers' truck, pulled 'em over and dumped out all of what they thought was blow, told them the cartel would be coming for it and would carve up their asses—" He was chuckling as he continued, "Wherever they are I bet they're still looking behind them. Then a turd burglarizing Latino houses, we had witnesses, illegals, that couldn't come forward so we did it to him too. A pedophile, when the girl's parents wouldn't let her testify. Joe and I paid him a late night visit and told him we were going to leak enough info to the press for people to figure out who he was and no one would do one damn thing to protect him. He was gone the next day."

She nodded. She'd had her own share of feeling maddening impotence when a preponderance of evidence didn't take dangerous criminals off the street. "Anything you know of along these lines that Joe might be doing now?"

He shook his head. "No idea, Kate."

"Anything he talked about when you camped? It could be important, Dutch."

"Wish I could help you there." He poured and drank more coffee. "I asked him a long time ago if he was running any of his vigilante stuff. He just laughed, said it was better if he didn't tell me anything. I sure as hell figured it wouldn't be with you."

"Only the one time."

"From what Joe said about you, I'm surprised it was the one time."

"So was I." She smiled at him. "You can take off my angel wings now."

He smiled back at her. "Thank God." He continued, "The pedophile, I called it quits after that. Told Joe I couldn't do it anymore and feel like I should keep wearing a badge. Come to think of it, that's probably why he didn't say anything to me when he up and moved along to LA."

She nodded. She liked Dutch Hollander and trusted her instincts about him. "You said something about Joe having a totally fucked-up family."

He sighed, looked up at the ceiling as if he didn't know how or where to start. "How much do you already know?"

"Damn little. He told me he lost his parents young—"

"Lost," Hollander repeated, and grinned sardonically and shook his head.

"He talked a little about his sister Jean, her divorce, her having the same miserable track record as him. Almost nothing about Jack. I've already tried to talk to Jean and she threw me out of her house."

He stared at her. "*Jean?* Did that? What the hell happened?"

"Beats the hell out me. All I wanted to know was about Joe. She was pure hostility. She also told me her son Jason was dead."

"*What?*" He was blinking rapidly, his face almost comical with incredulity and dismay. "*Jason?*"

She held up a hand. "He's not. This morning I found out from the next-door neighbor Jason is still very much in the here and now. Jean's boyfriend took him somewhere."

Staring at her, he ran three fingers through his bristly hair, leaving faint gray furrows. "The whole goddamn family's gone nuts."

"That's one explanation," she said drily. "I hoped you might offer a different take."

He just shook his head.

She was rapidly losing hope that she would glean much of anything from this boyhood friend of Joe Cameron's. She picked up her fork and ate more of her hash browns. "By the way, the neighbor happens to know you, Dutch. Dora Terhune."

"Dora?" His face changed and his chuckle held a hint of embarrassment. "Quite the character, isn't she? We're both into animals but I'm nowhere near—" He broke off but Kate knew he was going to say "as nuts." He added, "That house of hers—we all call her Jungle Jane."

Kate smiled. "I can see why. She let me know first thing that Jean packed up right after my visit and left in a very big hurry."

"I don't get this," he said in heated frustration. "I don't have one goddamn clue what's going on, Kate."

"The parents. You were going to tell me about them."

"You don't know anything about this, right?" His tone held hope that she might know and incredulity that she wouldn't.

She shrugged and said mockingly, "For being the closest friend Joe claims he has, I belong in the *Guinness Book of World Records* for clueless."

He sat back in the booth, his badge glinting under the fluorescent lights. "Joe was really close to his dad. His name was Jerry."

Kate couldn't prevent a laugh. "Why am I not surprised? Another J name. I've seen photos of the two of them in the desert."

Hollander nodded solemnly. "They were there a lot. When Joe was twenty-three Jerry found out his wife had been screwing his best friend from practically the day he married her. More than two decades."

Her first reaction, sympathy for Jerry Cameron, was swiftly overridden. "Joe," she said in a near whisper, "that's what happened with him and Janine."

He grimaced. "Yeah. You're right."

She was remembering the night when she and Cameron went out and got falling down drunk together, his trembling, incendiary rage at discovering Janine's perfidy. Now that she knew this history about his mother's betrayal of his father, she realized there had been so much more to his need to drown his pain than Joe had revealed to her...

Wrapping his hands around his coffee mug, Dutch continued, "Jerry Cameron got in his pickup and followed, chased his wife and best buddy till he rammed their car off the highway down into the bottom of a ravine. Died, the two of them. Then he drove his pickup on down to the cabin near Joshua Tree and walked into the desert. It was a hundred and fifteen that day. They never found his body. Coyotes, probably."

Shaking her head, Kate drank cold water to soothe a throat that ached with anguish over Joe's discovery that two beloved parents had so lost control of their lives that their children had lost all priority.

"I guess I see why he never told you," Hollander admitted mournfully. "Who'd want to open up that box of pain?"

"And what about Jack?"

"Down the tubes," he said succinctly. "Two years younger than Joe, drugs from the time he was a kid, hair-trigger temper, ran wild. Had a couple of DUIs before he was out of his teens, then a 501 with a mother and child in a crosswalk. They survived, but with his rap sheet he got sent up for the max, Solano that time, I think."

Which explained why Jack Cameron had left no trace of himself in public records.

Hollander shook his head and continued, "Made parole, did a 451 on his girlfriend and the kid he had with her. Thought she was cheating on him." He looked up at Kate. "The kid was Jason. Girlfriend was in the burn ward for weeks. He's in Folsom now, I think."

Kate responded to Hollander's information with a shake of her own head. Drug intoxication, felony vehicular with great bodily harm, felony arson... "Not much wonder Joe didn't talk about him."

"A very bad apple. Joe and Jean both testified for the prosecution at his trial."

Filing all this information, Kate nodded. "What a tragic family. What happened to the girlfriend?"

"Gone. I don't think she could deal with an autistic kid on top of everything else. Jean took him."

Which explained why Jean now had the boy but not why she would claim he was dead.

"This family cabin you mentioned, Dutch. Is that where you camp with Joe?"

"Nope." And added disdainfully, "A cabin would hardly be camping. Joe never went near that place again. I haven't been there since I was a kid. I don't remember, don't have a clue where it is. We always camp in the park by the rock formations."

"You don't remember anything about this cabin?"

He shrugged. "It was rustic, sort of a reddish exterior. There was a roller-coaster dip in the road just before we got there. Joe wouldn't be there, Kate. He'd never go back there no matter what."

Sally came by, check in hand. "You two all set here?" At their nods she dropped the check on the table and scooped up their plates. "See you, big boy," she said to Hollander and sauntered off.

Hollander picked up the check. Kate said, reaching for her wallet, "Let's go Dutch, Dutch."

"From what Joe says, you're not a woman to argue with," he said with a grin. And then he quickly sobered. "Damn it all, Kate, I've been no help to you at all."

"You have. I'm still piecing things together."

"So where from here? What can I be doing, Detective Delafield?"

"Sit tight," she told him in her most authoritative tone. "Not a word to anyone. Joe's future may depend on it." *Maybe his life.* "I need to do more checking to see what this is all about. I'll be calling on you, Dutch, you can be sure. I'll need your help—"

"I'll be here."

He dropped a bill on the check, again grasped her hand, and got up and strode toward the door of Rusty's Café.

10

Kate gunned the Focus toward the 15 and LA. She needed to keep an appointment, go to Silverlake Haven, strategize her next steps in finding Cameron and—based on her latest information—decide how much of what she'd learned she could, should or would share with Walcott.

The lessening of the immediate stress levels of the day had brought the beginnings of physical jitters and the unmoored and deepening anxiety that had become her daily companion. To distract herself from visions of the golden amber balm that filled many bottles on a kitchen shelf in her condo, she tossed a couple of pieces of sugarless spearmint in her mouth and bit down hard, exploding the hard sweet coating, and reached over to set the air conditioner at max.

The strategy around the next steps in finding Cameron she could think about right now—there weren't that many options. In fact only two that she could see. As she swung the car onto the 15 and merged into a sporadic stream of cars that would in a few hours congeal into rush hour traffic, she began a review of her actions of the past four days, a reassessment and reintegration of everything she had learned from her conversations with Jean, with Dora, with Hollander, with Walcott.

* * *

At home, she booted up her computer to begin option one. She searched for and located the website for the San Bernardino tax assessor for the Joshua Tree area. It was located in the town of Twentynine Palms. And was a dead end. The site would not take the name of a property owner; it required either the parcel number or street address to call up public tax records. She went to option two, clicking through the photos she had taken with her phone at Cameron's house and transferred to her computer. She was looking for the one of the mantel, hoping she had clearly captured one photo in particular on that mantel: twelve-year-old Joe with his father kneeling beside him, an arm around him, in front of a rust-colored cabin against a desert backdrop. But as she searched, a photo of the dining room arrested her: one of the paintings on the wall beside the table. A landscape, with a tiny cabin in the forefront of a desert butte. Aimee, she thought, why aren't you here to enlarge this for me so I don't have to cudgel my brains figuring out how to do it? Aimee, why aren't you here...But she knew the answer to that question.

She located the photo of the mantel, finally figured out how to enlarge the cabin detail on it and in the painting, printed out both screen images and compared them, squinting through a magnifying glass. They might be similar but were too indistinct for her to be certain. She had to be certain they were one and the same. She had to examine the originals. She needed to go back to the house.

* * *

Just before seven p.m., she entered Silverlake Haven, melting a few strips of breath-changing Listerine on her tongue as she approached the door. She had timed her arrival precisely, and after greeting Marla she strolled over to the furniture grouping beside the fireplace in the reception area and took a seat where she could watch the door.

Reaching into her pocket she withdrew a plastic pill container. She hunched over in her armchair to examine it, turning in her fingers the prescription she had picked up a few hours ago from a CVS Pharmacy on La Cienega, thinking about this afternoon's appointment.

When she had first walked into the office of the prescribing psychiatrist, the first sight of the woman rising to greet her had been somehow reassuring. A tall, thin woman nattily dressed in a light tweed jacket and russet pants, Dr. Natalie Sherman appeared to be in her seventies with gray-white hair in an unfussy hairstyle and an austere face that projected sagacity.

"Thank you for seeing me so soon," Kate said, gripping the hand extended to her.

"I had no choice," Dr. Sherman replied with a smile. "Calla insisted I fit you in. I've looked over the form you brought in. Have a seat."

Wasting no time on pleasantries, she directed pointed questions at Kate, leaning forward to gaze at her with shrewd hazel eyes as she absorbed Kate's replies. The questions were designed, clearly, to verify what Dearborn had related to Dr. Sherman as to Kate's state of mind and Dearborn's diagnosis and recommendation for Kate's immediate needs. Shrinking under the impartial gaze of this medical professional as the list of all her personal deficiencies unfolded, Kate wished she were somewhere else, anywhere else. Even hell would be preferable. Finally Dr. Sherman scrawled a prescription and handed it to Kate; it would be called into the pharmacy immediately and would be ready as soon as she could pick it up.

"I agree with Calla that you're experiencing severe stress and anxiety," the doctor had told her. "She'll keep me informed about any adjustment you might need in the dosage. It varies from person to person as to when you notice a difference, perhaps as long as a few weeks. But it will help, Kate. Also, I'm required to tell you not to combine alcohol with an antidepressant." She added quietly and with a trace of sympathy, "Try and do your best with that."

Outside the office Kate had been shocked when her watch told her she had been in the doctor's office a mere fifteen minutes. She had been evaluated, much too clearly seen and understood by another very smart and capable woman, and she still smarted from the humiliation. The goddamn pills had better be worth it.

Kate twisted open the top of the container and tossed a pill into her mouth and dry-swallowed it to join the shots of Cutty Sark she'd downed before she came here. All she could do was hope the medication would make alcohol less and less necessary.

At five minutes to seven a neatly dressed Latino couple, both of them portly, the woman in a flowery blouse and Capri pants, the man's blue-checked shirt tucked into pressed jeans, came through the tall oak doors and nodded a greeting to Marla at the desk. Kate waited until they were adjacent to her before she rose to intercept them.

"Pardon me," she said, "would you be Carlos and Josephina?"

The couple halted, nodded, and she looked into middle-aged faces filling with alarm, dismay.

"Ida is fine," she said hurriedly. "I didn't mean to scare you. I've been visiting her. Maybe she mentioned me?" Ida of course would not have had a chance to do so since the couple only visited her every Thursday at this time. "Maybe she mentioned a detective with the LAPD?"

"No," the two chorused, looking at her with surprise and interest.

"She mentioned something about the two of you expecting something from her when she passes on?"

"A painting." Josephina shrugged and added in slightly accented English, "Just a small painting we liked in her house." She held her hands about a foot apart. "Mexican art. We liked it. She gave us a deed of gift to make sure it came to us."

"It's just a painting," Carlos protested in a similar accent, his eyes darkening. He asked in testy suspicion, "What's the big deal?"

Kate had seen no apprehension in them at the mention of her LAPD affiliation, nothing to raise any suspicion whatever. She raised both hands. "No big deal at all. I just wanted to mention that I'm now a friend of Ida's too. If I can help."

She smiled and extended a hand, and both people warily shook it, then made their way down the hallway talking to each other in low tones. Kate went to Maggie's room.

Alice, in a light peach-colored dressing gown, was perched on the side of Maggie's bed and bent down to her; the two were conversing in low tones as Kate walked into the room. Kate could not see Alice's face, but Maggie, a hand patting Alice's arm, was smiling. Maggie as usual was hooked up to her oxygen but unlike the last time had more color in her gaunt face and seemed to be in no visible physical distress.

Maggie pointed to Kate, and Alice gave Maggie a push on the shoulder and shoved herself to her feet. "Go on, you old thing," she said jovially to Maggie. "Hello Miss Police Detective," she said in quavery cheer to Kate, and inched gingerly back to her own bed, waving away Kate's attempt to help.

"Alice," Kate said to her, "how are you?"

"Dying," she said matter-of-factly, "and wanting to get on with it."

Kate braced herself for fervent agreement from Maggie but instead she grinned. The grin was so filled with amusement that Kate realized it had been days, maybe weeks since she'd seen any such echo of the Maggie she'd known for decades.

Kate sat, taking Alice's spot on the bed, and leaned down to whisper, "Seducing your roommate, are you?"

From beside her on the blanket Maggie picked up the Karin Kallmaker novel Kate had brought her and waved *The Kiss That Counted* toward Alice. "I had her read a few passages so she'd know what she's been missing with all her stupid husbands. Now get off my bed and tell me what's been going on with you."

Maggie seemed so much better, was breathing so much more easily that Kate contrarily felt a sinking dismay: was this the proverbial Indian summer that terminally ill people sometimes experienced just before they died? *Get it together*, she ordered herself. *Appreciate the here and now.* She settled into the chair beside Maggie's bed and began relating in detail everything that had happened in Victorville.

"So what do you think?" Maggie asked, brows drawn in concern when Kate concluded her account.

"Joe can take care of himself and I think he's okay," she reassured Maggie. And herself. "I'm going to make sure he is." She asked, "Has Aimee been in?"

Maggie nodded. "Maybe an hour ago. And this afternoon some pals from the Nightwood Bar."

"It was like a party in here," remarked Alice.

In this small room eavesdropping was unavoidable, but Kate was especially irritated by Alice's presence because of what she was about to say. "Maggie…" She turned her back squarely on Alice. "I want you to know I've started seeing a therapist who thinks she can help. I'm taking some medication."

Again that "old Maggie" smile. Indian summer or not, Kate was glad for this, glad to have an image of Maggie to superimpose over the grim fatalism on her face over the past weeks.

Maggie said, "I won't say I'll die happy, but I'm glad to hear it. Do you have a pen? You can have it back tomorrow."

"A pen? Why?"

"Why else? Because I want to write something."

"Surely somebody in here has—"

"Of course, they do," she interrupted in exasperation. "I want yours. For the karma."

"You won't stab yourself in the jugular?" she joked and then could have bitten off her tongue as Alice barked with laughter.

"Now there's an idea," Maggie said, her eyebrows rising. She lifted a hand. "But not my style to go *that* particular way."

"I'll make sure she doesn't," Alice remarked.

Kate took out her notebook and pulled out the rollerball clipped over it and placed it on the side table.

"The very pen I want. You should go home, you look tired," Maggie told her.

"I'm not that tired."

"Let's put it this way. *I'm* tired. Come here." Maggie held out her arms.

Kate bent down to her, gently clasping her bony shoulders. Arms around Kate, Maggie bussed her on the cheek. "*This* is the kiss that counts. I love you, my dear friend."

Kate said through a thick throat, "I love you too, Maggie."

As Kate made her way from the room, eyes awash with tears, Alice called, "Don't you forget, Miss Police Detective—I still owe you."

Composing herself, Kate slowly walked on down the hall. She ducked her head into Ida's room. The Mexican couple had left.

Ida beckoned to her, then put a finger over her lips; Ida's roommate Mary appeared to be asleep. Kate went over to Ida's bed. Through the magnification of Ida's glasses she could see a coating of moisture in her blue eyes.

Kate touched her arm and said quietly, "I'm so very sorry about Carlos and Josephina—"

"Don't be." Ida took Kate's hand and patted it. "I understand. You were trying to look after me. You really upset them. They think it was a racist—"

"Of course they did. Especially with me being a cop."

"They actually offered to return my deed of gift. Thanks to you I know they're visiting me because they want to, not because they're looking to see if there's some other gain to be had from a dying old woman." She smiled. "It's fine, Kate. Don't trouble yourself further. I reassured them. They still have no idea what I'm leaving them."

"More than the painting?"

"No, just the painting. But it's a Tamayo."

Kate knew as much about painting as she did about opera. "Somebody famous?"

"Museum famous. I found him before everyone else did, in the early seventies. It's a very small Tamayo, but they'll faint when they see the appraisal report in the envelope on the back. I wish I could be there." She said mischievously, "My family will have a cow."

Kate grinned down at her. "I'll bet."

"So it's good you know about it, Kate. They deserve some good fortune for all their years with me, but you know how families can be. Just in case, can I have the three of you in touch with each other? Even if you're retired your connection with the LAPD will settle my family down."

"Definitely. If need be."

Ida again patted her hand and then released it. "I'd love more of a visit from you but you look tired. Go home."

"You're the second person to tell me that. I guess I'll believe it." She was indeed tired, so tired she felt weighted down with it. She smoothed white strands of Ida's hair back from her forehead, then impulsively leaned over and kissed her cheek. She turned and quickly left before she could see or hear Ida's reaction.

In her car she sat rooted, unmoving, feeling as if she had turned to stone. *What's wrong with me? Why am I such a fool?* Bad enough to have Maggie on the cusp of death, now she had been drawn irresistibly into a force field of affection for a woman named Ida who was also dying.

She really, really needed another drink. If only she kept a bottle in the car. But she hadn't done that since the night four years ago on her way home from Cameron's house when she'd been pulled over by a fresh-faced cop whose gaze had fallen instantly on a section of the pint bottle glinting on the seat beside her in the pulsing light on his motorcycle. She'd been too drunk to conceal it thoroughly enough in her shoulder bag. At his statement that her car had been weaving, and in answer to his courteous request to see her driver's license and registration and proof of insurance, she'd complied. At his next request to step out of the car she knew that although he was a Wilshire Division cop he did not recognize her name, so she produced her detective's gold shield. He'd looked again at the registration, asked if she was going straight to her address on Kings Road. At her affirmative reply he simply nodded and walked back to his motorcycle. But not so simply, it turned out. The next day she learned he'd quietly notified her lieutenant. To Kate's utter and lasting humiliation, Carolina Walcott had immediately put her on paid administrative leave. She'd already had a stint or two in AA but that had been her first time in rehab.

She would soon have that drink. At home. But only after she paid another visit to Cameron's house.

Dusk was descending when she pulled into the parking slot next to Cameron's RAV4 at the house on Hillcrest. She made her way through the gate and yard and around to the back of the darkened house. When she was here on Monday, not wanting to leave Cameron's house open she had left the deadbolt pulled back but the lower lock operational to secure the house. Now, she extracted a credit card from her wallet that would serve to lever back that lower lock.

She froze.

The door was closed, but not completely, and there were fresh splinters around the doorjamb. She backed carefully away.

Pulling her car keys silently out of her pocket, she returned to the front of the house with caution and then heedlessly sprinted for the gate, pressing her electronic door opener as she ran. She yanked open the passenger door and seized her personal gun from the glove compartment, flipping off the safety. Holding the .38 in both hands but pointed downward she shoved open the gate with a foot and returned to the house, around to the back.

Adrenaline surging, she touched a shoulder to the back door and quietly inched it open, slid silently into the house, stopped. For two full minutes she simply listened, trigger finger along the side of the gun so that an involuntary reflex would not cause it to discharge, trying to control her respiration as she inhaled an amalgam of faint must from a closed-up house, cleaning agents of the Marvell Maids, and an indefinable sourness that might be male perspiration.

The house was absolutely still. Which meant nothing. Someone might have heard her, seen her, and was also waiting. Turning her body sideways, gun again braced in both hands, she sidled her way through the laundry room. She edged into the kitchen, the room dimly visible in the remnants of dusk through the dining room window. The living room looked empty but someone could be crouched behind furniture or hiding in the bedroom.

She eased her finger onto the trigger. She opened her mouth to speak and then closed it again with the realization that she could not call out *"Police!"* She was no longer the police. She found herself in a ludicrous search for a word or phrase somewhere close to being as effective as that one infinitely descriptive and meaningful warning/identifier of a word.

"I have a gun!" she shouted. "If anyone is in here I have a gun!"

No response, no sound.

She had one advantage: having come in the back door, no one in the house could come up behind her. She removed her left hand from the pointed gun, felt along the wall beside her and flipped a light switch, simultaneously dropping into a crouch.

When she stood up her first thought was, *Joe will have a fit.* The living room and dining room floors were strewn with broken photographs and paintings. Cameron's desert scenes had been ripped from the walls in both the living room and dining room and judging by the splintering of the frames and cascades of glass, they had been repeatedly slammed and smashed into the floor. Everything on the mantel had been swept onto the floor. Other than a few pushed over dining room chairs the two rooms looked otherwise intact including appliances and other objects on the kitchen counters. Cameron's prized abstract sculptures on the fireplace hearth had not been touched.

With the kitchen light on she felt less vulnerable. The charge of adrenaline now expended, her instincts told her that no one else was here. But she moved silently down the hall adjacent to the living room with the gun braced and ready and looked into Cameron's bedroom. Pictures had been swept from his dresser, torn from the walls. She entered and surveyed the room, including under the bed, the closet. She proceeded to the den, the bathroom. Both seemed undisturbed.

She went back to the kitchen, sat on a barstool, placed her gun on the counter, opened and set her cell phone on the counter beside the gun, and contemplated the lighted blank screen awaiting her command.

Nothing visibly of value in the house appeared to have been taken. The destruction had been selective and meant to deliver a potent message along with clear identification of who had been here. And the rage she saw before her eyes gave ample evidence of why Joe had known to leave here. Told her, chillingly, the depths of the fury visited upon this house.

The question was: should she call this in? She had no proof of her suppositions about the perpetrator, only her pieced together scenario of what was coming down between Jack Cameron and the rest of his family. If he'd been remotely smart enough to wear gloves when he broke in, there would be no fingerprints. No evidence, no probable cause to arrest him. If she reported this B & E, she would need to explain her presence in this house. She would blow apart Walcott's attempt to quietly manage the situation with no lasting damage to Joe. She would violate Joe's intention to handle this in whatever way he had determined he must, based on his family history. She would end her friendship with him because of her own violation of his home and his privacy.

The cell phone she had been staring at startled her with its vibration, followed by the shrill ring.

Walcott, caller ID informed her.

She picked it up. "Yes, Captain," she said.

"How is your friend, Kate?" Walcott asked in a gentle tone.

"Better today. Thank you for asking."

"And you?"

"Doing as well as I can. I'm seeing Calla Dearborn."

"That's very good to hear. Are you home?"

"I left Maggie a few minutes ago," Kate replied smoothly. "My next step was to call you with an update."

"You have a lot going on with the situation with your friend," Walcott said. "I assumed there was no major breakthrough or I'd have heard. But you need to know that a Jackson Allen Cameron was paroled from Soledad Prison two weeks ago."

"So your hunch paid off, Captain," she said in warm tone, praising Walcott for what she herself had already deduced. "Good information. And way too much of a coincidence not to be somehow connected."

"I think so too, but it remains to be seen what a two-strikes felon with 501 and 451 convictions has to do with Joe dropping off the radar, even if this guy is a fucked-up family member. But if this is family business, that means Joe may be perfectly okay."

"He may be," Kate said mildly, her mind roiling with the knowledge that the news didn't mean that at all.

"Still, it doesn't explain why he wouldn't be getting messages, wouldn't call his captain back about the hit on the Carter case."

"No it doesn't," Kate said with all the gravity she felt. "I still need to find him. I have a lead on a cabin in the high desert where he might be."

"Which might mean his cell is out of range."

"It might." She hadn't thought of that. "How he went about concealing his disappearance makes me think we need to be really certain of the situation. I'd appreciate you giving me just another day to have a look-see and get an explanation to you for all of this."

"Well, I feel better about this now with a theory to go on. You have tomorrow and the weekend, Kate. No later than first thing Monday morning I report the FBI hit to Joe's partner and we contact the Carter family."

The Marvell Maids would be here Tuesday, find this scene, call the police, and it would be all over anyway. If she said anything to Walcott now about what she'd found here, it would be over immediately. She knew Walcott would feel duty bound to deem this a bridge too far, would call in the troops, take this off her hands. "Agreed," Kate told her.

Walcott clicked off.

Kate rose, pocketed the cell phone, restored the safety on her .38 and tucked it in the back waistband of her pants. Disturbing none of the damage, she made her way into the living room with the practiced evasive movements of a homicide detective who knew how not to contaminate a crime scene. She located the photograph she was after and carefully plucked it from its mangled frame. It was marred by slashes from glass damage but its details were visible. She found the painting she was looking for, compared it to the photograph. The cabin depicted was so much smaller in the greater perspective of the painting with the butte in the background that she would again need to look at it with a magnifying glass. But it seemed a similar shape and color as in the photograph. She looked at the signature: Jerome Cameron. So it was the same cabin in the photo and the painting. Jerome Cameron—the artist was Joe's father. Joe had never mentioned his father was a painter. But then Joe had not mentioned lots of things. From her limited knowledge, Jerome Cameron seemed a pretty good painter.

Home, she could finally go home. She really, really needed a drink.

She closed up Joe's house as best she could and went back to her car carefully carrying the photograph and the painting, knowing they were her one and only and last chance of finding Joe Cameron.

11

Gasping, Kate lurched upright in her bed tearing frenziedly at her T-shirt. She instantly collapsed back onto her pillow, felled by lightning strikes of pain in her head.

"Oh Christ Jesus," she muttered.

She realized the T-shirt was drenched in sweat, not blood. And that last night's bottle of scotch had given her a head full of excruciating pain without the usual tradeoff of rendering her sufficiently comatose to prevent dreams. The worst dream yet, her house awash in blood with more pouring from the ceiling, this time with Cameron's body at her feet, spilling its own crimson into the warm coppery-smelling blood that rose over her feet toward her ankles...

In infinitesimal increments she turned her pain-strobed head to see the clock: 6:15. She lay perfectly still again, waiting for the agony to subside enough to allow her to grope in her side table drawer for the bottle of Excedrin. She dry-swallowed four tablets, wincing at the ashy astringency filling a mouth that already seemed stuffed with cotton. Again she lay quietly, waiting for the pills to hit her bloodstream.

Why had she dreamed? Had her newly prescribed medication somehow interfered with the effectiveness of the scotch? Highly unlikely. Not this fast. What on earth would she do if her companion Cutty Sark, so dependable, so faithful over the years, was beginning to fail her...

It was after seven a.m. when she was able to sit up and strip off her damp T-shirt. She picked up her cell phone and selected a number.

To her surprise—and utter dismay—the phone was physically, not electronically picked up. She did not want to talk beyond leaving a message. Her caller ID was blocked to anyone she called, and her finger hovered over the disconnect key.

"Hello? Is anyone on the line?" asked Calla Dearborn.

"Kate Delafield." A throaty semblance of her voice had somehow managed to emerge from her dry mouth and throat. "It's too early for you not to have your answering machine on."

"You're right. I need to be more thoughtful about this working from out of my new home office. What's happening?"

"I was calling to make an appointment," she responded more normally, her vocal chords having finally unpacked themselves.

"Okay, we'll do that." Dearborn repeated, "What's happening?"

"Another dream. Worst yet. Maggie's better but I don't believe that's good news. I'm taking the antidepressant and wondering if it's making things worse."

"It's had no time to have any effect," Dearborn said in confirmation of Kate's assumption. "Can you come over today?"

"Not till next week. I have to—"

"You're calling me at seven o'clock in the morning, Kate. What I'm hearing tells me it should be today."

"I have to be in the high desert today. I have a friend in bad trouble."

"*You're* in bad trouble." Dearborn's voice had picked up more than a degree of vehemence. "This once, think about putting care of yourself ahead of what you think are higher priorities."

"This one's higher than a high priority. Someone's life is at stake."

"Aimee's?"

"No." She would not elaborate.

After more moments of silence Dearborn asked, "When do you leave?"

Kate said honestly, "I'm having a very rough morning. As soon as I can pull myself together."

"I know I won't convince you right now that it's not wholly up to you to save anyone's life but your own. So how about we compromise? How about you spend some of that pull-yourself-together time here? Will half an hour make that much of a difference? I'm right on your way to the freeway."

Kate looked at the crumpled, still-damp T-shirt on the floor. "I'll need coffee."

"I'll have it. Strong and lots of it."

* * *

Just after eight o'clock, Kate pulled up in front of Calla Dearborn's house. She had showered and felt better for it, her head pain had subsided, but she still felt internally shaky and nauseous as she took the pathway around to the cottage/office. The door was open, the aroma of coffee permeating the yard and a gloomy fog-shrouded morning serenaded nonetheless by a chittering symphony of birds.

Dearborn was at the sideboard pouring coffee into oversize mugs. "I heard you on the pathway," she said, handing one of the mugs to Kate and going to her armchair. "You'll find it really strong even for a cop. I'm not a morning person either," she said, her dimple emerging with her smile. "Help yourself to all the coffee you want."

Want? *Need* was more like it. The visage in Kate's bathroom mirror had looked ashen and ill. But Dearborn's gaze showed no judgment; her face was serene. "Thank you," Kate said, and sat down and welcomed a burning swallow of bracing brew from her mug. It wasn't like Cutty Sark coursing down her throat, but at this moment it felt like a close second.

"How are you doing, dealing with Maggie?"

"Just dealing." She gulped more coffee. "Well, not exactly. I've compounded my troubles. I'm visiting a wonderful old woman at the hospice and of course she's dying too."

"I'm sure she's grateful for the visits."

"She is. I think we both are—but I like her and don't want her to die, either."

Dearborn picked up her pen and pad from the side table and made a note as she asked, "How is Maggie dealing with herself?"

Kate was struck by the question. "She seemed better last night, and the last couple of visits she's stopped asking me to help kill her."

"Has she indeed. What do you make of that?"

"Well, I'm glad of it, I guess." Kate warmed her hands around the coffee mug. "I suppose it's resignation. She finally believes I can't do it. Or accepts she's close enough to death that it doesn't matter."

Dearborn didn't react beyond a brief but thoughtful silence. Then she said, "Tell me about your dreams, Kate. The one this morning and the other ones. Everything you can remember."

As Kate haltingly described the nightmare sequences in her blood-drenched dreams, her heart began to pound, her skin crawled, she found herself having to take deep, sometimes gasping breaths. Dearborn made very few notes, just listened. And her acute attention, her sympathetic murmurs and occasional wincing, her quietly voiced questions, drew Kate's trust and elicited more and more background details in the dreams, details of milieu, of smells and textures. She gradually calmed, and was feeling better for talking about the gruesome images and dragging them into the light of this misty morning, feeling better for the coffee. Drinking her second mug Kate thought to look at her watch; she was surprised to see that twenty-five minutes had flown by.

Seeing Kate's glance at the time, Dearborn told her, "I do respect that you feel you have to leave. You do that when you think you must, Kate."

Dearborn took another drink of her own coffee and said in commiseration, "Those dreams are so horrific. You describe them so well it would be hard—for me at least—to imagine anybody spending sleep time in a worse reality. In the time you're willing to give me right now, would you tell me what you make of them?"

Kate managed a bleak smile. "Isn't that what you're here for?"

Dearborn's smile in return was warm. "Detective Delafield most definitely doesn't get to deflect this particular question. Can you be specific in terms of what you feel while you're having these dreams?"

"I feel frozen," Kate answered immediately. She held up a hand to forestall any response from Dearborn while she sat back to think. She continued tentatively, "I don't feel fear exactly, because I want to *do* something, I *need* to *act*. So it's more like frozen horror because there's nothing I can do to stop anything. I feel...futile. Inundated with feeling...helpless..." She foundered, not sure how to go on from there.

Dearborn was making notes. She nodded. "That's very descriptive, actually. What do you think these repetitive messages from the subconscious signify about your life?"

Kate said slowly, "I'm no longer a cop and the dreams only started when I was no longer a cop. So are they about Maggie? What she's dredged up with her dying? Maybe about my parents, Anne, everybody I've lost..." *Or might lose.* She had not and could not mention Cameron.

"Are you telling me you feel the death and dying in your dreams refer only to personal loss?"

"'Only'?" Kate echoed with a shake of her head.

"Bad choice of words. I meant that several of those dreams have you in a squad car. And you were a homicide detective. Very unlike the work most other people do."

"Yes." Hadn't she been reminded enough of that through the years. People she met reacting as if her profession placed her in the ranks of the utterly strange and exotic, their interest in the gory details of her investigations often bordering on the prurient. "The job," she said.

"'The job,'" Dearborn repeated in clear disdain for the term. "You were on the front lines of law enforcement in the second largest city with the smallest number of police per capita in the country. Would a soldier in Iraq call what he does 'the job'?"

Kate shrugged. "We all of us call it that. I grant you, Iraq's an apt comparison. We're the thin blue line and all LAPD designations of rank are military—befitting a city where that thin blue line barely holds."

"'The job,'" Dearborn again repeated and shook her head. "So sadly consistent with my experience with the lot of you, that macho minimization of risk all of you adopt about putting your lives on the line."

"It's what it takes, Calla," Kate stated. "We're comrades who buck each other up because we're the ones who walk into the situations everyone else runs from." But she had been thinking, turning over in her mind Walcott's comment about her daily life as a homicide cop. "The dreams…maybe they actually have to do with the job."

"What are you thinking, Kate?"

"I lost my parents, Anne, comrades I had in Vietnam, and now it's my closest friend—"

"Heavy losses," Dearborn interjected.

"But all the death I saw over all my time on the job…" She faltered.

"Tell me more."

"The accumulated weight of it all over the years…"

Crossing her arms, Dearborn said firmly, quietly, "Your job may not have everything to do with the dreams but from what I know now I believe it has to be the major component. You saw so much death, so much loss—"

"It was the loss, Calla. More than the murders. The victims, they're dead and gone, their bodies tell us what people are capable of doing to each other. But the people around the people who are murdered—that's what's so hard. You have no idea," Kate said, expelling the words. "Really no idea. Murdering someone is so much more than murder. It's a devastating assault on the survivors too. Death by heart attack or cancer or even an auto accident, families and friends get to bury that person and assimilate the loss as best they can and get on with their lives. A murder, it goes on and on, years, forever. Survivors relive and relive all those images all through the investigation and afterward, whether we catch someone or we don't."

Dearborn was nodding. "And so do the investigating detectives," she pointed out, intensity in her gaze.

"Yes," Kate conceded, thinking not so much of herself but Joe Cameron and his Tamara Carter case. "Very much including us." She again glanced at her watch.

"Kate, as the detective you are, I want you to deduce something. Why, after all that time on the job, after all you saw over all those many years, why only now has it been translated into these dreams? How would a detective look at this?"

Kate said immediately, "The first thing a detective would look at is what's changed."

"And?"

"The job's gone."

"So how is the loss of the job connected, Kate? What's different there?"

Kate was silent for some time before she said slowly, "I don't have new cases crowding out the old ones."

Dearborn's eyes held such a glow that Kate felt as if she'd correctly answered a key question on a vital test.

"Kate, tell me this. On the first day when you were called to a new homicide, what did you do with yourself when you came home that very first night?"

"Ordinarily I wouldn't come home that night. The first twenty-four hours of a homicide, you run collecting facts. Run like hell with what you've got."

"Okay. When you did finally get to come home, what did you do with those images imprinted in your brain?"

"Drowned them," Kate said immediately. "If I didn't have to get up and go again on the case in just a couple of hours, I usually told myself I needed sleep and I had some really stiff drinks. The worst ones, I had to. There was the stabbing death of a gay man," she said, suddenly immersed in memory, "so gory and hate-filled I was just numb from it and that night I made love to Aimee just to make myself feel alive." She realized what she'd just blurted out and added in embarrassment, "You asked."

"I did. You can tell me anything in here. I'm glad to have so honest an answer." Dearborn spread both hands on her lap. "Have I understood what you're telling me? To make it possible to fully function on your job you opened a cupboard in yourself and put your cases in there. You came home and drowned the worst impressions the day they happened. You took one case after another and stuffed them in that cupboard, the next case pushing the last case further back in the cupboard. Is that what you're telling me, Kate?"

Dearborn fell silent. And let the silence grow as Kate absorbed what she knew was truth.

"Until…until I didn't have any more cases to stuff in. My career ended. And the dreams started to leak out of my full-up cupboard."

Dearborn did not respond for a time, simply looking at Kate as if she wanted that thought to marinate. She finally said, "All your cases were pushed not only out of your sight but out of the sight of all the people you love—"

"*God damn it!*" Kate flared, jerking forward in her chair. "So I never told anyone. So I didn't talk about what I did, what I saw. How I felt. Aimee said I should. Maggie said I should. You said I should. I tried and one look at Aimee's face, Maggie's face, and I *couldn't*."

"Of course we would react, Kate—"

"You civilians, you don't have a goddamn clue," Kate barked. "You don't know what you're asking when you want to know what I do."

"But isn't that up to us decide? After all, we already have some reference points, we have books, films that convey—"

"*Convey?*" Kate flicked the word away with a contemptuous wave. "No matter how convincing the acting is, it's acting. However real the blood looks, it's fake." She said heatedly, "People don't *know* how it is to see someone's eyes when they hear the person they love most in the world is dead. And worse, *murdered.* To see a *real* body bled out, a *real* black bullet hole through somebody's eye, some woman's breasts hacked away…" She choked to a halt.

Calla Dearborn did not speak, only shook her head. Finally she said, "Yes, I truly hear you. I truly see why you believe that. But isn't it true that this belief means you placed taking care of the people you love ahead of taking care of yourself?"

"And you're telling me that's a bad thing?"

"I'm not putting a value judgment on it, Kate. You made a choice. You paid and are paying a terrible price for everything about yourself that you chose to submerge. That's not what *I'm* telling you, that's what your *dreams* are telling you."

Dearborn picked up her coffee mug and sipped from it, her dark eyes contemplating Kate over its rim.

"I hate fucking therapy," Kate muttered, sloshing coffee around in her mug. "All questions and no fucking answers except my own."

Dearborn looked at her with the faintest of smiles.

Kate drank more coffee. "Doctor Sherman said I had stress and anxiety but didn't give me a diagnosis."

Dearborn said quietly, "Doctor Sherman's confirmed Post Traumatic Stress Disorder. I hope you won't be offended when I tell you you're textbook. You were a front line soldier, Kate, in Vietnam and now here. Soldiers put their bodies through extreme stress and danger to serve their country, suffer horrendous physical and mental trauma and in return we give them lousy pay and mostly untreated PTSD. We gave you better pay and a pension to go with your PTSD. Which in your case we can and will treat."

"How?"

"We go back and do a rerun."

"Are you saying…"

"I help you unpack the cupboard. We take your cases out and look at them again. And this time you and I talk about them. In detail."

Kate mumbled, "My therapist will need a therapist."

Dearborn chuckled. "It may surprise you to know I have one. And a consultation group. I do take care of myself, Kate."

"It will take forever," Kate grumbled.

"I'm not going anywhere."

Unlike everybody else in my life.

"Kate, what I'd like you to do as soon as you can is to take a case and write out all you can about it. Bring it in and we'll talk about it."

"Calla, I have a larger problem that revisiting my cases won't help. It's what the hell I do with the rest of my life."

"I know that, Kate. We'll get into that another time. I have some thoughts." Her dimple showed as she said, "Some people might even call them answers."

"Like what?"

"Not now. Another time. You have enough to think about. You look to be up for your drive to the desert now. Be on your way, Kate, go save that life you need to save. I'll see you next week."

12

Heading toward Victorville, Kate fed herself occasional bites of the muffin she had picked up at Starbucks along with another large coffee. She still felt queasy and nauseous, lurking head pain threatening to break through a full load of painkiller she had taken earlier. She was hoping the efficacy of more caffeine and the muffin she was managing to get down, along with her body's healing properties, would improve matters as the day unfolded.

Traffic was sparse at this hour, and she reached for the phone as a distraction from her physical miseries. She never used her cell phone while driving, even hands free, and despised the reckless idiots who did. But she was weary of yet again having to traverse this same long road into the high desert, and since music and news had turned out to be irritants it might actually be safer to distract herself by making the call now instead of when she arrived in Victorville. Additional rationalization: she was stopping in town only for gas.

Roberto answered the phone at Silverlake Haven. Marla would not be in till ten, he informed Kate. Maggie had had a restless night, been given opioids to make her comfortable and was now asleep. Kate made certain that Roberto had her cell phone number and that Marla was informed she would check back in early in the afternoon.

When she finally reached Victorville she was feeling somewhat better. After gassing up the car she soon turned off onto the one and only road that led from Victorville toward Joshua Tree, Highway 18 toward Apple Valley. Noting she was now on Happy Trails Highway and crossing Dale Evans Parkway, she imagined her parents' bemusement at all this commotion over the life and times of one of many movie cowboy heroes from the fifties. She had never been on this road and was surprised it was so populated with houses and shopping malls and the standard commerce found in any city or town in America, planted as it was amid an uninviting expanse of sand and sagebrush, a colorless dusty landscape on a featureless plain within a circle of low, distant hills. Yet it made sense. Hot dry desert weather and cheap land made possible a healthy and decent life for families with limited money, for retirees living on Social Security.

Joshua trees came into view, increasing in density, and she absorbed the sight as she drove along, each tree bristling with vivid green spiky branches twisted into the singular, striking, captivating distortions that distinguished this ancient species from all others. The individuality of each tree evoked images of people buffeted and shaped into all manner of personality distortions by outside forces in their lives just as each of these sun-blasted trees had been whipped and torn by wind into its own shape and identity. A scattering of homes overlooked this growth of trees, but did so from a respectful distance on low sloping hills.

She was welcomed to the Lucerne Valley, and all the commerce and houses vanished entirely, replaced by a vast valley that ended at far distant hills with only power lines and the occasional Joshua tree dotting the intervening panorama.

Highway 18 became Highway 247 and Johnson Valley. This much closer to her destination she paid attention to the horizon details on each side of the narrow two-lane road cutting through what had become a dead flat plain that reminded her of Death

Valley. Reddish brown hills appeared, splashed with patterns of black, all of it so otherworldly she could be driving on the moon. Four decades of living in California, she reflected, and she had yet to see whole swatches of a state whose landscape was as varied as the people who had found their way here from every country on the globe.

The temperature was in the low eighties and her light khakis and short sleeve shirt made for comfortable driving with the windows down. The road became virtually empty of traffic, and beyond the ubiquitous power lines there was no sign of human habitation for miles to come. She felt isolated on this road, only partly reassured by her full gas tank: this would be one hell of a bad place to break down.

But the first signs of civilization were most unwelcome: arresting, naturally artistic formations of large pale rocks defaced by huge initials, splotches of chalk and paint and graffiti. She seethed at the sight. *Morons. Idiots. Assholes.*

Rustic structures appeared, became an increasing encroachment, and with them, ever closer to the road, rolling hills to which she paid acute attention as she drew closer to Yucca Valley. A single flat-topped formation that reminded her of the mountain in *Close Encounters of the Third Kind* came into view, and she pulled over to the side of the road. She picked up the damaged Jerome Cameron painting from the seat beside her to study it, comparing it with the land formations around her. Nothing matched, and she drove on. Several times she pulled over to allow traffic to pass; she had to drive slowly enough to study the topography and could not risk a mistake through inattention or distraction.

Miles later she was feeling the first pangs of dispiriting doubt, wondering if Jerome Cameron had been a figurative rather than literal painter, wondering more basically if she was on a wild goose chase of the first order. But the road began to rise and fall with the rolling of these foothills and when she came over a rise and rode down a pronounced roller-coaster dip, her spirits performed a countering soar. It had to be the dip Dutch Hollander had experienced when he came to the Camerons' cabin as a child.

She had gone only a few miles farther when she spotted the formation she'd been watching for, a pair of buttes with a cleft between, their sides deeply scored, the tops covered by overhanging caps of green. As depicted in the painting. A sizeable scattering of dwellings, perhaps several hundred, sat at the base of the formations amid a plethora of Joshua trees. This indeed seemed where a desert aficionado like Joe Cameron's father, a lover especially of Joshua tree country, would decide to buy or build a cabin.

Kate sighed at the size of the settlement. She might need to search the entire area. Pulling over to the side of the road, this time she studied the photo of Joe and his father, examining details of the cabin behind them, door and window location, roof line, chimney. It showed the cabin isolated at the base of the butte. It was quite likely other houses would have been built around it in the intervening years. Again she sighed, this time at the unwelcome but real possibility that the cabin might no longer exist.

She pulled into the first road she saw off the highway, a dirt lane identified as Luna Vista. Inching along the dry, dusty, bumpy road, she examined every single dwelling, a collection of cabins, trailers and RVs and manufactured housing, some of it boarded up. Most appeared to be vacation homes, but modesty of structure might not necessarily be an indication that people lived elsewhere for the hottest months of the year. She came to the lane's end, turned and bumped her way back to the highway. She repeated the process on the next lane, N. Wood, and then Steffenson. Then she turned down Kelley.

A few minutes later Kate stopped, idling the car, gripping the wheel. That she had come to the end of the road was more than metaphorical. Before her sat the cabin in the photo, in the painting. Clapboard, its original rust color weathered to gray and visible only in faded patches, but the same location of windows, same chimney, same door location exactly centered. Still isolated by hundreds of feet from nearby structures and well off-road. The frontal perspective on the cabin in the photo and painting was slightly misleading—it not only abutted but was built into a scoured, earthen outcropping of butte. Looking at the scored and weathered wood of the cabin, its single door and no way out the back, the surrounding terrain liberally dotted with dry bush and a scattering of Joshua trees, remembering Jack Cameron's felony arson conviction, Kate thought: *It's a firetrap.*

A car was parked off road on desert sand on the far side of the cabin, and as Kate drifted her car past the cabin she saw that the Toyota Corolla appeared to be Jean's with the license plates removed. Kate pulled her own car in beside it, automatically picked up her cell phone from the passenger seat to stuff in her pocket. No service, read the screen. *Maggie*, she thought. Hating the feeling that she was now out of touch with Maggie, she got out of the car.

The cabin door opened. And closed behind an unsmiling Joe Cameron. He walked toward her on sandaled feet, wearing a Dodgers T-shirt, hands shoved in the pockets of his khaki shorts.

Halting a few feet from her, he said, "If anyone figured out how to find me it was bound to be you. I wish I could say I'm happy to see you."

Suddenly roiled with emotion, fiercely angry, fiercely relieved, Kate shoved her hands into her own pockets. She wanted to leap at him and pummel him, she wanted to leap at him and wrap him up in a hug. So intent had she been on her pursuit it had not occurred to her to consider her emotions when she found him. Not knowing what might come out of her mouth if she spoke, she just stared at his unshaven, drawn, tense face. He looked thinner. He looked exhausted.

"How is Maggie?" he asked.

The question made her angrier. With so much at stake, so much trauma happening for both of them, no matter what he thought or believed about the depth of their friendship, how could he have just walked away? Still unable to speak, she shrugged.

"Still with us?"

She nodded.

"Kate," he said. Then stated firmly, intensely, "You need to leave. This is not your deal. You have to trust me on this. I have a situation—"

"I know all about your goddamn situation," she snapped. She demanded, "Why didn't you tell me?"

He looked only momentarily taken aback. "If you know what it is then you know it's *my* problem."

"I'm supposed to be your friend, Joe. Your *friend!*"

"Which is why I couldn't tell you. Or anybody. But especially you. You don't pull friends into this kind of deep shit."

She planted her Nikes firmly in the sand, feeling heat on her head and shoulders, the sun beating down on her. "You owe me more explanation than that." Whatever his doubts about her and her own culpability in this situation, she had to hear him finally voice them.

"I need to take care of a problem. The way it figures to go down, I'll do it my way. A way you can't deal with."

"Why wouldn't you let me decide that?" A similar question Calla Dearborn had posed to her echoed so resonantly through her mind she had to push it aside.

"You already decided it, Kate. When we were first partners. When I helped you with that friend that was being stalked. I saw how you were with that. I didn't know enough about you or I'd never have roped you into that. Made me feel like I raped a nun."

Kate couldn't prevent a snort of laughter. "Do I really come off like that? I've never been anything near a saint. And now I'm no longer a cop."

"You are still a cop, Kate. Always will be in the ways that matter. I know you. Nothing about you or your code has changed."

"I'm here, Joe." She took a step toward him. "I'm here and I'm staying."

"Fuck," Cameron muttered under his breath. "How did you find me?"

"Long story. Later."

He pulled his hands from his pockets, braced them on his hips. "You don't have a fucking clue what you're getting into. What the fuck this is about, what you're even talking about."

She squelched her trained, ingrained investigator's impulse to challenge him to tell her what she was talking about. Far more important that he understand what brought her here, what she knew and that she had chosen on the basis of that information to be here. To not have it appear she was making any sort of on-the-spot decision based on what he revealed to her.

She said, "So let me tell you what—"

The cabin door flew open and Jean Velez, wearing pink short shorts, a tank top and tasseled cowboy boots, stalked out. The pings, bells and whooshing sounds of a computer game emerged with her. "What's going on? What the fuck is *she* doing here?"

"It's okay Jeanie, I've got this covered. Go back inside."

But Jean, a hand on one hip, stood unmoving. "How the hell did you find us?" she yelled at Kate.

Cameron held a hand up to forestall a response from Kate. "She's a detective," he called back as if that explained everything. "Go back inside, Jeanie. I'll be there in a minute."

"She must be fucking Sherlock Holmes," Jean fumed, retreating, slamming the cabin door behind her.

"You have an interesting family," Kate said.

"Tell me," he said.

"I will." She glanced at the cabin door. "Want to take a walk while I tell you?"

"Not far, Kate," he said, and set off at a stroll, his sandals kicking up puffs of fine dust from the sand. "We'll need to stay within sight of the cabin."

She was only momentarily startled to see the shape of a gun under his T-shirt, shoved into the back waistband of his shorts. Of course he would be armed. At all times.

"I understand," she said, glad to stretch out her body even minimally after the rigors of the morning, to have sun on the shoulder that had taken the bullet years ago and now ached from the drive. The warm, crystalline air, redolent with aromas of unadulterated plant life warmed by unfiltered sun, the pristine sand, felt rejuvenating. She was beginning to understand the affinity some people felt for this arid, forbidding, primitive terrain.

"This is about your family," she said to him. "About your mother, father, sister and brother—how what happened to them changed your life. I found out why you left your hometown. What turned you into the kind of cop you are now. Your parents. Sam Raddich, his massacre of his family. This dropping out of sight, it's entirely about your family. I know about your parents, Joe, I found out when and how they died."

His arms were swinging slightly as he walked, his hands clenching and unclenching as he listened. "How do you know all this?"

"Long story. Later."

"So you're here because now you think you know all my secrets." His tone was flat, laced with bitter resentment.

"Not all of them I'm sure. Just the ones friends should be telling each other. Just the ones I should have known all along."

"I had damn good reasons I couldn't tell you. Where did you get all this shit about me?" he repeated, his voice rising with the demand.

She ignored the question. "I know the deaths of your parents changed everything. Probably had a lot to do with your brother's substance abuse—"

"Not probably. Everything."

"—and I know he's been incarcerated most of his life. I know he has two felonies, DUI loss of life and attempted murder by arson, and you and Jean were on the prosecution's witness list at his second trial. I know he was paroled week before last. I know—in fact I now have proof—that he's coming after you. And I presume Jean as well."

Cameron halted. "What kind of proof?"

Kate pulled out her otherwise useless phone and located the two photos she had taken yesterday of his living room and bedroom, handed him the phone.

Standing immobile he stared at the first picture, the wreckage in his living room.

"Nothing is damaged except what you see."

His face twisted as he looked at the violation of his home, the destruction of his art works. "What the fuck were you doing in my house?"

"Long story," she said, then, seeing his eyes darken dangerously she added, "The Marvell Maids were there."

He flicked at the photo on the phone with a fingernail. "Was this called in?"

"No," she said, "I made sure of that."

Cameron shook his head. "Fuck," he said again with even more feeling, and looked at the next photo of his bedroom, scratching at his growth of beard. "Guess I'll consider myself lucky he didn't burn the place down."

"Probably would have if he hadn't wanted to leave a clear message he was there."

Cameron said thoughtfully, "So he thinks I'm still in LA."

"Maybe not, Joe. Maybe all that desert art he tossed around gave him the same set of clues it gave me."

He nodded grimly. "He'd eventually come here anyway."

"What I can't figure out is how he found your house."

"Jack is a screwed-up disaster but unfortunately not stupid. He had lots of time, prison computers, public records."

"I take it he's after Jean too."

He nodded. "All of us. We never let Jason visit him, too confusing for the kid, so in his eyes Jason's turned against him too. We didn't just testify at his trial, Kate, we were always at his parole hearings. One of the hearings, he told us he'd come after us, screamed it right out."

"Jesus. Why was he paroled?"

He emitted a short, cynical laugh. "You just said it. He found Jesus. Plus time served. He finally wised up, started claiming reform at the hearings. We both know overcrowding is so bad the release standards keep falling. The death he caused was a DUI and his arson didn't take lives so the state rationalized he wasn't that violent a felon." He shrugged. "I had to keep this from you, keep my secrets all these years—this was sure to happen, it was only a matter of when. We kept him in there as long as we could."

They had circled back to where the cars were parked, and Kate leaned against the hood of her car, feeling the hot metal against her hips and back but needing to brace herself for what, as a matter of principle, she had to ask. Cameron also leaned back beside her.

"Joe," Kate said, "I do need to ask why you can't bring regular law enforcement into this."

He took a step forward from the car and turned on her, his face twisted in fury. "You need to ask?" he spat. "What a fucking stupid question. You of all people know how fucking stupid it is. No one can protect us—you know that. We're the ones with the rules. He can't be arrested till he does something. You know that, I know that. He knows that. I'm going to protect my family. He's not going to be another Sam Raddich, not while I have a breath left in my body." His voice was strained with intensity as he struggled to keep from shouting at her. "Did you actually come here thinking you could stop me?"

"No," she said.

He leaned toward her, brought his face close to hers. "I'm going to kill him. Understand, Kate? *I'm going to kill my brother.* That's why you can't be here, God damn it."

Kate held up both hands. "I hear you. Loud and clear. But why make a stand here, Joe? Why *here*?"

He gestured at the terrain. "Look at this. No else one around to get hurt, only three sides, I can defend this for as long as it takes. I'm a trained police officer, I can defend my family here. What's left of my family and such as it is," he added in a mutter.

"How? You can't guard this place all day and all night by yourself."

Again he gestured at the terrain. "In the day he can't approach without me seeing him. At night, motion sensor lights. Soundless perimeter alarm. From dusk till dawn it wakes me if it's triggered. So far I've drawn down on a roadrunner and a kangaroo rat."

Kate smiled. Realized it was the first time she'd done so since she arrived. "I take it Jason is here too?"

He nodded, again leaned back against the car.

"Why? Bringing the boy—"

"This is the only place where I know he's safe. Besides, Jeanie wanted some time with her latest knucklehead boyfriend. I get it, Jason's more and more a handful. I told her she wasn't safe anywhere in town even with that bozo Brandon riding shotgun." He chuckled humorlessly. "You panicked Jeanie. The fact you found her and mentioned Jack, that did it. Brandon came here with her, stayed a day, sized up the situation, decided getting his ass shot off maybe wasn't his scene, took off." He grinned, shook his head. "Jeanie can sure pick 'em."

She grinned back at him. "So you always said, time and again. She told me Jason was dead."

He chuckled. "Yeah, she said she got a crazy idea in her head she might protect Jason if you found Jack—you'd pass on the news that his son was dead." His expression sobered. "No way is he going to hurt that kid," he said in a tone of granite. "He's a sweet little kid, Kate, innocent as a kitten."

He crossed his arms. "Another reason you have to leave—we have no room, Kate. Simple as that."

"You have a floor, a place on it is all I'll need. Simple as that. But you'll have lots of room when Jean leaves."

"Leaves?" He looked at her incredulously. "So where's she going?"

"To my condo. She and the boy will be safe there."

He began a protest, stopped. Then said thoughtfully, "Yeah, they actually would. It would be so much easier. That much less stress not having to worry about them. Especially Jason if the worst-case scenario comes down."

She pushed herself away from her car to confront him. "Joe, you're not facing your brother alone. I won't let you."

"You can't do this, Kate. Take my family and go. You can't be here with me. This is against everything you believe."

"You're my friend. I protect my friends. As best I can."

He shook his head emphatically. "You have to live with yourself. I have to live with myself, too."

She stared into his eyes. *Without Aimee, without Maggie, if anything happens to you I don't care if I live or die.*

"Joe, if you ever believe anything I ever say to you, believe this: whatever happens, whatever comes down, I can live with myself."

He searched her face. Then asked, "Are you carrying, Kate?"

There was only one reason he would ask. She was elated. "Of course. Always. You know how paranoid I am."

"We all are. We're cops."

"It's in the car. But I have to leave you here now to take them to the city." She gestured toward the cabin.

He frowned. "What's your plan?"

"You need a car. I assume this is your only car—"

"Yeah. I dropped off the rental when Jeanie got here."

"I need a car. I'll have to leave if Maggie..." Her voice quavered. "She's in hospice care, Joe."

"Christ, Kate," he said, his face crumpling. "I'm so sorry. Something else I owe Jack for," he seethed. "That I couldn't be there for you with this. How long has she got?"

"Days. Speaking of Maggie, where the hell do I get cell phone service around here?"

"You don't. I have a landline. Put it in when Jeanie turned up. Can't have Jason here without a phone."

"Thank God," Kate said fervently. "I'll take Jean and Jason in, get them settled, see Maggie and give her a version of what's going on, give the hospice the number here, be back tonight."

He didn't respond, just looked at her for some moments, digesting this information.

He held out his hand. Kate gripped his, and they stood looking at each other, hands clasped hard.

"Kate, I can't tell you how tough it's been. Having all this going down. Having you here, I can't tell you how great it feels. You're a better partner and better friend than I ever deserved."

The praise from this introverted, taciturn man warmed her more than the sun. She gripped his hand in both of hers, then released him. "Not true, but we'll debate that some other time. I have one additional piece of news, Joe. Important news. About the Tamara Carter case."

He blinked at her.

"The FBI got a hit on the palm print."

"No fucking way!" He leaped away from the car, his body electric, his face galvanized into an amalgam of elation, confusion, frustration. His body jerked as if he wanted to jump into Jean's car and speed off to LA. Which, Kate knew, he probably did.

"What do you know?" he asked eagerly.

"Not much. The guy's on ice. Somewhere in the prison system, don't know where."

He was silent a beat or two. "Good thing for him. What he did to that little girl, give me the chance to arrest him, I'd rip his junk off."

"He's an animal," she agreed. Worse than seeing the murder book were the photos Cameron had shown her.

"No he's not. Any animal's better than him." He was staring at her. "How do you know this much?"

"Walcott," she said. "She's been trying to reach you. She contacted me."

"Has she—"

"No. Nothing's been done. Rasmussen knows nothing. She gets how this case is for you and we have till Monday when contacting the family is a must."

"The parents...Tim...Donna...I should be the one to tell them." He raked both hands through his hair. "Goddamn it, I have to get out of here."

"Yes you do. And I have some ideas," Kate told him. "Let's get rolling."

"Jean!" yelled Cameron. "Get out here!"

The cabin door slammed open and Jean flounced out. "What!" she yelled back.

He beckoned to her. "It's important."

She marched toward them, her boots kicking up dust, her large breasts bouncing in the tank top, her gaze shifting between her brother and Kate. She halted, crossed her arms. "What," she repeated.

Kate held a hand up to Cameron. This had to come from her. "Joe is my friend and I'm here to help and I'm here to stay. I want to take you to LA, have you and your boy stay at my condo."

She gaped at Kate, opened her mouth to say something, and Cameron said, "Jason will be safe."

Jean closed her mouth and looked at Kate. Wonderingly. "You're okay with this?"

"I'm fine with it. All you have to do is feed my cat."

"We love cats, the both of us. We'd have one, but the trailer's too small and there's dogs and coyotes all around. You sure you're okay with this? I haven't exactly—"

"The place is yours," Kate said. "For as long as you need it."

Jean raised her eyebrows, shook her head. "I'll go pack."

13

As Kate entered her condo, its serenity and coolness, the tree-shaded muted light, fell over her like an embrace. Even with all the changes she'd so recently made the place was so utterly and gratifyingly hers that she momentarily regretted her offer to house Jean Velez and her son. No one besides Aimee had ever stayed here and she felt vague apprehension that somehow this mother and son might imprint themselves and alter the atmosphere that had become almost spiritual to her over the years. She could not imagine ever selling this place, she realized. She could not imagine ever living anywhere else.

"Nice," Jean Velez said, looking around, setting down a suitcase.

"Wow," said Jason, depositing his knapsack. "Do we get to stay here, Mom?"

"For a while, honey," Jean said, ruffling the boy's thick, dark hair. "Only if you do your part to prove to Kate we'll take very good care of her place."

On the drive to Los Angeles Kate had begun to modify her opinion of Jean Velez. Picking up the 10 Freeway out of Yucca

Valley west of Palm Springs made for a longer drive back to LA through heavy traffic but Kate had felt little awkwardness during her two and a half hours with mother and son; Jean had sat in the backseat playing games with her son, doing her best to keep his hyperkinetic activity and occasional screams of triumph tamped down: "Cool it, honey, Kate needs to concentrate on driving."

And she had needed to concentrate, especially on the changing array of traffic in the rearview mirror, until she was completely certain that Jack Cameron had not somehow concealed himself near the cabin and identified her car and its occupants and was following them.

"I won't be here nights so you can have the master bedroom," Kate told Jean. "Everything's in walking distance, grocery stores, lots of places Jason might like. You bring the rest of the stuff up from the car, I'll stay here with him and change the sheets on the bed."

"You need to go," Jean said firmly, grabbing Jason by the tail of his Big Bird T-shirt as he was about set off to explore the rest of the condo. "If all three of us unpack the car, I can change the sheets. You have things to do and you need to get to them."

Kate nodded. The preparations for leaving the cabin had taxed her to her very last molecule of patience. First had come the necessity for each adult to offer persuasion that it was a very good thing for Jason to come to West Hollywood where he could look for movie and TV stars. He absorbed all these assurances, his guileless eyes switching uncertainly from Kate to his uncle to his mother, fearfully studying all three adults coaxing him, before finally voicing a doubtful, "Okay, I guess." Packing up what mother and especially her needful son demanded he had to have for an indeterminate time at the condo—which meant everything—had taken more time. Then more reassurances from Jean into the renewed resistance of her son as to why he had to get into a stranger's car when their own car was *there*, he pointed, *right there*. Combining this with the drive back, the day had devolved into late afternoon and her nerves felt stretched to snapping, especially when she could not have a drink. She still had to see Maggie, then return to Yucca Valley.

She and Cameron were in agreement that she would stay dusk to dawn at the cabin and as much of the day as possible.

It took little intuition or skill to extrapolate years of wrathful planning in a prison cell to implementation of what would be a well-coordinated attack. Without doubt he would launch it in darkness. Not just for concealment but to allow ease of approach, few if any witnesses, and more time to inflict the most vicious and primitive terror Jack Cameron could devise as vengeance for what he viewed as years of incarceration at the hands of his family.

On the drive, finally assured that she wasn't being followed, she had totaled up a few more facts and suppositions. Jack would have left prison prohibited from ever driving a car or ever owning a gun. He would have funds consisting only of minimal wages he may have earned in prison shops over the years plus the small allowance when he was released. None of these limitations would stop him. He would immediately steal a vehicle, and no one knew better than she did that his prison associates would tell him where he could easily and cheaply get a gun. He could and would rob for any money he needed and probably had, since he'd neither taken nor searched for anything of value from Joe's place. He had already committed a felony by breaking into and damaging his brother's house—if he had not worn gloves his fingerprints would be everywhere. He was a man with a broken life. A disastrous past, no present, no future. He was a man with nothing to lose. *Like me*, she thought.

Although she had not yet been able to voice the opinion to Cameron, it was her belief that Jack Cameron, his plan already in place, would be coming after his family sooner rather than later. The destruction in Joe's house depicted a man possessed of far more fury than patience. He was probably already in the high desert, and the strike would quite likely be tonight. If he felt more need to reconnoiter the cabin, then tomorrow night. There was no rationale, no tactic in waiting. He was coming after his family, they knew it, and he knew they knew it.

She would do a daily commute, here to spend time with Maggie, then back to the cabin to keep watch with Cameron.

Jean had not changed the scant clothing she wore at the cabin, and now, as she sashayed down the third-floor hallway in her short shorts and cowboy boots, Kate was amused by the glances cast at her by Ramon and Ernesto who were waiting for the elevator, Ramon visibly wrinkling his nose as her floral perfume arrived in advance of her. Jean Velez would find limited interest in her wares here in Boystown. Kate's neighbors grinned at Jason, Ernesto's elbow-flapping imitation of Big Bird on Jason's shirt making him laugh.

"I know we got off to a rocky start, I've been a real bitch," Jean told Kate in the slow-moving elevator, oblivious to the witnesses to the conversation. "What you're doing for our family—I owe you big time."

Remembering Alice's avowals of "I owe you, Miss Police Detective," Kate smiled.

"Joe doesn't deserve what our fucked-up brother's done to his life," Jean said.

"None of you do," Kate said.

Jean shrugged that off, saying, "Joe's the best of us. The best brother anyone could want."

"I can say the same about him as a friend," Kate said as the elevator doors opened on the first floor.

Jason said to Kate, "Do you have a gun in your pants too, like my Uncle Joe?"

Without missing a beat Ernesto answered, "Sure, kid," as he and Ramon got out of the elevator on the first floor. "Everybody does." He winked at Kate. "They call this the Wild West Hollywood."

Smiling as she pushed the button for the garage, Kate asked Jason, "What would you think if I did?"

"I'd be glad," he said somberly. "To keep us safe."

"People don't need guns to be safe," she said with confidence, wanting it to be true. "Nothing will happen, Jason, I promise. Your mom, your uncle—we'll all keep you safe."

"I'll be so glad when this is over," Jean said, sliding an arm around Jason's shoulders. "Whatever happens."

Kate kept her silence. Depending on what happened when Jack Cameron tracked down his brother and how out of control events might spin, this might not be over for a long time. If ever.

With all three of them carrying boxes of Jason's games and plastic bags holding their other possessions, they emptied Kate's car in one trip.

The condo phone began ringing as they made their way back in the door. With a frisson of alarm Kate saw that it was Silverlake Haven. She dropped her bags and moved quickly to pick it up.

"Kate," Marla said.

And Kate knew.

She flashed back to her visit with Maggie, Maggie asking for a pen, Maggie's embrace, her whisper, *"I love you, my dear friend."* Every sense she had ever developed as a detective, her every intuition about Maggie, were raising hairs on the back of her neck.

"I'm so sorry," Marla whispered.

"Did you reach Aimee Grant?"

"I called you first."

Kate glanced at her watch. Aimee would have just left work. "You'll need to call her cell. I'm on my way."

Kate slammed down the phone, grabbed her car keys and ran to the door shouting at Jean, "I have to go."

She did not wait for the elevator, instead racing headlong down the stairs. Wrenching open the door she leaped into her car.

Kate sped heedlessly toward Silverlake Haven, weaving around traffic, wishing she had the flashing rear window light she'd once been able to activate that scattered cars from her path as she commandeered her way through the city in an otherwise unmarked police vehicle. She cut off an oncoming car, its brakes screeching, to pull off the road in front of the hospice.

Marla was waiting for her, standing inside the door.

"What in the name of God happened?" Kate strode down the hallway, noticing vaguely that Alice was in the reception area in her wheelchair and gesturing to her.

Marla said from behind her, "The doctor we use is on his way but it'll take him awhile to get here from County General."

"Did you reach Aimee Grant?"

"She's on her way."

The door to the room was closed. "Stay here," Kate ordered Marla, opening the door and closing it behind her on whatever reply Marla was making.

Then, only slowly, she approached the bed.

Maggie lay on her back, head sunk deep in the hollow of her pillow, arms neatly along her sides, the dandelion fuzz on the very top of her head illuminated in a waning ray of sunlight slanting through the window. Her eyes were closed, her mouth slightly askew, her jaw lax. Her oxygen tube lay on the other side of her pillow. Kate stared at the tube and then her chest, willing it to rise and fall, her throat filling with anguish at the stillness before her, implacable, irreversible. Her gaze became liquid, blurring as she stared, her eyes burning with tears.

She walked over to the bed, placed her hand on Maggie's chest, warm through the soft flannel gown. She raised her hand to Maggie's face, stroked her cheek; it felt feverish. She leaned over and kissed Maggie's forehead, caressing the fine soft hair on her head, aware of a slight powdery smell from the bedclothes mixed with a faint acidy earthiness that might be urine.

Only gradually did she acquire wider awareness, hear a stirring and realize that Marla had come quietly into the room and was slightly behind her. Kate turned blindly to her.

"I'm so sorry, Kate." There were tears in Marla's voice. She briefly touched Kate's arm. "We all came to love her."

"Thank you," she managed.

Remembering her last time with Maggie, looking again at the oxygen tube, she felt her investigative impulses awaken, even in the presence of the body of her dearest friend. She did not resist them. *I owe her no less.*

"Did you touch her?"

"To take her pulse."

"Nothing else?"

"No. Kate...she was dying. She had a DNR. It's our policy besides." Marla's face and voice were calm, but the hands clasped at the waist of her white scrubs washed each other incessantly. Kate wondered fleetingly how the men and women caring for the clientele within these walls could contend with death and impending death on a daily basis.

Kate nodded. "Has anyone else touched her? Or anything?"

She shook her head. "I left the room and closed the door. Came out to make the call to the doctor and then the two calls to you and Aimee Grant." Her dark eyes were fixed on Maggie.

"No one was with her? Alice—"

"Was in the hallway. I told her she'd need to wait for a while in reception."

"Marla," Kate said quietly, "when you last spoke with her did she seem alert?"

She nodded.

"Medicated? What was her speech like?"

"Normal. She was very alert, Kate. Same as always."

"Did she have visitors today?"

"Yes, but a lot earlier, not too long after I came in, maybe noon. Some of the ones who come every few days. An African American woman, a Latina, and a very…mannish woman."

Kate nodded. Raney, Tora, Patton, from Maggie's days at the Nightwood Bar. Kate too had known them for decades and she could not imagine any of them doing anything, it seemed an impossibility that one of them would give Maggie anything to…

"Marla, how long have you been in hospice work?"

"Sixteen years."

"In your experience," Kate asked, "does something like this…happen? Someone terminal says goodbye, yet seems to be very okay, and then just…passes?"

"Kate…remember…she was dying," Marla said, looking at her in compassion. "But yes it does, and something like it actually happened to a close friend of mine. She was in Cedars for tests for persistent back pain. Turned out to be terminal spinal cancer. Her doctor told me all she said was, 'The hell you say,' and that night she walked all over the hospital and that very same night she died. The will to live—who knows?"

This did not apply here, Kate thought, or Maggie would have willed her death. She nodded. "Thank you, Marla."

"Shall I give you some more time…to be with her, Kate?"

She was peering anxiously at Kate, and for the first time, because of a drop of moisture landing on skin inside the collar of her polo shirt, Kate realized her face was wet. "Please," she said, wiping the tears from her face with both hands. "I'd appreciate it. I don't know if you could get word to me when Aimee Grant arrives—before she comes in here—but if you could…"

"I'll do my best to watch for her."

Hearing the door close, Kate pulled a chair up beside the bed. "What did you do, Maggie?" she whispered. "I know you did something. What did you do?"

She took Maggie's forever-stilled hand in her own, clasping it. Welling emotion from twenty-three years of friendship flowed through her as she gazed at Maggie for what she knew would be her final time alone with her, and she gave in to everything she felt.

Sometime later Maggie's battered old coffee mug caught her eye and she released her hand to pick it up from the side table. Wiping her eyes with a sleeve of her polo shirt, holding the mug as if it could help her divine the secrets held in this room, she noticed dregs of tea half dried in its bottom. She replaced the mug and got up to look over the room.

The wastebaskets were empty, in this room and the tiny bathroom. No surprise, the room had been cleaned before Marla called her. If someone had brought in something in packaging, that packaging was now gone.

Back at the bed, after first placing a hand on Maggie's shoulder as if asking permission, Kate adjusted the position of Maggie's arms enough to lift the blanket and peer under it to where Maggie's stick-thin legs extended down the bed, then restored the blanket and, reverently, the position of Maggie's arms. She looked at the pillow, the oxygen tube, then again at the side table. Aside from Maggie's mug there was a small bottle of Arrowhead water, its seal unbroken. If Maggie had had anything to drink within several hours it was not apparent, unless Charlie had cleaned away a finished bottle of water...

Kate heard a sound, the doorknob turning, saw the door edge open aided by the insistent wheel of a wheelchair.

"Alice," Kate said quietly, "don't come in. You can't come in here."

"I have to explain," Alice said in a quivery voice. She pushed her chair through the door and into the room. "I told Marla I was coming down the hall to visit Ida and Mary."

Alice gazed at Maggie, not Kate; then closed her eyes and with her eyes still closed she said, "I told you I owed you, Miss Police Detective."

Kate felt her heart stop.

Her blood stop.

Every nerve in her body stop.

She stood rooted, paralyzed with horror.

Her voice came back first. A croak: "You—you—"

Then her body galvanized into action and she leaped toward Alice.

With a shriek Alice threw both hands up, her head jerking to the side, her body shrinking back into the chair. "Before you kill me!" she screeched. "Look!" She was shaking one of her raised hands.

In that hand was a book: *The Kiss That Counted.*

"Maggie said I should give you this book. She said you'd be acting like this at first—"

"*At first?*" Kate seized the book. Flung it. It slammed against the wall and ricocheted onto Alice's bed. Kate pulled Alice's wheelchair into the room. Knelt down in front of the wheelchair and with her hands gripping the cold metal arms of the chair, she looked directly, fiercely into Alice's watery blue eyes, the whites veined yellow with jaundice.

"Listen to me, Alice. Tell me what happened in this room—"

There was a soft knock on the door.

"Stay out!" Kate bellowed. "Stay the hell out!"

"She said you couldn't do it." Alice gripped her robe closed at her throat as if to protect it from Kate's hands. "She said it was what you needed." Her withered cheeks sank inward as she spoke, but her voice suddenly acquired force. "She said you'd do it if you could but you couldn't. She said it's the best thing I could do for you even if you didn't know it. You didn't want to see how she would die and remember it. She said it was her very last days and it would be a gift for you not to see them. It was for you. She said I could never in your life do anything better for you. I did it for her. I did it for you."

Kate collapsed back on her ankles and thought she might faint. *Please God stop me from killing her...*She gripped her head between her hands and closed her eyes to try to gain equilibrium.

"Alice," she said heavily, "tell me what you did."

But she already knew. She already understood how she had done this. The removed oxygen tube had said it all.

"Over this week we got it all planned out. Maggie made her goodbyes to you and that pretty woman, that other close friend last night—"

Again remembering Maggie's embrace of her, her kiss, her soft, sweet *"I love you, my dear friend,"* Kate took a deep, shuddering breath.

"—and more people today. Charlie cleaned the room and helped me get in my wheelchair and I went into the hallway. As soon as I saw him go back down the hallway I came back in and she pulled her tube away and I got my pillow and just put it over her face and held it down and just leaned on it as long as I could."

Kate dropped her head into her hands, squeezing her eyes shut as if that would block out the images.

"She didn't fight at all. She never moved. Look at her, Kate," Alice pleaded. "She wanted this. With all her heart." She put a shaky hand on Kate's arm.

Kate shook it off. But she lifted her head. And did look.

There was no struggle for life reflected in that body. Maggie had closed her own eyes in welcoming the pillow that brought death. In that face was only acceptance. Only peace.

"You can arrest me," Alice said in a nearly inaudible voice. "But my liver function is down to where the most they give me is two weeks."

"You and Maggie," Kate said bleakly. "You really had this worked out."

"We were friends."

Kate looked into the rheumy, lemony eyes of Maggie Schaeffer's killer.

Friends. In a week.

As if hearing the thought, Alice said, "Anytime we met in our lives we'd have been friends. Who knows, I could have gone the way of my gay nephew with her, maybe we could have been more."

Kate looked away, and her gaze was caught by the book on Alice's bed. *The Kiss That Counted.*

"She wrote something in there," Alice said, following Kate's gaze. She reached into the pocket of her dressing gown. "She said I should give this back to you."

Kate got to her feet, took the pen she had given Maggie the night before and slid it into her pocket. "I need to get you out of here," she told Alice.

"What are you going to do with me? Arrest me? Kill me?"

"Kate? Kate?"

Aimee's voice, from the hallway, other voices, a rapping on the door.

A hand on the doorknob, Kate looked back at the peaceful, forever stilled figure on the bed. Never to see that face again... never to look into those eyes...never to hear that voice that always, always brought wisdom into her life...

As she opened the door, loss in all its finality descended on Kate in a consuming pall of desolation and darkness.

14

Kate surfaced from black fog to find Aimee's arms supporting her, protecting her, grounding her. She was still in Maggie's room but had no memory connecting this close, full body embrace with Aimee to the initial sound of Aimee's voice calling her name and the opening of the door to the room.

"I'm so, so sorry, Kate," Aimee was whispering brokenly, her arms tightening, her face wet against Kate's. Whether from her tears or Kate's, Kate did not know; her own body was heaving with involuntary sobs. Aimee moved one arm, but only to stroke and gently pat Kate's back as if she were soothing a child.

Gradually Kate regained control, and Aimee gave her one final pat and eased the tightness of her embrace, stepped back from her. She looked searchingly, almost wonderingly at what she saw in Kate's face, took both her hands and squeezed them hard before releasing them. Then made her way over to Maggie's bed, Kate following. Aimee gazed down at Maggie, her slender shoulders slumping. She leaned down and cupped Maggie's face in both hands and kissed her forehead.

Pulling tissues from the box on Maggie's side table, Kate wiped her face and blew her nose. She glanced around the room: Alice was gone, Marla nowhere in sight.

Aimee, her blue-violet eyes a gloss of tears, turned to Kate and reached for her hand. "She looks like she just slipped away. She looks very peaceful."

"Yes," Kate conceded, "she does."

"What was all the commotion in here? Marla said you were angry—told her to stay out. Something going on with you and Alice?"

Kate took temporary refuge in a vague, "I don't know, I was upset…" An inner voice combined with an investigator's innate sense of caution told her to marshal her thoughts more coherently before saying anything about Alice to anyone, even Aimee.

"I understand," Aimee said softly. "Marla told me you couldn't understand how she could seem so much better and then…" Her voice choked and she looked down at Maggie. She asked, barely able to formulate the words, "Kate…do you think…could she actually…do this to herself? Take something? Is that…what's happened here?"

"Aimee…The doctor's on his way. We'll know more then."

But she was already recognizing two realities. The doctor would arrive only when it was convenient: this was a hospice and people in here were expected to die. And from decades of experience in homicide she knew that by far the most difficult cause of death to determine was suffocation. Excruciatingly difficult to prove in its most common and tragic manifestation, infant crib death, and probably impossible in a woman with terminal lung cancer who not only did not struggle but welcomed her death. Experience told her the doctor, in the absence of very obvious evidence to the contrary, would issue a death certificate for one Magda Schaeffer with cause of death listed as lung cancer and manner of death respiratory failure. As for Alice…

"I called Raney on my way in," Aimee intruded into her thoughts. "She'll let everybody know. They're coming over to be with her—and us."

Kate nodded distractedly, still deeply preoccupied by a decision she must make and make quickly while she still had extreme grief as a reason for her reticence thus far. Revealing that Maggie's death was actually a homicide—what would happen? What if Alice denied what she had confessed? Beyond that, what would bringing an accusation actually achieve? Beyond adding a deeper layer of shock and grief and exacerbating everyone's anguish? Beyond damaging the reputation of a hospice providing outstanding service and which bore no responsibility for what had happened here?

Her entire belief system told her, ordered her to report what had occurred: it was a crime. Cameron was right—she was a cop to her soul. Her experience and reputation as a former homicide detective would lend not just credibility but muscularity to an accusation. But speaking to her out of common sense and common humanity was the stark and leavening wisdom that a woman only days from death had advanced its certainty aided by another woman only days from her own death. Assisted or not, this was a suicide.

She brushed her fingers over Maggie's forehead. *You old fox. What did you write in that book?* She needed to confiscate it before anyone else might find it and open it by happenstance. She released Aimee's hand and moved to Alice's bed.

"I'm taking this," she told Aimee, picking up and displaying *The Kiss That Counted.* "The last book she was reading, I brought it in for her."

"Sure," Aimee said with a fleeting, unseeing glance at the book.

Kate came back to the bed and reached to the side table and cradled Maggie's ancient coffee mug in one hand. "More than anything I want this," she said softly. "She used it every day of her life."

"You're the one who should have it," Aimee told her. "You should have anything you want. There was never anyone closer to her. Months ago I asked her for the sign from the Nightwood Bar."

Kate was surprised, touched by this revelation, vividly remembering the lavender script of the discreet sign that had identified Maggie's bar. "I wondered where it was. Let me put these in the car," she said. And make some phone calls while she had a few moments of privacy.

"Want me to come with you?" Aimee asked, looking at her in concern.

"Please stay here with Maggie," Kate said quietly. "She shouldn't be alone. I'll be okay. Some air would be good and I need to make a phone call before...everyone gets here and everything begins to happen."

"I'd like the time to make my own goodbyes," Aimee said in a subdued voice. She pulled up a chair beside the bed.

At the doorway Kate looked back into the room at the two women who had been the fortresses in her life.

Aimee, seating herself in the chair, elegant in her work clothes, her body subtly ripened into even more feminine grace over the years since the day Kate had first held her in her arms. Her hair parting as always into currents with the movements of her head, threads of it glinting silver under the ceiling fluorescents as she bowed her head and reached to the bed to place long, delicate fingers on Maggie's arm.

And Maggie. Once so robust, now so tiny, a virtually shapeless presence in the bed...Not a presence at all, really, her indomitable spirit having finally taken flight, abandoning the shrunken, ineffectual, foreign body she had long since rejected. That spirit winging its way—to where? In the nebulous spiritual belief system she shared with Maggie, Maggie was free. And that was enough.

Eyes again blurred with tears as she made her way down the hallway, she heard her name called and recognized that it was Ida. She ducked her head into the room.

"Kate, please come in—for just a moment."

Ida, face creased in sympathy, raised herself on her bed and reached to Kate, took her hand, lay back and clasped it in her two. "I heard. My very deepest condolences, my dear Kate. As often as you visited I know you loved her very much."

Touched by the distress on Ida's kind old face, Kate said, "Thank you," her voice unsteady.

"I'm guessing you won't be back. It would be so hard for you to come back...I just wanted to tell you I'll miss you, tell you how much you've meant to me—"

"If you want me to come back, Ida—"

"More than anything."

"Then I'll be here. I promise."

Feeling her control slipping further, Kate squeezed Ida's hand, released it and left the room.

Wiping her eyes, she walked unseeingly through the hospice and out to her car, halting when she saw skid marks leading to where she had come to a heedless stop, the car all but in the bushes of Silverlake Haven. She swore at herself for not having had the presence of mind as she came to Maggie to at least point her key ring at the car and lock the doors. In the glove compartment her loaded .38 had been accessible to anyone curious enough to get into what seemed an abandoned car.

She got in and placed the mug on the seat beside her, held onto *The Kiss That Counted*. She contemplated the book, the intense face of the tousle-haired woman on the cover. Riffled its pages.

Not now, Maggie. No matter what you wrote I just…can't deal right now.

She placed the book next to the mug and took out her cell phone. Embarrassed, ashamed of her need, she punched in the number she had to call first. She held the phone close to her ear, taking refuge in Calla Dearborn's calm, measured tones instructing her to leave a message. "It's Kate. I wanted you to know Maggie just…passed. Thanks…thanks," she repeated, her voice breaking. Realizing she could not think of a single other thing to say, she clicked off.

She dialed the cabin in Yucca Valley. Dreading the news she had to relay, she asked heavily, "Everything there okay, Joe?"

"Everything here is okay. You sound like you're not okay."

"I'm at the hospice. Maggie just passed."

"Oh my God, Kate. I am so sorry. I hope Aimee's there with you?"

"Thank you, Joe. She is. I can't leave right now. Maybe later tonight but right now I don't think I can drive—"

"Don't even think about coming here tonight. You taking Jean and Jason with you, it's the world off my shoulders. You have a lot to take care of there. I just wish I could—the timing on all this just sucks big-time."

Tell me, she thought.

"Go be with Aimee and Maggie. Don't worry about me. Trust me, I'll be fine. And Kate, you have my deepest condolences." He hung up.

Kate started the car, moved it further down the street to park it properly, and sat rubbing her face, feeling herself on the knife edge of yet another crucial decision, one as meaningful as what she had just faced about Alice, as meaningful as when she'd risked Joe's friendship by entering his house without his knowledge or permission.

The last thing on this earth she was willing to trust was Cameron's assurances that he would "be fine." Not alone, not with so lethal an entity as Jack Cameron stalking him. Joe was all alone in confronting his brother for one reason only: he saw no other choice. With Maggie already gone, how could she get through this night fearing she might be losing another close friend because she couldn't be there with him? There was really no choice to be made.

She pulled out her wallet and extracted Dutch Hollander's card from one of its compartments.

"Dutch," she said when he picked up his cell phone, "it's Kate. You offered to help—"

"What can I do?" he broke in, his voice firm, resonant.

"I need you to absolutely trust me and I need to absolutely trust you."

"I'm right there on both of those."

Remembering his hand gripping hers so firmly on the restaurant table, she plunged on. "I've found Joe. He's in bad trouble and facing it alone. His life may depend on us. On you."

"I'm right there," he repeated. "Where are you?"

"Long story and I don't have enough time to explain much of anything except I can't be where he is, not till tomorrow. I need to tell you what's going on with him and I need you to do exactly as I say and not one thing more. Are you in?"

"He's my friend, Kate. And I totally trust you on this. I'm totally in."

A few minutes later, having filled in Dutch Hollander on the situation at the cabin, seeing Aimee come walking down the street toward her, Kate hurriedly concluded her instructions to him, uttered, "I have to go," and signed off.

Aimee leaned in the window. "Are you okay?"

"Yeah. I was just about to come back."

"Who did you have to call?"

"A friend of Joe's. I had to tell him where he is—"

"Which is?"

"The high desert, out of cell phone range. How to get to him there."

Whatever her judgment about Kate going to this much effort to notify Cameron of Maggie's death, Aimee's nod acknowledged that she accepted it was important to Kate. "The gang's arriving," she said.

"Yeah. I saw." During her call to Dutch Hollander she had been peripherally aware of two cars driving past whose occupants were friends.

"So let's go be with Maggie," Aimee said, and pulled the car door open. "With our family."

A fractured family, Kate thought, climbing out and taking the hand Aimee extended to her. A splintered family. The heart and soul, the glue holding together what little family she could lay claim to over the last twenty-three years was gone, had departed from that bed in the hospice. Aimee, for all her supportive behavior under these circumstances, was estranged from her. And Cameron…what might be happening to Cameron this very night?

In Maggie's room, Raney was first to come up to her, her dark eyes wet, her ebony face anguished. Hugging Kate, she told her, "I know how you feel."

"I know you do, Raney," Kate said, hugging her in return.

The loss of Raney's partner from breast cancer—it was another compelling reason for letting pass the truth of Maggie's death. Unlike Maggie, Audie had retained sufficient agency with her illness to take her own life, and even though she had shown in every way she could to everyone who loved her that her overdose had been a rational act, not an act of despair, Raney to this day remained haunted by a decision made independently of her and a death that seemed all the crueler for her life partner's usurping whatever days remained to them.

Patton was next to pull Kate into a bruising, hip-clanging hug. "Nothing will ever be the same," she muttered, her weather-beaten face coursed with tears. Patton looked oddly different, and Kate realized that Audie's funeral had been the last time she'd seen Patton in anything but baggy jeans and a T-shirt, long or short-sleeved depending on the season. In what passed as her most formal clothing, she now wore black khakis and a gray shirt and was hatless, her trademark yachting cap resting on Alice's empty bed.

Ash and Tora were at Maggie's bed, banking flowers all around her, bouquets of sunflowers, Mexican daisies and dahlias. "Maggie's favorites," Tora said, turning her tear-streaked face to Kate.

"I know." They were the flowers Maggie had planted and tended in the miniscule yard of her tiny house in Pacoima. "How wonderful of you and Ash to do this."

"The flower stand on Melrose," Ash said, "I bought everything they had of these. We checked, Kate. Whatever we leave here with Maggie can be included for her, her…"

Everyone nodded mutely, as if no one wanted to name the process that would transmute the woman on the bed from her human form into gray ashes.

Patton went over to Alice's bed and picked up her yachting cap, battered and threadbare with age. "Take this…this piece of me with you, Maggie," she said brokenly and placed the cap reverently at the foot of Maggie's bed.

Ash, finished with the flowers, arranged gay pride flags on Maggie's pillow on either side of her head. From a backpack Tora removed a rainbow-hued T-shirt, unfolded it and placed it tenderly across Maggie's legs; it read CHICANA PRIDE and Kate recognized it as the shirt that Maggie had bought for Tora at a gay pride parade they had all gone to well over a decade ago. Tora tried to speak, could not, and backed away, into Ash's arms.

Aimee, who had been searching for something in her shoulder bag, was next. Lifting Maggie's hand, she slid onto her wrist a bracelet of stones the colors of the pride flag. Kate had been with Aimee the weekend she had bought the bracelet at one of West Hollywood's pride festivals.

Kate was looking wonderingly at the group of women, all of them with hard life history seared into their faces, Patton's once-dark hair bleached to snow…It now seemed all so brief, their time together in the sun when Kate had found her community in Maggie's bar. When they had all been young and hanging out together, this little band of friends, Latinas, African Americans, Caucasians, defiantly queer and defiantly in-your-face to the world. Save for herself, a closeted police officer, and Audie, a closeted kindergarten teacher…Who among them could ever have imagined this day…Imagined themselves this much older… This much beaten up by life…

Maggie had minced no words in her opposition to a memorial service being held for her, and so nothing had been planned beyond this meeting here tonight, beyond the cremation that would occur no later than Monday morning. But Kate had never given any thought to this night, these moments directly after Maggie's passing, what might or should be happening. "I don't have anything for her," she said helplessly.

"You already did what we're doing," Patton declared. "You put her in here, made sure she had the best of care up till the moment she left us."

I put her in here, she thought, and made Alice possible.

Then she thought: *Let it go.*

"You're in her heart, Kate," Raney told her. "She's already taken that with her. She loved us, loved my Audie, and she loved you more than any of us."

"More than all the rest of us put together," Aimee put in, adding a brief, pointed smile.

The thought was still reverberating in Kate's head: *Let it go.* She was also thinking: I do have something to leave with her.

"So sorry to interrupt," Marla said from the doorway, "Doctor Patel has just arrived."

"If you wouldn't mind," Kate said, her gaze encompassing all the women in the room, "could I have just a few last moments alone with Maggie and then remain here with the doctor?"

With sympathetic murmurs of acquiescence and a pat on the arm from Aimee, everyone filed out of the room.

Kate reached into her pocket, took out her LAPD detective's badge. Then she covered Maggie's hand, the one with Aimee's bracelet on it, with her own. The hand was still warm; her body had not yet begun to cool.

The doctor walked in, a handsome older man of Indian heritage, carrying a medical bag and wearing a suit and tie, Kate was pleased to see. "Doctor Patel," she said, "I'm Kate Delafield, the decedent's closest friend."

He responded with a handshake and a fleeting smile flashing white against the warm dark tones of his skin. "You are also LAPD?" he asked in a slight accent, his gaze catching the badge in her hand as she had intended.

"Wilshire Division homicide. Retired," she said, and fully displayed the badge. "It's a replica. I'll be leaving it to be cremated with my friend."

He was surveying the bed, the flowers, the flags. "Along with other tributes, I see. Your friend obviously meant a great deal to people in this world."

"She did," Kate said thickly, struck by the phrasing and the truth of it. Maggie had indeed meant a great deal in the sphere she had inhabited.

He opened his case, removed a penlight, placed the case on the floor by the bed. He held a middle finger to the inside of Maggie's wrist for a few moments, then touched palpating fingers to Maggie's face. "Were you here for her passing?"

"Afterward. Only moments afterward."

In a single fluid instant he lifted one of Maggie's eyelids with a thumb, splashed his light into it and flicked the light off, lowered the lid. "Everything seemed as it should?"

"She had stage four extensive lung cancer," Kate offered in reply.

"I'm very sorry for your loss, Detective Delafield," the doctor said as he gently lifted the neck of Maggie's gown. "A very great loss, to pay her such a tribute as giving her your police badge. Why don't you lay it right here over her heart. Seems that's where it might go?"

"Thank you for your kindness," Kate managed. She placed the badge over Maggie's heart, precisely on the expanse of bare skin the doctor had exposed. Dr. Patel restored the neck of the gown.

Again the reverberation within her: *Let it go.*

The doctor put his light back into his case, closed it up and without another word left the room.

Kate stood beside Maggie's bed, her body again heaving with sobs, telling herself again and again, *Let it go.*

It was time to let Maggie go. It was time to let the badge go. The job go. It was time to let many things go.

15

"Neither one of us should be alone tonight," Aimee had told her. Adding, "We shouldn't go to the condo." Kate had noted the neutral language: nineteen years they'd spent together in what they had always called "our home" or "our place" and now it was "the condo."

The reason they should not go there was starkly apparent: on this night of loss, tangible reminders of themselves together during happier times would be excruciating. At least Kate did not need to explain why the condo was off limits anyway, with a mother and son in residence.

After Maggie's body had been removed from Silverlake Haven, everyone who had come to be with her had afterward gone to a Thai restaurant on Silverlake Boulevard where they had spent several raucous hours gathered around a table of communal food and drink, reminiscing and sharing stories and memories of Maggie, laughing and crying. Even though Kate had consumed only iced tea she could not remember anything she'd said or any food she'd ordered or consumed.

And now here they were in West LA, off Overland Avenue near Olympic, on their way into the guest cottage that Aimee was renting from a friend and colleague at her law office.

As Kate followed Aimee down the side path she thought of the cottage/office behind Calla Dearborn's house, and she thought of another cottage nearby—the one in which Herman Layton had lived a fortress-like existence until his murder became the fateful first case when she and Cameron had become partners, when Cameron had lost his fundamental trust in her.

Aimee's place was unlike either of those other significant dwellings, resembling in miniature the house it sat behind, beige stucco with arched windows, occupying its own patch of ground delineated by a white picket fence no more than a foot high, its tiny lawn consisting of thick ivy, a wave of scarlet bougainvillea along one side of the house spilling over onto the Spanish tile roof.

Kate followed Aimee into the house and scrutinized Aimee's living space and, even more acutely, how she occupied it.

On a polished bamboo floor, a small sofa along the front window and two small leather armchairs formed a grouping with an end table and coffee table arranged between them. Behind a counter fronted by two barstools, an alcove kitchen looked to be well equipped with apartment-size appliances. Accordion doors were closed across an entrance that presumably led to a bedroom and bath.

A coffee mug and a plate with a scattering of crumbs sat on the kitchen counter, several magazines beside the plate, the top magazine folded over to the article currently being read. Here, apparently, was where Aimee had her toast and morning coffee. All the mornings when they had been together, Aimee had taken the same items back to bed on a tray, along with orange juice and a big cup of fresh brewed coffee and a muffin for Kate.

Behind the counter a cupboard door was ajar and the dishwasher door agape, a tray of plates and glasses pulled partially out as if Aimee had been interrupted or run out of time while putting dishes away. Salt and pepper shakers and other condiments, along with bottles of olive oil and vinegar, were strewn along the counter beside the stove, and a loaf of bread sat tucked in beside the toaster as if that were Aimee's casually assigned place for it.

In the living room, books and magazines were heaped in haphazard stacks beside one of the armchairs. A blue UCLA basketball T-shirt Kate recognized had been flung across the back of the other chair. Aimee's favorite slippers had been kicked off beside the sofa where another stack of magazines lay in disarray, a plate on top of them, beside a floor lamp.

Aimee had been observing her, arms crossed. "I guess I can no more expect you to stop being a detective than that proverbial rooster not crowing at sunrise."

Was she being funny or sarcastic? Kate chose her words: "It's a nice place."

Aimee shrugged. "Now you know my dark secret. I'm a slob."

"You don't remotely qualify." But she was surprised. More than that, deeply unsettled. They had lived together in neatness and order, and she had never questioned the assumption that her own habits and predilections were Aimee's as well. Now she wondered how much it had cost Aimee all those years to live in deference to Kate's standards.

"Can I get you anything?" Aimee asked, moving toward the kitchen with an easy ownership of this space that made Kate's throat ache with regret.

"Maybe some water." This would give her a few moments longer to look around.

By the time Aimee returned with a bottle of water from the fridge Kate had satisfied herself that everything she saw appeared to belong to Aimee or was part of the furnishings of the cottage. Of course she had yet to see the bedroom…

"Why don't you go ahead and take your shower," Aimee said. "Towels are in a chest in the bathroom. I'll be there in a few minutes."

Only Aimee would know that she showered at night as well as in the morning. "Sure," she said.

Kate pushed open the folding doors, closed them behind her, and then stood rooted, suddenly hesitant to take another step. If Aimee were indeed seeing someone…This day had already been filled with such turmoil, such anguish, she could not bear to have anything more…

"Everything okay?" Aimee called, apparently having heard her footsteps halt on the bamboo floor.

"Yeah, sure," Kate said. She squared her shoulders and walked into the bedroom. And again stood rooted. Closed her eyes, inhaled. Aimee's perfume mixed with soap and shampoo had always permeated the bathroom at the condo, but here in a much smaller space it had penetrated the bedroom...

Get a grip, she ordered herself.

On the bed a quilt of multihued yellows Aimee had taken with her from the condo, so much too large for the double bed it now covered that it reached the floor, had been carelessly pulled up, pillows tossed in the general direction of the wicker headboard. A storage bench at the foot of the bed was covered with folded clothes; more clothes lay in a disheveled pile in a corner, jeans, tops, underwear, presumably laundry. She hoped Aimee had access to facilities in the owner's house and did not need to use a Laundromat. Kate reflected guiltily that even though she hadn't been the one to walk out on their relationship, Aimee was the one now living in diminished circumstances, crammed into this tiny place, while she herself had the upscale, spacious condo. Aimee's one and only gain seemed to be a shorter commute to her law offices in Century City...

A utilitarian blond nightstand held a lamp, a clock radio, a book. The small flat-panel TV that used to be on a stand in the den of the condo opposite Aimee's desk now sat directly on that same desk alongside an iPod speaker system. Thinking ruefully that she was getting too used to feeling and acting like a burglar, Kate stole into the walk-in closet. Along with a solid wall of unpacked boxes stacked ceiling high were double racks of clothes Kate mostly recognized, and a maelstrom of shoes Kate also mostly recognized. Sweaters and sports attire crowded a shelf above the highest clothes rack.

She went into the tiny bathroom. It was, as she expected, redolent with scents of Aimee. The tiled counter and its single drawer and the medicine cabinet shelves were all crowded with the usual bath accoutrements and Aimee's cosmetics, all of which she recognized. Satisfied, her spirits lightening because there seemed no evidence anywhere in this place of another woman, she took a towel from a plastic chest that also held changes of bedding, and turned on the shower. She pulled her clothes off, wondering if there was anything of Aimee's that would fit her in lieu of pajamas, and walked into the shower cubicle.

The water was cold but she did nothing to adjust the temperature; she was again thinking about Maggie, and her spirits once more plummeted. Maggie was at the crematorium now, awaiting flames, and here she was, standing under cold water, trying to feel something like what she used to feel in a world that no longer had Maggie in it.

As she was toweling off, Aimee walked into the bathroom, handed her a packaged toothbrush. "Thought I had one of these somewhere, finally found it."

Even though Aimee had seen her naked countless times, Kate hastily wrapped the towel around herself and took the toothbrush and uttered the first thing that came to mind: "What time is it?"

"I didn't notice. Does it matter?"

"Not really." She asked, "Pajamas?"

Aimee shrugged, repeated, "Does it matter?"

As Kate took refuge in a shrug of her own, Aimee turned and left the bathroom.

When Kate walked naked into the bedroom a few minutes later, Aimee, wearing a short white terrycloth robe, pushed blindly past her into the bathroom blowing her nose, her eyes newly reddened from crying.

Soon Kate heard water running, the sound of an electric toothbrush, and five or so minutes later Aimee reappeared wearing white pajamas. She turned out the bedside lamp and got into bed under the light sheet that covered Kate. Turned to Kate and, snuffling, put an arm around her.

Kate gathered her in and was barely able to smother a moan, so overwhelmed was she by the achingly familiar, pliant softness of Aimee's body filling her arms, melding with the curves and hollows of her own body, the warmth of Aimee beginning to permeate the cool fabric of Aimee's pajamas along the length of Kate's bare skin. As Aimee buried her face in her shoulder, a skein of hair, soft as feathers, brushed Kate's cheek and fell onto her throat, peach and apricot aromas from Aimee's face cream and hair intoxicating all her senses.

Aimee slid a hand over Kate's shoulder, fingers delicate, almost tentative in their touching then suddenly sinking into her flesh and convulsively squeezing, Kate feeling each imprint of finger and fingernail as warm tears wet her bare shoulder. Aimee did not audibly sob but Kate felt tremors in her body and tightened her arms.

Aimee's hand left her shoulder to come to Kate's face and then both hands clasped and held and warmed her face, then traveled up to encircle her head. Thumbs resting on Kate's temples, Aimee sifted Kate's hair through her fingers in separate, erratic patterns.

Every nerve alert and ragged with desire, Kate lay in a stillness of tension, on a razor's edge of anxiety that a wrong movement would rupture the membrane of what was unfolding. Whatever happened or did not happen, she knew with certainty that it had to be what Aimee needed, had to be Aimee's initiative, and that her own response could be no more than what Aimee wanted.

Holding her close as the tremors continued, Kate felt Aimee's fingers settle into an arrhythmic stroking of her hair as if seeking solace in its texture. Kate remembered the collection of smooth stones Aimee had gathered over the years, how she sometimes selected one to hold and stroke between her thumb and index finger. "The shape of the stone," she had told Kate, "it soothes me." Kate hoped the texture of her hair was like one of those stones.

Aimee's fingers stilled, and her body stiffened, stirred until Kate understood and loosened her embrace. Aimee moved down from her pillow to lay her head briefly on Kate's chest, then buried her face between her breasts. Kate cradled Aimee's head, feeling the heat of her face, the heat of her breath, penetrate her chest, the corn silk of her hair in her hands and in spreading filaments over her throat and shoulders. Aimee was crying silently again, wetting her breasts, and Kate drifted a hand down incrementally, cautiously, and then caressingly over her neck and shoulders, her kneading fingertips tracing the triangles of her shoulder blades.

She did not speak; did not know if she should; did not know what she could say if she did speak beyond, "Are you all right?" And of course neither of them was all right.

Aimee grasped Kate's arms and pulled her body away from Kate's, but only to turn her back to Kate and then again seek her, fitting herself closely into her, burrowing in so tightly that her back was flattening Kate's breasts, the back of her kneecaps fitting onto Kate's knees, her hips plush and malleable on Kate's upper thighs. Aimee took Kate's arm and pulled it around her, then sighed, whether from sorrow or comfort Kate could not tell. Aimee's hand, still clasping Kate's forearm, slid down its length to cover the back of Kate's hand; then she pulled Kate's hand under her pajama top and cradled its palm and fingers over her breast, her hand holding Kate's hand in place.

This was how they had slept together, whether or not there was lovemaking, for nineteen years. Exhaustion descending from all the emotion of this day, her face buried in Aimee's hair, her hand overflowing with the sweet heavy warm curving creaminess of Aimee's breast, inhaling through the apricot scents of her shampoo to the essence that was pure Aimee, her entire body imbued with warmth and softness, Kate thought: *I would do anything, anything to have this back.*

Distantly, vaguely, she heard a question from a voice that might have been Calla Dearborn's: *Then why don't you?*

* * *

When Kate woke up, the bed was empty of Aimee, sunshine was streaming through a window, the cottage was aromatic with coffee and toast. The clock radio on the nightstand read 9:10.

A few minutes later, having pulled on her polo shirt and briefs, Kate padded barefoot into the kitchen.

Dressed in exercise clothes on this Saturday morning, Aimee was sitting at the counter drinking coffee, munching on a piece of toast, looking graceful and beautiful in navy pants with a white stripe down the side and a matching top, her hair still damp from the shower. Kate could not imagine how she could have slept through the sound of Aimee showering.

Kate said, "Good morning."

Aimee glanced at her and then looked away, as if waiting for something else to be added, then responded, her face tightening, "Same to you." She got up and tossed the coffee remaining in her mug in the sink and put the mug on the counter, turned and nodded, almost curtly, to the coffeepot. "There's lots of coffee, bread if you want toast. There's eggs if you want them. Help yourself. I have to go."

Kate smothered the automatic *Where to?* She no longer had any right to know.

Aimee strode into the living room and picked up her shoulder bag. "Stay as long as you need to. The door locks behind you."

Aimee was at the door when Kate said to her, "I never realized you loved Maggie so very much."

Aimee stopped in mid-step. Turned and stared at Kate. Both hands convulsing into fists, expelling a breath explosive with frustration, she said gratingly, "Last night was all about *you* loving Maggie so very much. It was about me with *you* about *Maggie.*"

Kate gaped at her. "I never—"

"You fool." Anger was suffusing Aimee's face, her eyes sparked with fury. "You've always been such a *fool.* You always think you have to be everyone's protector. You always think you have to decide what everybody else is supposed to feel. Or need. You actually believe *none* of last night was about me and what I feel about you." Her voice rose. "You actually think you miss me more than I miss you." In a ferocity of rage she spat, "You stupid stupid *stupid*—"

She was gone, the door slamming savagely behind her.

16

Numbly, Kate went into the kitchen alcove. Picked up Aimee's mug and slopped coffee into it and took a deep swallow heedless of its temperature. It scalded its way down, resembling the burning rawness of that first scotch of the day. That first scotch being something she had not experienced yesterday, for the first time in months. She could not remember how many months.

Anne. Aimee. Three decades. And I still don't seem to know the first goddamn thing about women. Aimee's right. I am stupid stupid stupid.

And now she couldn't go to Maggie any longer for her counsel. As for Calla Dearborn, how could she even begin to fill Maggie's shoes?

Focus, she told herself. It was imperative that she focus. Compartmentalize. Right now she could not afford to think about any of it, especially the accusations Aimee had hurled at her. Maybe on the way to Yucca Valley.

Yucca Valley…Swallowing more coffee as she strode back into the bedroom, she located her cell phone in the pocket of her pants.

Three messages. Hoping her prickling of dread was not a premonition, she punched in her password. The first call had come in last night, Calla Dearborn, shortly after Kate had called her.

"Kate, I'm so sorry about this great loss in your life." The voice was soft, pitched so low with compassion that Kate pressed the phone to her ear, straining to hear it. "Come in and talk about it when you can. I could make time for you tomorrow. Call me when you're feeling up to it."

Tears welling then overflowing, Kate wrathfully clawed them away. How could a few kind words from this woman dissolve her like this? How had this woman become so quickly and embarrassingly important to her?

Kate took a deep, shuddering breath, let it out, and listened to the announcement that the next call, the second message, had come in at 6:55 this morning.

"It's Dora Terhune."

Kate had to think a moment before remembering Dora in Victorville, Jean's next-door neighbor, Dora the bitch.

"I just called the cops. I figured you'd want to know—Jean's trailer got trashed. I heard some real loud banging in there sometime last night but you know, I was dead asleep and I thought it was Jean and her beefy boyfriend making their usual racket. Then this morning I see a car go screeching away and it isn't Jean's or the boyfriend's truck so I go over there. Just to make sure everything's okay, you know. So the door's wide open and inside…well, whoever this guy is, he's really smashed up the place. Looks like a hurricane went through. Mack that owns the trailer, he's gonna shit himself. That's pretty much all I know, I never saw anybody, but this is scary stuff, Kate. Somebody's really coming after Jean, I just hope to hell she's okay and he doesn't come back. So you call me if you want to."

Sitting down heavily on the bed, Kate waited for the final message. It had come in only five minutes later, at seven this morning. Dutch Hollander, and she could tell from his first word, his tone, that there would be no bad news.

"Nice night under the stars," he reported in an easy, laconic tone. "I found a real good reconnaissance spot." The rest of the message was equally concise: "Nothing suspicious, I did a good canvass. Had to drive five miles to get a damn cell phone signal." She heard traffic noises; he was driving. "I'll get some breakfast and keep checking for a call back. Let me know when you get here, Kate."

Sagging with relief, she called the cabin in Yucca Valley.

When the phone was picked up she asked without preamble, "Everything's okay?"

"Everything's okay," Cameron answered calmly. "How are you doing, Kate?"

"I'm okay, Joe. Sorry to be so late checking in with you. I just heard from Dora Terhune. Jean's trailer was trashed last night. Dora didn't see anyone, but we know it's him. He really wrecked the place, lots more damage than in your house."

Cameron let out an audible breath. "Jesus."

"Seems he's a lot angrier at Jean than he is at you."

"He isn't," Cameron said shortly. "He hasn't found us yet, is all." His voice was grim. "He's in a rage, he's escalating. Does Jean know?"

"I just picked up the message."

"Don't tell her. She's crazy-dumb enough to want to go back and not having a car won't stop her."

"I agree. Let's keep her and her boy completely safe."

"Kate," he said somberly, "this isn't somebody wanting revenge, this is Jack gone right off the rails. I know how he is when he gets like this—he doesn't care about consequences, self-preservation, anything. This figures to be his very next stop. Don't do this. Don't come here—"

"Nothing's changed for me, Joe," she interrupted decisively. "I'll be there. As soon I can." If anything, Maggie's death had sharpened her resolve, given more urgency to being there with him.

"Kate…then take whatever time you need, my friend. I know this is a very rough patch for you."

"Thanks, Joe, see you early afternoon," she said, and clicked off, no longer trusting her voice.

She wanted to call Calla Dearborn, set up an appointment. Mostly, she admitted, to again have the comfort of even brief contact with her. But with no idea when she might be back in the city, with no intention of filling her in on her present circumstances and running the risk of Dearborn attempting to divert her from the path she was bent on taking, of course she could not...

She called Dutch Hollander, who was apparently again out of cell phone range, and left a message to call her as soon as he could.

She gulped the rest of her coffee, used her borrowed toothbrush, and dressed, thinking that she could not remember the last time she had not showered in the morning. She wanted to carry the feeling of Aimee on her body along with the memory of their close connection throughout the night for as long as she could into this day. And the coming night in the high desert.

She was on her way out of the cottage when her phone rang with Hollander's call back.

"Dutch, thanks for all this," she said earnestly. "I owe you."

"You owe me nothing," he said emphatically. "Thanks don't apply here, Kate. Joe's been my friend since we were kids."

She couldn't argue with that. "I'm leaving now, should be there early afternoon. There's been a development..." She informed him of Dora Terhune's call, the destruction in Jean's trailer.

"This guy is the fucking worst of bad news," he muttered.

"You might just drop back into town and check in with Dora," she suggested.

"Kate, I won't leave you and Joe with this. I can—"

"I really get that," she interrupted him, "but what he did to Jean's trailer gives us a shot at stopping him. Jack has to be driving a stolen vehicle and if Dora can give us the make of what she saw taking off from the trailer, you can check the most recent stolen car records of locales where he's been sighted and maybe get a match, a license plate. And if anyone nearby is an actual eyewitness to Jack Cameron going into or out of that trailer we can put out an APB for him and his vehicle, pick him up before he even begins his act three."

There was a lengthy silence while Hollander considered this. Then he said, "I can see why Joe thinks you're a great detective—"

A great detective who just let someone get away with murdering my best friend.

"—and it's a good plan," he conceded with clear reluctance in his tone. "Picking him up for grand theft auto and felony destruction of property would put him right back in jail. The best outcome. By far."

A long shot, she could almost hear him thinking. But one that had to be explored, given the alternative.

"I'll get on it," he promised her.

"One more thing." With a chuckle of embarrassment she admitted, "I feel like I'm chasing a shadow. Except for a photo of Jack when he was a kid, I have no clue what he looks like."

He laughed. "Me either, after all his years of incarceration. I can only tell you what he looked like last time I saw him. Five-ten maybe, brown eyes, broken nose, dirty blond hair in a ponytail, scrawny, fidgety as hell—drugs, you can bet—a few razor-thin horizontal scars on his forehead and chin from the accident, his felony DUI. He might have beefed up in jail—"

"He'd get drugs there as easy as on the street," Kate interjected.

"Sure. Never saw him in anything but knee-length shorts and ratty T-shirts."

"Thanks, Dutch. Let me give you Joe's landline number in the cabin. If you pick up this guy or whatever, let it ring twice. I'll get back to you. Somehow."

"Got it. Bring some warm clothes with you, my friend. It gets cold here in the desert at night. Good luck, Kate."

"You too, Dutch," she said fervently.

She left Aimee's cottage, closing its door without a backward glance. She would drive to the condo to pack for the cabin and change clothes. Leave the ones she was wearing in the donate pile for Goodwill. She could never look at them again without thinking of Maggie, without remembering the churning despair of that drive to the hospice, her first sight of Maggie's lifeless face…

* * *

As she unlocked the door and came into the condo, Miss Marple flew down the corridor from the bedroom and wound her meowing self around Kate's ankles. It seemed days since she'd seen her furry companion, had left Jean and Jason here with Miss Marple who, Kate was sure, was spending much of her time sulking under the bed. The place was cool, quiet, empty, for which Kate was inordinately grateful. The absence of her visitors saved her from having to explain her abrupt departure last night, from having to make conversation with Jean while concealing her knowledge of the devastation to the place in Victorville they called home. Maybe Jean had taken Jason out to look for movie stars, she speculated, remembering how his earnest, guileless face had lit up at this particular blandishment to leave the cabin and travel here with his mother.

She leaned down and gently picked up Miss Marple, cradling and stroking her as she checked the food and water bowls, which were full, then looked approvingly over the living room which showed no evidence of her visitors, and finally walked on into the bedroom. The bed was made, the room was neat. The suitcases and clothes and games that had taken possession of the room and closet had done so in an organized manner.

With Miss Marple climbing onto and sitting on each item Kate laid out on the bed, she packed a duffel bag with thought and care for what she might need at Victorville. Including her new prescription. Including a bottle of Cutty Sark she grabbed from her stash in the kitchen. *Medicinal*, she told herself, stuffing it in the bottom of the bag. She did not know how long she might be holed up with Joe, how long she could hold off her need, and she would be of no use to him with her concentration fractured by a serious case of the jitters. She left a note on the counter that she would be staying with Cameron indefinitely, and included Aimee's cell phone number as a close-by emergency contact. If it became necessary for Jean Velez to dial that number, explanations to Aimee as to who Jean Velez was and why she and her son were here in the condo would hardly be necessary. Unless she and Cameron could figure a way to prevent this onrushing, seemingly inevitable disaster, it would be all over the news.

With one final pat to Miss Marple, one final look around at this place she loved, her refuge from the world, Kate let herself out of the condo.

A few minutes later, making her way down Santa Monica, Kate realized she had one more very necessary stop to make before she headed for the 10.

Though La Brea was a major thoroughfare in Wilshire Division, it had been years since she'd driven down one particular stretch of it. She'd always instead chosen Highland or Fairfax for reasons having everything to do with avoidance of memory and emotions too inchoate and too laden with the potential to overwhelm her. A reluctance made up of unwillingness to resurrect the tragedy of the murder she had investigated here, unwillingness to see what changes had occurred along this street from when the Nightwood Bar had closed, unwillingness to learn what had become of the one place where she had been able to put aside the isolation of her police career, where she had spent some of the happiest and most convivial evenings of her life with her little band of lesbian friends in the warm glow of Maggie's genial presence.

Traveling down La Brea from Santa Monica, she noted that the street itself hadn't changed all that significantly over time. However rearranged the conglomerate of small independent businesses might have become over the years, they were still the same auto repair shops, furniture stores, bank branches, antique dealers, fast-food outlets. Only the cellular phone stores, a Petco, a Trader Joe's at Third Street outwardly reflected cultural mutations of the new century.

As she approached the streets below Olympic, she felt a leaden justification for her resistance to driving along here. What had been a welcome landmark for her, a cheery bright yellow beacon of a place offering fried chicken and biscuits and gravy, was gone. She had never been in it, could not even remember the name. The only eatery on La Brea she could recall patronizing was Pink's, a long-standing LA landmark for chili dogs that her first partner, Ed Taylor, had loved, his touchy digestion be damned.

She wondered when the chicken place had been torn down. The buildings along the block opposite the Nightwood Bar had changed so much in configuration that she could no longer even distinguish exactly where it had once been located on the street.

She pulled into the crescent-shaped drive that for a single short block veered off and then back onto La Brea. It had been six years since Maggie had held court in her bar up on the hillside behind the businesses on this block, twenty-three years since the murder of Dory Quillin had first brought Kate to the Nightwood Bar, and to her community. She parked, and sat for a time, unable to stop the grief and melancholy washing over her. Then she got out of her car and walked along the shabby block, her memory indelible of that very first step in the investigation of the murder, when she had written in her notebook the names of the businesses that used to be here. A car rental agency, she recalled, a travel agency, dress shop, mailbox rental, an auto repair shop. The Casbah Motel and its restaurant with its window sign simply announcing Turkish Food.

All were gone. La Brea Center, read a sign over the middle doorway. The "Center" housed two hair salons, a photo shop, offerings of guitar lessons and readings from a psychic, a dusty window bearing a For Lease sign. In place of the Casbah was a featureless pink stucco motel.

She was brought to a halt by a discovery she had never imagined. The driveway that had once led up the hillside behind the motel had vanished. It had been flattened and incorporated into the parking lot for the motel. Much of the hillside behind the motel had been leveled and a retaining wall now supported the structures on what remained of the hill.

The Nightwood Bar was gone.

Completely, utterly gone. Vanished as if it had never existed. Maggie gone...Her bar gone...

She stood rooted to the cracked sidewalk, assimilating this new reality, trying to peer beyond the phalanx of faded stucco storefronts into her imagination and memory of where the bar had once been. Gone, all of it was gone. As if it had been nothing but a mirage.

She closed her eyes for a moment, shook her head, turned and trudged back to her car, remembering and trying to take comfort in Maggie's mantra: "Everything changes, Kate, nothing stays the same."

As she got back into the Focus, she again shook her head, this time over the conversation with Maggie that had led her to what had turned out to be the invisible grave of the Nightwood Bar. Maggie telling her: "I don't care what you do with my ashes but you know how much I love the sun, Kate, so please don't dump me into the cold wet ocean…"

Kate had thought the environs of the Nightwood Bar would be the perfect place, would be where Maggie's ashes should appropriately go.

No way in fucking hell would she ever put Maggie here.

17

Wearied by the sights and sounds of freeway traffic on yet another interminable trip to the desert, weighed down and on edge with not knowing when she could have a drink, assailed by a jumble of thoughts about Aimee, about Cameron, about Maggie and about that other passing—the Nightwood Bar— Kate punched on the radio to a news roundup on KFWB. The lead story was Barack Obama for the first time edging ahead of Hillary Clinton in committed delegates for the Democratic National Convention. A momentary gladness swept over Kate that Maggie had lived to see the first African American and the first woman as front-runners in an American presidential primary. She hoped Maggie would be right in her forecast that in November the country would choose one of them as the next president.

Turning off the radio, she inserted into the CD player her self-assembled collection of oldies that had played on the jukebox at the Nightwood Bar, the songs that over the years women newly in love or newly looking for love constantly played for each other. She was able to listen to "When You're in Love with a Beautiful Woman," "Wrapped Around Your Finger," "You Make Me Feel Like Dancing," "Slow Hand," "Loving Her was Easier," "If You Could Read My Mind" and "Every Breath You Take" before a mixture of teary nostalgia and throat-aching grief forced her to switch off the CD player.

She cast another desultory glance at the cityscape flying by, a virtually unbroken sequence of light industry interspersed with giant malls, sprawling auto dealerships and innumerable fast-food outlets, and then at a mileage sign that placed her past the city of Ontario and coming up on the cutoff to Yucca Valley.

Maggie. Everything was different, the world was off its axis without Maggie, and it was disconcerting that life was going on and looking exactly the same. A line from a classic film came into her mind: "There are eight million stories in the Naked City." The reference was to New York City, but Los Angeles County qualified with its own nine million stories. On this freeway it was hard to imagine any of them, hard to envision lives holding anything but the most desolate of drama along this interminable, characterless, soulless corridor stretching from LA into Riverside County. She was glad to see the sign for Highway 62 to Yucca Valley, and soon afterward, the clean welcome vista of wind-smoothed foothills and an occasional Joshua tree with angular limbs jutting every which way like a creature in a mad solitary dance over sunlit sand dotted with desert scrub.

A call came in on her cell phone on the passenger seat. She did not answer because she was driving but did glance at the caller ID. And disgustedly smacked herself on the forehead. Immediately after the call was finished she listened to Dylan's message.

"Aunt Kate," her nephew told her in hushed tones, "I got Aunt Aimee's awful news last night about Maggie—"

Bless Aimee for knowing to call him, she thought wryly. For knowing full well I'd be too *stupid stupid stupid* to do it.

"I know Maggie was really sick but she seemed pretty good last week, really happy about me and my surgery. I'll miss her so much…"

Dylan cleared his throat. Twice. And Kate understood that he had something significant to tell her.

"I couldn't call last night because I heard from Mom and with this just happening about Maggie I didn't want to upset you more. Mom and I had a really long talk. Aunt Kate, she's coming here for my surgery. Which is great but…The really big news is, she's walked out on Dad."

"Wow," Kate uttered, glancing at the phone as if a vestige of Dylan inhabited the instrument along with his voice.

Again he cleared his throat. "Yeah, can you believe it? She says she's done a lot of praying and thinking and reading and she says Dad doesn't know God's plan for me, no one knows except God, and she's okay with me changing my body because it houses my soul and my soul isn't what's changing. That's what she told me, Aunt Kate, and this is what she said, here's the best part: 'I'll love you as my son every bit as much as I did when I thought you were my daughter.'" His voice broke.

Kate stared ahead at the freeway with moisture blurring her vision, moved by the words Dylan's mother had spoken to her child, knowing how much they meant to Dylan because she herself had never held a hope for any kind of family acceptance.

Several seconds passed before Dylan continued unsteadily, "I'll be so glad to have her here for the operation but I feel like shit about this, Aunt Kate. My parents have been married twenty-six years and I'm the reason they've split up…" Again his voice broke.

Anger instantly roiling through her, Kate rolled down her window and shouted at the cars and trucks around her: "HE'S the reason they've split up! Your father is a pigheaded bigot! He doesn't deserve either one of you!"

She cast her seething thoughts at her brother: *See what you get for thinking you have the one and only answer, Dale? You come right ahead to LA, you pinhead, I'll be the one doing the ass kicking!*

Calmed by the explosive release of anger, she rolled up the window. Maybe, she thought, maybe I shouldn't feel all that superior. Maybe this *stupid stupid stupid* business ran in the family.

"…talking to my shrink," Dylan was saying. "He wants me to come in Monday. So don't worry, Aunt Kate, you just call me when you can. I'm so sorry about Maggie...You take real good care of yourself."

What a good kid he is, she reflected, clicking off the phone. The world of psychotherapy was trying to save the day for them both. She felt suddenly grateful even in the face of her grief over Maggie. With or without Maggie, life went on.

* * *

Half an hour later, she pulled onto the dirt road leading to the cabin. She drifted the car along the road and explored and inspected the entire area, including all around the cabin, scrutinizing every dwelling, many of which appeared to be occupied this weekend, taking note of the cars and trucks parked by them. She stopped several hundred yards from the Cameron cabin to assess its setting and environs.

A dilapidated shack sat well across the road from the cabin, two weathered planks nailed crisscross over its only window, beside it an old Toyota pickup. She hadn't noticed either the shack or the pickup before, but she had been entirely focused on finding the cabin when she was first here. The shack was several hundred yards distant and in any case the pickup was so coated with dust it might have been sitting there for months. Two other derelict cabins flanked the Cameron cabin, each of them a hundred or more yards distant. She had driven by both of them, twice. Both appeared unoccupied if not abandoned.

Ground cover was a scattering of Joshua trees on terrain generously speckled with brush and creosote bushes and other scrub and a few scraggly cactus. Sufficient, she judged, to offer zigzagging cover to a man approaching low to the ground. Especially in darkness, when lighting in the desert would consist of the night sky and whatever very faint ground illumination was emitted from area buildings, light that would extinguish when the residents went to bed. A quarter moon or less, or even thin cloud cover, would render the night virtually pitch-black.

She examined the butte abutting the cabin. Well over a hundred feet high, its side descended gradually and gracefully in vertical rocky ridges formed into a concave curve by centuries of weathering. The flat top had become a grassy overhang, so a man trying to lower himself on a rope would dangle in midair much of the way with no possibility of purchase for footing. From one of the photos she'd seen, Joe and Jack had been rock climbers, would have had many opportunities to be among the avid devotees who scaled the spectacular rock formations within the nearby confines of Joshua Tree National Park. Hard to imagine, though, that today's Jack Cameron would have the wherewithal to obtain the necessary equipment or possess the training and physicality to make such a midair descent.

She pulled up in front of the cabin, took her .38 from the glove compartment, flicked off the safety, climbed out of the car. Holding the weapon at the ready in both hands she glanced all around her, including at the cabin, then restored the safety and tucked the .38 in the back waistband of her jeans under her loose T-shirt. Her shoulder stiff from the drive, she stretched out her body, arms taut against the car, flexing and loosening her bad shoulder in the bright sun, and did a few deep knee bends, appreciating the dry heat of the early afternoon.

The cabin door opened and Cameron, wearing only a pair of plaid shorts and tennis shoes without laces, looking even more hermit-like with his unshaven face and straggly hair, sauntered toward her, smiling, hands shoved in his pockets. She watched him approach, concerned that his face seemed even more gaunt, his eyes red-rimmed with exhaustion. Without a shirt covering his chest the loss of weight was evident.

"Good trip?" he inquired, his eyes searching her face as closely as she was inspecting him.

"Only the last thirty miles," she answered. "I'm beginning to see why you love it out here away from the LA ant heap."

"Kate..." He gripped her shoulders, and then awkwardly pulled her to him. "Kate, I'm so sorry about Maggie."

"I know, thank you," she murmured, enormously touched by this uncharacteristic display of affection from him. Inhaling and for perhaps the first time in her life not minding male sweat, she hugged her friend back, tightly.

As they released each other he asked with a faint grin, "Is that a gun I feel, or are you just glad to see me?"

She grinned back. "Both." Then in realization she asked, "Where's yours?"

He jerked his head toward the cabin. "In there. Jean and Jason are gone, thanks to you. Crazy as Jack is, he won't want to just shoot me dead. He'll want to do a lot more than that."

She concealed her incredulity, feeling doubly glad she'd made a show of her weapon when she got out of the car. Maybe he was just too tired to realize that unless weapons were observable Jack could just walk up and shoot out a kneecap on both of them and proceed to inflict whatever mayhem he damn well pleased on her as well as his brother. Or, she thought, maybe this *stupid stupid stupid* business has become a contagion.

"Let me get my stuff and let's go inside," she said abruptly. Even with a gun in her belt she felt exposed where they stood.

"Sure," he said, yanking open the back door of Kate's car and grabbing her duffel bag. "Jeanie make a total mess of your condo yet?"

"Not yet. They've been very neat, very respectful."

"No shit." He barked out a laugh. "What did you do, pistol whip her? Jason's always picking up after his mom—the poor kid needs order. But Jeanie, she seems addicted to chaos. Drove us all crazy when we were kids. You must have her totally intimidated."

She shrugged. "May it continue."

She pulled a small box of supplies out of her car and preceded Cameron, nudging open the door of the cabin with a foot. Now that Jean and her son had taken away their mess along with most of their possessions and Cameron had tidied up the place to his own standards, she could look around much more observantly.

From behind her she heard a smothered yawn. She turned to him. "When was the last time you had a decent sleep?"

"The day before Jack's parole. Catnap is what I do these days. Last night the alarm and the lighting system kept getting triggered. The desert gets real, real quiet at night."

Dutch, she thought, good old Dutch doing his "canvass."

"Go get some sleep," she ordered. "Let me look around, get my bearings." She smiled. "Without you and your preconceived ideas."

He grinned back. "I could use a few solid hours." He shifted her duffel bag to his other hand. "Put this where you'll be sleeping?"

"Sure." She added as he trudged to the sleeping area, "Joe, don't worry. I've got your back. Depend on it."

The cabin, she decided as she gazed around, was like a crayon drawing a child would make, especially the exterior. Peaked roof with a pipe chimney, a front door placed precisely between two small front windows, a window on each side of the cabin. She estimated the interior to be perhaps fifteen by fifteen. Its walls consisted of sheets of nailed-up plywood aged to gray and curling up at the edges, the flooring unfinished thin planks that felt solid but emitted faint squeaks with each footstep. Although another plywood wall beginning inside the door separated the sleeping quarters, the wall extended only partway in, and the cabin was basically one room, its roof supported by a half dozen evenly spaced four by sixes. The slapdash pebble and concrete fireplace, firewood stacked beside it, had been built against the back wall so that its chimney would discharge smoke harmlessly against the butte that the cabin adjoined. In front of the fireplace stood a flimsy card table and four cheap plastic chairs. On the table were Cameron's nine millimeter Beretta 92 service weapon and his personal Glock.

Kate placed her box on the table, pulled her own weapon out of her jeans and added it to the gun collection, and took a look at what comprised a kitchen. A rickety cupboard with crooked doors was set beneath a worn Formica counter that held a hot plate, a miniscule microwave and what appeared to be the receiver set for the alarm system Cameron had rigged around the perimeter of the cabin. The corroded metal sink had only one cold water tap, dented and even more corroded. A mini refrigerator that looked new sat beside the counter. Looking more closely at the appliances, she saw that all were new and of course they would be; Cameron would have had to buy them all. This cabin had been abandoned for years and anything of value would surely have been taken by squatters and thieves.

Moving as quietly as she could over the squeaky floor, she glanced behind the partition and saw that Cameron was already dead asleep in a face-down sprawl on one of two bare mattresses on the floor, arms outflung, head buried in a thin gray pillow, a faint sheen of perspiration on his back glistening in a shaft of sunlight from the window. Her duffel bag sat on the mattress next to him. On the other side of that mattress a flimsy plastic partition provided minimal privacy for a tiny compartment holding presumably a toilet and perhaps a cold-water shower. She backed away as silently as she could, although she suspected only something like a gunshot would awaken Cameron now.

After performing a precautionary reconnaissance from one of the front windows she went into the kitchen carrying the box she had brought into the cabin. She checked out the cupboard under the sink. Instant coffee, a few cans of organic chili, and Cameron had raided the earthquake supplies at his house for several dozen aluminum pouches of ready-to-eat hash, beef dishes, pastas and soups. He must be going nuts without his salads and fruit, she thought, rueful that she had not thought to stop and get these instead of bringing potato chips and packaged nuts and crackers from the condo.

Plates, cups and cutlery were stacked and arranged neatly in a metal tray, everything plastic except for a can opener. There was a box of candles and a butane lighter. A roll of paper towels and a half-full quart of Arrowhead water sat near the tiny sink. Every space in the mini fridge was stocked with more bottles; three more cases sat on top. This is the desert, she reminded herself, where water was by far the most essential commodity. Amazing that a municipal water line extended into this area and out here to the cabin when no water whatever was to be had only a few scant miles away in Joshua Tree National Park. But that miracle aside, any water coming into this cabin through pipes that had collected God knew what toxins over the years—she too would prefer not to have to sample it.

A transistor radio the size of a cigarette pack sat by the window over the sink. At least one electrical outlet served the kitchen appliances, but there was no TV here, no iPod— Cameron could afford no distractions. He was a reader, but had brought no visible stash of books either—again, he could not become absorbed in anything that rendered him even

momentarily unaware of his surroundings. That included booze.
None of that here, not so much as a beer. With only a transistor
radio connecting him with the outside world, with no cell phone
service, how had he not gone crazy? Jack Cameron had, in effect,
put his brother in prison. To await his executioner.

This primitive cabin and the way Cameron occupied it
generated a renewed and sadder awareness in her. It was the
most eloquent possible testimony that since the murder of his
mother and suicide of his father, putting an end to the hell that
had engulfed his family was the most powerful of incentives, was
worth any price to him.

But not to her. With four to five hours stretching before
her until she could wake Cameron, with nothing to occupy her
during those hours except keeping watch for an attack that she
was virtually certain would occur after darkness fell, she knew
what she had to do. While she had this impulse of resolve and
the wits to do it.

She stepped as quietly as she could into the bedroom, grabbed
her duffel bag and brought it out to the card table. Fished out
the bottle of Cutty Sark.

Carrying her .38 in one hand and the bottle in the other, she
let herself out of the cabin. Went around to the side, to the rock-
strewn foot of the butte. With one sharp stroke she broke off the
top of the bottle against a rocky outcrop, then, wincing, looked
away and listened to the contents glug out over the rocks, telling
herself she had to keep watch on the sun-bleached landscape
around her. Turning her back to the butte so that she could face
the desert, gun held loosely, she crouched down to the rocks
and set down the empty bottle to pick up the top she'd broken
off. And remained on her haunches, deeply inhaling the richly
pungent fumes of scotch wafting to her in the hot dry air. With
a sardonic smile, she thought maybe she could make frequent
pilgrimages out here and breathe in what she needed.

When she stood, she remained where she was, again sniffing
the air, this time intently. The odor was faint, but it had to be
some sort of petroleum product. Could Jack— She looked all
around her, envisioning gasoline as an accelerant on this highly
flammable landscape and the firetrap that was the cabin.

Ridiculous. There was no way Jack could get this close to lay down gasoline or anything else without Cameron seeing him. Not with Dutch having been here last night too…

Where could the smell be coming from? Light wind was blowing toward her—some distant oil spill? The creosote bushes—didn't they smell something like this? Or was the creosote that built up in chimneys the kind that smelled like tar and not the creosote plant? She shrugged. How would a city slicker like her know, anyway? This was Cameron's bailiwick.

As she came back around to the front of the cabin the odor faded and vanished. Maybe just a passing old car or truck, a smog burner of which there seemed to be plenty out here. After another surveying look around, she went back inside.

* * *

Two hours and fifty-six minutes. Seated on one of the plastic chairs, her gun on a chair beside her along with a bottle of water, staring out a front window into the shimmer of the desert, Kate pulled her gaze away after what seemed about twenty more minutes and once again studied her watch. Two interminable hours and fifty-*eight* minutes had now ticked by. And there were still two more hours before she should awaken Cameron.

She had already begun railing at herself for her rash dumping of the scotch. If she hadn't been so fucking *stupid stupid stupid* she could have rigidly rationed herself. Poured herself only enough of a drink to take the edge off, consumed the ration only one small sip at a time. Given herself a rigid time limit to have the next drink—if she even needed one. Stashed the bottle out in one of the bushes to further make sure she'd discipline herself.

A voice whispered to her, a voice that sounded like Maggie's: *Discipline—you really, actually, honestly think you have discipline around alcohol?*

Impatiently, angrily, she retorted aloud, "I would in this case. Two lives depend on it."

How dependable are you when you'd actually bargain to use a substance that dulls your senses? The challenge coming from a voice that sounded like Calla Dearborn's.

194 Katherine V. Forrest

Fists clenched, Kate stared out into the desert in agitated fury that she had nothing to smooth out her edginess, worse still, nothing to deflect these useless, invasive thoughts.

Now it was Aimee coming into her mind, accusing her…

You never talked to me. Even when you promised, you'd talk a little and then stop. You kept it all from me, the career that took up more than a third of your life and meant everything to you.

"You know why," Kate answered sharply. "I had to protect you from what I saw, what I had to do on the job."

Bullshit. Maggie's voice. *Talking to Aimee meant you had to think about it, Kate. About bodies, death, blood, grief, suffering, all the agony and tragedy and loss that tore your guts out. Telling her about it meant living it again and that meant feeling it again.*

"Shut up, Maggie," Kate snarled with a backhand flip of her hand. "You're supposed to be dead."

Being dead won't shut me up. The truth is, protecting her was never what it was about. Protecting yourself, that's what you were doing.

"Shut up," said Kate.

Not wanting to open up feelings—that's what it was always about.

"I couldn't face it. I couldn't do it. Maggie," she pleaded. "I had to drink just to get through the night. Talk to Aimee? I couldn't break down in front of her. I couldn't let her see me like that…"

Swiping tears away she shifted on the hard plastic of her chair, her body aching, her head pinging with the pain she knew so well, the pain of sobriety. The cabin had filled with afternoon heat that smelled of dust and dried her skin and her eyes and was exacerbating the rawness of her nerves.

"This bloody godforsaken desert," she muttered, glowering out into the wavering yellow haze on the horizon. "That's what this is. I'm in the desert. I'm hallucinating."

As if in answer a sighing breeze rustled the desert flora, bringing with it whispers she wished she could swat out of her mind like an attack of mosquitoes.

Why are you here, Kate? Why, exactly?

This question startled her. Where had it come from? Whose voice was this? She almost looked around before she could stop herself. She felt ridiculous. She snapped back, "To help my friend. Who's now my closest living friend."

Why are you so willing to abandon the oath you revered as a police officer? Willing to abandon your conscience and the beliefs that guided you all your years as an officer of the law? The law you swore to uphold?

"I haven't," she insisted. "This is about a friend. This is different. And who the *hell* are you?"

You just called it. Hell. Where you're going. You've stacked another value onto the conscience and conduct you're willing to abandon: you've put your life on the line. A value that's no longer a value because you've come to the place where it's now worth nothing to you.

"So what," she muttered.

And that's the truth of it, isn't it. When you really don't want to live anymore, conscience and conduct no longer matter because your life no longer matters.

"I don't care. What difference does it make?"

Maggie asked for the means to end her own life. Calla Dearborn's voice sliced into her mind like a knife. *You wouldn't do it and you sat in judgment when someone else did. What are you doing here, Kate? Is it because if you die tonight it will be considered a death with meaning? Because you'll be dying for a reason? In defense of your police partner? Isn't that what you're doing here?*

She leaped to her feet. "God damn it to fucking hell," she snarled. She paced, the silence of the cabin penetrated by the moaning of the wind and punctuated by the squeaks of her footsteps.

But she could not prevent Maggie's voice from coming into her: *Why didn't you tell Aimee you were coming here to do this, Kate?*

"She'd have stopped me."

Just like you did me when I wanted to put an end to it all. This woman who's loved you for twenty years of your life, she has no right to know what you're doing? What you're putting on the line?

"She does have a right," Kate muttered, "I just can't tell her. She'd stop me."

Calla Dearborn's voice: *How can you be so absolutely sure what she'd do?*

The question reverberated.

Aimee's voice: "You *actually believe* none *of last night was about me and what I feel about you.*" Her voice rising. "*You actually*

*think you miss me more than I miss you. You always think you have
to be everyone's protector. You always think you have to decide what
everybody else is supposed to feel. Or need."*

What she told me in the cottage this morning, Kate thought,
it's the absolute truth of me. But I *have* to be here. I *have* to do
this.

*Granting that…*Calla Dearborn's voice. *Why have you not
allowed yourself one thought of how Aimee—or Dylan—will feel to
learn you've been killed out here? Not given Aimee one clue about
what's going on, even your legitimate reasons for having to be here?*

"She's used to this, Calla. She knew every day I walked out
the door to go be a cop that it could be my last day."

You were a homicide detective. Maggie's voice. *Not on a SWAT
team.*

"Shut up," Kate muttered. "Just shut the fuck up."

Aimee's voice: *"You actually believe none of last night was about
me and what I feel about you. You actually think you miss me more
than I miss you."*

Kate ripped open the cabin door and stalked out into the
desert.

"Shut up!" she screamed. *"All of you!"*

The voice from Hell said, *You don't need anyone to interpret
what she said to you. She told you she still loves you. And you're doing
this to her. You're out here and she doesn't know it, and you could die.*

"No," Kate shouted. "No, goddammit, I won't die. That is
not going to happen."

In the desert heat she felt suddenly as stone-cold sober and
clearheaded as if a bucket of ice water had been poured over her
head. She looked wildly around her, aware of where she was.
Outside. No gun. Exposed.

"For Christ's sake," she snarled, stalking back to the cabin,
"how the fuck did I end up out here without my gun?"

She marched inside, picked up her .38, jammed it into her
belt. Went to the doorway of the sleeping area and quietly,
grimly addressed Cameron's comatose form: "We're going to do
this, Joe. And no fucking way are we dying out here."

She returned to the window and once again took up her post.

18

Kate woke Cameron, calling his name and shaking a shoulder until he came groaning to consciousness, groggy and disoriented.

"...the hell time is it," he mumbled, turning his head on the pillow, one bleary eye peering out the window.

"Showtime. Almost seven." She had let him sleep as long as she dared; sunset was approaching.

She realized she had never before seen him without his Fossil watch. Given her own ordeal with the passage of the hours till she could wake him, she understood why he would not want to wear one during his own endless days here. Maybe he'd brought his precious watch with him, she thought, and had stomped it flat and hurled it into the desert. A day or two more here and that's what she'd probably be doing with her Timex.

He swung his legs over the side of the mattress and sat bent over, yawning, elbows on his knees, rubbing the stubble on his face and running his hands through his hair.

"How do you feel, Joe?" Kate asked. "Any better?"

"Yeah, actually." He sat up, patted his chest over his heart. "A lot better for the sleep. Like I've got a few more wits about me. Weird, though. Even dead asleep I thought I heard voices."

"So did I," Kate said, deadpan.

"This place will do that to you." He got up, slid his feet into his tennis shoes. "Those forty days Jesus fasted in the desert, no wonder he came out believing he was the messiah." He flung out his arms in what could have been either supplication or a stretching of his body. "Christ, could I ever use a beer."

"Yeah, well, here's what you get." She reached down and handed him the cold bottle of water from the refrigerator she'd set on the floor beside his mattress.

He unscrewed the top and downed half of it without stopping, rivulets running down the dark blond stubble on his chin onto his chest. "Thanks. You have to drink lots of water here."

"Already figured that out." Kate had consumed a bottle of her own, and after one look at the toilet in here, had gone out to the side of the cabin to add urine to the aromatic scotch deposit.

He asked, "Want something to eat?"

She shrugged. "Whatever. We need to talk."

"For sure." He went to a duffel bag that sat up against the plywood partition, lifted out a neatly folded long-sleeve black T-shirt and pants. He looked at her sharply. "I wear dark clothes every night—so should you. I've got extras." He pulled the T-shirt over his head.

"I brought my own." She'd anticipated the need. Fortunately. The area wasn't exactly crawling with Laundromats and Cameron's clothes by this time had to be close to the stand-up-by-themselves stage of cleanliness.

"Good," he told her. "Aside from anything else it gets cold here."

"I noticed," she said, and went to her own duffel bag on the other mattress.

"I'll give you some privacy," he offered.

"Don't be ridiculous," she said, unzipping her bag and yanking out a sweatshirt and sweatpants, a baseball cap.

He turned his back anyway, took down his plaid shorts, displaying his thin naked flanks, and pulled on a pair of black mesh pants with a baseball cap folded into one pocket. Then he edged past her, around the partition into the main room. She quickly stripped off her jeans and shirt. Donned the navy sweatpants and sweatshirt, sat down on the mattress and laced on matching navy sneakers. Folded and stuffed the baseball cap into a pocket.

Walking into the main room she saw he was in the kitchen alcove. His gaze shifting to her, he nodded approval at her outfit. Then, with arms crossed, he studied the chairs she'd set up in front of the window. "It's not a big window," he remarked, "but I'd feel like a target sitting there. You're braver than I am."

"Not braver," she joked, "dumber."

But she was mentally shaking her head. The cabin was nothing less than a sitting duck. Isolated from any immediate help, it might as well have a neon bull's-eye on its roof. How could he have stayed in here waiting, night after night? She'd feel less exposed in a sleeping bag in the desert. Better to worry about desert sidewinders than Jack Cameron shooting or burning up the place.

Cameron fished out several aluminum pouches from the cupboard under the sink. "Which of these scrumptious offerings would you prefer for your last meal?"

She pointed to her box of supplies. "I'll have what I brought."

He peered into the box. "Potato chips? Crackers? Cashews?" He pretended to clutch at his heart.

Grinning, she raised a middle finger to him. "If it's my last meal I'll eat something I damn well like. That means potato chips."

"That's my girl, unhealthy to the end." Cameron tossed the aluminum packets back in the cupboard. He pulled the bag of chips out of the box and ripped it open, tore two paper towels off the roll, took two bottles of water out of the small refrigerator and put everything on the counter. He carried the card table to the window, then placed his and Kate's guns on the table, ceremoniously arranged the chips and water and towels in the middle, and sat down on the other plastic chair. "Dinner is served," he announced. Picking up his bottle of water, he offered the bag to her. "Bon appétit."

200 Katherine V. Forrest

Laughing, Kate took a handful of chips and reached for her water and clicked plastic bottles with him. She felt no fear—at least not yet—about the coming night, only determination and purpose, and was glad to see she had somehow communicated that to him. Watching him reach into the bag, she wondered when Cameron had last contaminated the temple that was his body with a potato chip. Probably not since he was a boy in this very cabin.

They ate half the contents of the bag in companionable silence, the two of them keeping watch out the window, Cameron consuming his fair share of chips with apparent enjoyment. Then he asked easily, "Any ideas?"

"More possibilities than ideas, Joe. He's your brother so you tell me. Any way he might have help?"

Cameron took a swig of water while he considered. "Plenty of like-minded company in prison. But I'm betting he's basically still the loner he always was. And this is his deal. Him and me. Why would anybody want to help?"

"Okay," Kate said. That didn't eliminate the possibility—some people could be talked into anything—but it lowered its likelihood. "Next question. Assault weapon. Think he could get one?"

"He'd have to steal it."

"Would he?"

"He's been incarcerated most of his life, he's never used one and Jack doesn't have much imagination beyond what he knows. What he'll do figures to be what he knows."

"Which is?"

"Handgun."

"Rifle maybe?"

"Maybe. He's used one, we both did as boys. But doubtful. Hard to conceal."

Unless he had one in a car. But she chose not to mention the point. "Anything else?"

Cameron sat back, let out a long breath. "I've had a lot of time to think about how this will go down. He wants Armageddon. So, he's thinking maybe pin us down with gunfire and try and burn us out. I figure a Molotov cocktail—it's the most portable."

She nodded. On her way here she had envisioned a similar scenario among other possibilities. "Trying to burn out his girlfriend and his son, that was vengeance too—fire would seem to be his MO."

Looking at the man sitting across from her, so intelligent and rational, so attractively male despite the hair in need of a barber and the growth of scruffy beard and a body in need of a bath, a figure of slender elegance in his black clothing in spite of it all, she wondered how he could ever have ended up with such a monster for a brother. But families did. Any family. She'd spent a career looking into the stupefied faces of mothers, fathers, siblings, friends who'd borne witness to inhuman savagery exposed in someone close to them, someone they'd been certain they knew.

"Where we are, he'll trigger the lights coming in here," Cameron was saying. "Even with no imagination he'll see he can't get near enough without us spotting him."

She doubted the lights would be sufficient coverage. Or deterrent. "Moonlight, how much can we expect?"

"A quarter moon, so not much. More stars than Cher has rhinestones. About as helpful."

She asked, to cover all bases, "What about him coming down from the butte?"

"Entirely possible."

"It is?" She stared at him in astonishment.

"It is. He was a rock climber. A damn good one."

"Even so, wouldn't he have to come down on some sort of rope pulley?"

"Nope. We never used ropes in Joshua Tree. We learned to climb with handholds, footholds, special gripping shoes."

"Then how—"

"If you take a look at the butte, it's vertical rock ridges—"

"I did look, I saw that."

"He'd come down between two ridges in the narrowest channel he could find—" He demonstrated with his hands and feet, "—use one side for handholds, the other to brace his feet."

She shook her head. "Seems impossible."

"It's possible, believe me. Dangerous but possible…" He was smiling at a memory, a memory that quickly picked up an edge of pain reflected in his eyes. "We did it as boys, Jack and I. Dad saw us when we were halfway and he and Mom screamed at us all the rest of the way down. It really was dangerous, we could have broken our necks…"

"Christ," muttered Kate, more interested in the fact that they'd lost the advantage of their rear flank being inaccessible than in Cameron's near-death experience two decades ago.

Cameron had been studying her face. He said reassuringly, "If he tries that we'd hear him. It's an ancient rock face. He couldn't possibly come down without dislodging rock. You can hear a pin drop in the desert at night."

She nodded but was only partly mollified. Even if they did hear him, if he too were wearing dark clothing, in the limitless black of a desert night he would be invisible on that wall of rock.

"So, any theories, guesses, bright ideas, Kate?"

She sat back, nibbled on a chip, gathered her thoughts. "All that time in his jail cell, we have to believe he was planning this. But not *this*, here. From his movements since his parole, he thought you'd be in your house. Probably lay in wait for who knows how long because you left your RAV4 parked in front. Figuring you'd be back." Probably watched me go in that first time, she realized with a prickling between her shoulders. She continued, "He finally decided you were gone, broke in to see what he could find, saw all those photos on the wall, lost it and trashed them. Then he tracked down Jean, who knows how—"

"Maybe asked around in the local bars," Cameron muttered.

"—and did the same for her and her trailer. My theory is this is the last place he'd made any plans for."

He was nodding. "Given the timing it all fits."

"So his plan of attack will be pretty simple. He's obviously stolen a vehicle. If I were him, if I were planning this, I'd drive it straight into the cabin."

Cameron whistled, gesturing around him. "If he's in a truck, he'd take this cardboard box down without denting a fender."

She did not respond; she was too astonished that he had not thought of this. Finally she asked, "See any vehicles around today, stopping anywhere around here, driving by?"

"Nothing I didn't recognize. The ones I saw." He picked up his bottle of water.

"I smelled gas or something like it a while ago. Outside."

"Fuck," he said, his bottle suspended halfway to his mouth. "You're telling me now? When was this?"

"A few hours after you went to bed. I don't know that it's anything. I went outside to...look around," she hedged. "The smell was distinct, then faded. I didn't see a thing. I take it it's not some friendly little desert plant letting off unfriendly fumes?"

He shook his head. "No such thing as a friendly desert plant. Everything here is tough as steel, loaded with needles. To survive."

She looked out at dusk falling over the landscape and felt a rash of goose bumps along with a growing chill in the air. "Joe, we need to get out of the cabin," she said.

"I agree."

"I mean now."

"Not yet," Cameron said, surprising her with his tone of authority. "If he's down on the ground somewhere with binoculars, he's watching the door." He pointed to the windows. "I haven't been totally sitting on my ass since I've been here, Kate. I knew I might need to get out fast, some way that wasn't the front door and didn't make a lot of noise. The side windows, they pull out. A few more minutes and we'll have good shadows to go out a window and move along the bottom of the butte."

"Great, okay," Kate said, liking this development, revising her judgment of him. "Let's leave some light in here, give him a target, every reason to think we're in here."

"Good idea. Maybe a couple of candles."

"Just the thing," Kate said. Flickering candles would suggest movement, presence.

Cameron sprang to his feet. Donned his baseball cap and pulled it down low on his face, tightened the drawstring on his pants, picked up the Beretta and shoved it in the front waistband, his Glock in back. He located the box of candles in the cupboard and lit one with the butane lighter, held it horizontal over a plastic plate to form a liquid base to hold it, did the same for two more and set them all on the counter.

"The place might burn down without Jack doing anything," she offered. The candles were of a size, she estimated, to last only several hours.

Cameron muttered something indecipherable and peered out the window at the darkening landscape. "What were you saying about showtime?"

For the first time she felt a surge of adrenaline at the peril this night would bring. "We should split up," she told him. "You out one window, me the other. Improves the odds."

"Yeah, well..." Fists on his hips, he looked at her. "We both go out the same window. Me first."

"And this would be what, partner," she said, an edge in her voice, "some sort of chivalry?"

"When was that ever an issue between us, Kate?" he snapped. "My turf, my rules. Something happening to you was never ever supposed to be part of this deal. Besides..." He managed the briefest of grins. "You being shot right out of the gate would bother my concentration."

"Ditto you." *And I'd empty all three guns into your worthless son of a bitch of a brother.* She shrugged, gestured to the window. "After you, my dear Alphonse."

"The one over by the mattresses," he said. "It's got the best cover."

She nodded and rose from the table. "After we get outside—" She bit off the rest of her words and waited. His turf, his rules.

"We'll go with what develops," he said crisply. "For now you follow, stay low. Absolute silence. I'll get us behind the best cover I can find." He added, "Don't touch any part of any plant or you'll spend the night wishing you hadn't."

"Got it," she said, moving toward the sleeping area. "Let's roll."

Beside his mattress, feet braced, Cameron gripped either side of the window frame, rocked it slightly, soundlessly lifted it out. Behind Kate, dim light flickered from the three candles in the fresh air currents. Outside the yawning window frame the desert lay cloaked in deep gray dotted with the inky shapes of Joshua trees and scrub brush making skittering sounds in a gusting breeze.

Beretta in hand, Cameron braced a foot on the windowsill, crouched and vaulted over it. Kate donned her cap and then used the same technique, and chivalry or not, grabbed for his outstretched, steadying hand as her feet hit the sand hard.

His back up against the butte, Cameron stood perfectly still to take his bearings, as did she. There was no sign of any movement anywhere that was not a part of the natural landscape. The night air, mild with lingering hints of the heated day, was aromatic with dusty peppermint scents of the desert. The breeze was stronger than she'd thought, with intermittent gusts sufficient to ruffle the hair extending from under her cap. A dim quarter moon had already unveiled itself high in the sky along with a few emergent stars, prime among them Orion, its four corners bold and vivid. But none of the skyward show cast any luminescence onto the desert floor. Cameron was right. This would be one very dark night, so dark that she was already grateful for her idea of leaving light in the cabin—it would be her one point of reference on an alien, treacherous landscape.

Crouching, gun at his right side, Cameron felt his way along with his left hand, taking small careful steps amid the rock debris from the butte, Kate following close behind, guided more by the faint scuffing of his sneakers than the inky shape of him in front of her. Any sounds their footsteps made in the rocky gravel were being smothered by the rustling of the brush in the breezy winds. She saw no reason to draw her gun since Cameron had his in hand; given her awkwardness on this terrain she could maneuver better with hers in her waistband.

Cameron led the way to the derelict shack that sat a hundred yards or so to the left of his cabin, a misshapen monolith against the butte, before turning forward into the desert. She deduced that he had taken this pathway to avoid tripping his own alarm system. Crouched even lower to the ground, he inched his way among the bushes and scrub. Reaching behind him, gripping Kate's arm, he hunkered down beside a bush that seemed dense with leaves, pulling her down with him.

On her haunches on sand still radiating warmth from the day, she reached for her gun. But Cameron seized her left wrist. It took her a moment to realize he was unfastening her wristwatch: its hands and numerals were phosphorescent in the dark. Cursing herself, she snatched it from him and jammed it in her pocket, wondering if it had been at all visible while they made their way here. As if this possibility had occurred to

Cameron as well, he moved off in a zigzag pattern a few yards distant to another thick bush, then sat in a signal to her that this was where they would wait. As nearly as she could tell, they were angled away from the cabin, had positioned themselves closer to the road. A good tactical spot, she realized, to overlook the road and the cabin. Still smarting from her latest iteration of *stupid stupid stupid*, she sat beside him on the sand, gun at the ready in her lap, knees slightly raised so that she could quickly rise.

Even with her eyes fully adjusted to the dark she was essentially blind, yet she felt individual air currents buffeting her face and hands, the contours and coarse texture of the sand under her hands, even the subtle heat emanating from Cameron's body. She heard his breathing, the rustle of separate leaves in the bush concealing the two of them, smelled the rain-like aroma of the leaves beside her, thought she could even taste their earthiness. This acute alertness, the preternatural sharpness of her four other senses—she wondered if the absence of alcohol was a factor, whether raw nerve ends had opened her to a new sphere of awareness. If so, she was grateful.

The moon was higher, the sky now a glittering canopy much too hard and cold to be anything like Cameron's comparison of it to Cher's warmly glitzy rhinestones. Far more like diamonds, she thought, five- and ten-carat solitaires, with the varied scatterings of diamond dust around them looking like careless discards from their creation.

The sand under her hips was yielding but increasingly chill, and she began a quiet, virtually motionless version of isometrics, shifting and flexing her knees and ankles to prevent any stiffening from prolonged stillness, aware of Cameron doing the same. When the two of them had to react it would be sudden. Their bodies had to be ready for the adrenaline rush.

When would Jack Cameron make his move? As she had so many times in her investigations, she tried to project herself into the mind and motivation of a perpetrator. A logical plan would take the attack into the deep dark dead of night when exhaustion took its toll on anyone waiting, when watchfulness became boredom and then inattention—maybe even dozing. Between three and four in the morning. But from what she had gleaned about a man whose name was all she had known until two days ago, Jack Cameron's lack of impulse control would cause him to throw logic to the wind. If he was here now, the moment he felt ready he would put his plan—if he even had anything as cogent as a plan—into motion.

Like the ordeal of the afternoon, again she felt disoriented in time, finding herself wondering how many minutes had passed and constantly telling herself the answer had no relevance. But unlike the ordeal of the afternoon she did not crave a drink. Not here, not now.

Beside her Cameron stirred again, settled back. She reached to put a companionable hand on his arm, then jerked it away as an electric charge of adrenaline shot through her along with the explosion of sound rocketing through the silence of the night.

The starting of an engine, she realized. "Where?" she said under cover of the noise, seizing her gun.

Cameron was up on his knees. "Across the road."

"The Toyota pickup?"

"*What* Toyota pickup?" he said, almost savagely.

"An old pickup parked next to that cabin—You said you recognized all the vehicles—"

"I never saw it. I can't *see* that cabin from mine."

Of course not. Neither could she, during all those hours she'd spent in and around the cabin. "Christ," she spat.

"Makes no difference, Kate. He's here."

"Where?" Hearing the crunching of tires she looked around wildly.

She did not hear the answer from Cameron and did not need to. Jack Cameron had stolen the least noticeable vehicle he could find, he was in that dusty pickup she had assumed belonged to the cabin across the road. Driving with lights out and using the light from his brother's cabin as his beacon.

"Fuck fuck fuck," she snarled and started to rise.

He grabbed her. "Stay down!"

She obeyed. He was right. They were not in the cabin and not yet visible. She felt more than saw him pull both guns out of his waistband.

The sound of the engine unaccountably lessened, seemed to be moving away from them. Then the sound grew subtly louder—the vehicle had apparently turned. The engine louder and louder, Kate tensed, crouched but braced, leaning forward on the balls of her feet, gun in both hands, ready to leap. The pickup, rattling over and crushing impediments in the desert terrain, approached and invisibly passed them. Then the smell reached her, blown to her on the wind, the same smell as earlier today.

"Joe, he's dumping gas!"

He dropped his guns and leaped to his feet. "Run!"

She was instantly up and running, tossing her gun to run faster, understanding that Jack Cameron had laid down a semi-circle of gasoline around the cabin—and them. To her far left she saw an arc of brightness. A lighted something thrown out of the pickup's window.

The desert lit up. With the sudden flare of headlights. With wind-driven fire racing toward and flashing past them, torching the dry brush, an instant inferno.

She knew there was only one chance and she was already on the dead run beside Cameron heedless of impeding brush as he screamed, "*Run! Run!*"

He grabbed for her and missed as they reached the wall of fire but she understood what they must do.

She thought: *Aimee.*

Then with a last deep gulp of breath she drove herself forward in a headlong leap into the fire.

She felt such intense searing from head to foot that she knew her skin must be burning off. Then she landed on elbows and knees on bone-crushingly hard sand.

"*Roll roll roll roll!*" she heard and did not know if the scream came from Cameron or from her.

She rolled perhaps six times until she slammed into a bush, its branches like spears, her body in agony from any number of piercings. Then she realized she was in the clear, she still had clothes on and as nearly as she could tell she had most of her skin, and she did not care how much she hurt: what she felt seemed to be caused by the hard landing and body rolls and not fire.

"Kate!"

"Joe!" she yelled back.

"Over here! You okay?"

"Yeah." Getting to her knees, too shaky and flooded with adrenaline to test her legs, she scrabbled and crawled toward the sound of his voice, aware of throbbing in both knees, the sand raw on her hands.

Where was Jack? Then, with profound relief, she knew. From the retreating sound of the engine in the pickup. Jack was gone.

In the illumination of the fire behind them she spotted Cameron about ten feet away, also on his hands and knees. "You okay?" she called.

"Yeah. Ass full of needles," he muttered as she reached him. Kneeling, he ran his hands down his chest and thighs.

Looking at her he grabbed for her but it was to rip the baseball cap off her head as he yanked off his own. Both were faintly smoking, and she understood as she grabbed her hot hair that he had just saved both of them from head burns. She could not imagine how their caps had stayed on running through the fire and after, but without them their hair would have ignited.

She stared at Cameron where he knelt, his face strobed by light from the fire. His pupils were huge and black, his face streaked with sand and bloody from a wide scrape on his cheekbone. Blood dripped from his chin, his T-shirt was a mass of tears and his mesh pants were shredded at the knee. She looked down at herself: a blackened sweatshirt covered in sand and torn out at the elbows, pants ripped at the thighs and torn out at the knees. She could not imagine what her face looked like and everything else hurt like hell. All she knew was without the wind blowing toward the cabin they would now be dead— or dying and wishing they were dead—because the wind would have followed them. They would not have been able to outrun the fire. Their charred corpses would have been found by police colleagues callously calling them crispy critters—

The jumble of thoughts was wrenched to a halt by Cameron grabbing her. She grabbed him back and they hugged with a fierce savagery, rocking back and forth.

"Thank God," she breathed to the deity she did not believe in. "Thank God you're all right."

"You too, Kate," he said in a husky, shaky voice, his vise-like grip finally loosening.

"Jack," she said.

"Gone," he grated. "Fucking gone."

The multitude of aches in her body was quickly escalating to orchestral sites of pulsing pain. She focused on the friend in her arms. "Thank God," she said again. "He thinks you're dead, Joe. It's over."

You had to be out of your mind crazy to do this, she raged at herself. *It's a fucking miracle you survived being so* stupid stupid stupid *with your one and only life.*

"It's not over, Kate," he said, his voice a despairing wail in her ear. "He's in the wind."

"He's *done*, Joe!" She pulled herself furiously away from Cameron. Had the fire made him brainless? "It doesn't *matter* that he's gone. You did what you had to do, he's made his move, he's *done*."

He looked at her in bewilderment. "Kate, he's not done. He'll still—"

She started to jab a finger at him, then flung herself at him and seized his shoulders and shook him. "Joe, it's *over*! As soon as we report what he did here, there'll be an APB for him and the Toyota and we'll get him. *Don't you get it?*" she yelled. "You did this because the police couldn't do anything till he did something. He did something! We're *cops*! It's the police family he's attacked, he'll have everybody in law enforcement in the country on his ass, we'll *get* him!"

"But Kate, we never actually saw him here—"

"Jesus." She heard the sound of approaching cars, a siren. "We didn't?" Again she shook his shoulders. She wanted to slap his face.

"What am I saying?" He broke away from her, clapped his head with both hands. "Did we switch identities going through that fire? Of course we saw him."

Finally, finally he had his wits about him. She told him soberly, "I'm glad you didn't have to kill your brother, Joe."

He closed his eyes. "Oh God....you have no idea. I am too."

From behind her she heard a series of gunshot-like pop pop pops.

"Our guns," he said. "The bullets."

"Jesus." Then she heard a loud *whuuump*.

"Either Jean's car or yours," Cameron said, sitting back on his heels with his hands on his thighs, staring into the fire and smoke. "Fuck."

There was another *whuuump*. "Either your car or Jean's," Cameron repeated. "Shit, Kate."

"Insurance," she said succinctly. Adding, "Who cares. We're alive."

The two of them, sitting on their haunches, watched the conflagration, five torches twisting in the wind, the three cabins, the two cars. She felt worse for the loss of the Joshua trees, the foliage. Especially the Joshuas. Jack Cameron, she thought viciously, should get the death penalty for those trees. Each one of them was worth a hundred of him on his very best day.

She could smell the fierce heat, hear the powerful whoosh and crackle of the fire. The rancid smell emanating from her clothes made her wish she could rip them off. In the distance she heard indeterminate sounds, vehicles probably, people in the area reacting to the sight of the flames. With the direction of the wind the fire would not spread beyond the confines Jack Cameron had laid down with his trail of gasoline. It was already expending itself against the bluff.

"The cabin," she said and stopped, not knowing what else to say.

He shrugged. "Paid the taxes every year, I had to...but could never ever come back and see how things used to be..."

"It's gone now, Joe. They're gone, Jack's gone, it's all over."

"Kate..." He visibly pulled himself together. "We need to get our stories straight. Before everybody gets here..."

A few minutes later, a fire truck pulled up, siren wailing, followed by a cavalcade of cars, and Kate found herself in the glare of a multitude of headlights, heard the shout, "Hey, are you folks okay?"

Cameron called back, "Can you give us a hand?"

* * *

Several hours later, they were still being checked out in the ER at Hi-Desert Medical Center in Twentynine Palms. Both had had treatment for first-degree burns on their faces, hands and knees and for various cuts and contusions, and four stitches had been taken in Cameron's chin. Now they were back in their beds in their hospital room while X-rays were being evaluated. The pain in Kate's body had been alleviated by an injection, and she had six Vicodin in an envelope on her bedside table, an equal amount having been doled out to Cameron by a young, shaven-head ER doctor who'd cheerfully assured them both they would feel like the wrath of God for the next few days.

Two hours earlier their injuries had been photographed and they had given statements about the events at the cabin to a deferential and respectful young police officer from the station at Joshua Tree, which like Victorville was under the jurisdiction of the San Bernardino County Sheriff's Department. A beefy crew-cut young man, the officer was so clearly impressed that they were both LAPD and Kate was an ex-Marine, nearby Twentynine Palms being home to a Marine Corps base, that he skipped over the procedural nicety of interviewing them separately.

She had come to the high desert, she told Officer Barnes, to be with her close friend and former police partner after the death of a dear friend in Los Angeles. Cameron was on leave from LAPD, here for the first time in years in a cabin owned by his family. He was worried about his recently paroled brother who had threatened him and his sister, to the extent that his sister had taken up residence in Kate's home in Los Angeles. Thus, even though they did not expect him to come to the cabin, they were both armed. They heard the pickup truck but did not realize what was occurring until they smelled gasoline. Carrying their service weapons they came out of the cabin and saw Jack Cameron throw lighted material out of his Toyota pickup and speed off. They'd managed to dive through the fire...

"Some piece of work, this brother," Barnes commented, finishing up his report.

"He's done it before," Cameron told him calmly. "Arson, attempted murder. Trying to kill his girlfriend and son."

"We'll get him," the young cop had promised as he rose to leave. "He'll never get out of Riverside County."

Kate now said to Cameron in the bed beside hers, "I still can't figure the gas I smelled this afternoon. How the pickup got here without you seeing it—"

"That part's easy. Jack knows this terrain, knew I'd be watching, so he didn't use a road, came in right over the desert. How this went down, my guess is he bought a bunch of gas cans, got here before you did, made himself at home in that cabin and what you smelled was him uncapping those cans and putting them in the front seat—"

The door to their room swung open with emphatic authority and in strode Dutch Hollander in full uniform including his hat, which he promptly doffed and tossed onto a chair.

"Dutch—what the hell are you doing here?" Cameron blurted.

Kate simply stared at him.

"Just happened to be in the neighborhood." Grinning, he strolled over to Cameron's bed. "I could ask you the same question, but I already know what the hell you're doing here. How you doing, buddy? You look like shit. You too, Kate."

"Thanks. Doing great, Dutch," Cameron said, laughing, "the both of us. Good to see you, buddy. Can't shake hands, a few scrapes and burns. Kate saved my life."

"Not true," she said, sitting up in her bed in glad welcoming of the sight of him. "Joe saved mine."

"Either way I believe you," Hollander told them with an even wider grin. "Thought you'd like to know a piece of news. We already had a BOLO for a stolen Toyota pickup—" He winked at Kate. "Then this little escapade of yours comes over the scanner about one Jackson Allen Cameron wanted on suspicion of violating every code in the book and driving a Toyota, so we called in the cavalry figuring he'd be on either the 62 or the 247 and we boxed him in on the 247, drove him right off the road in that piece of shit he was driving, no sweat. Arrested his ass, took him in."

Jerking upright in his bed, Cameron said unbelievingly, "You got him…"

"We got him. For good. Jack had what, two strikes?" Hollander said jovially, "So this caper he just pulled would be what, strikes three, four, five…?"

"Nine that I can think of offhand," Kate offered drily.

Hollander nodded. "So no possibility of parole this time, Joe. I was damn glad to be able to personally assure the chickenshit dirtbag that you survived and were in great shape."

Kate looked at Dutch Hollander, hoping the gratitude she felt showed on her face. He grinned, tossed a thumbs-up, added another wink. "What I hear," he said, "you guys lost two sets of wheels so you might need a friend to drive you back to LA tomorrow. A friend like me."

"Dutch, thanks…what can I say?"

"No problem, Joe. I have to leave you two. Paperwork, you know the drill. They tell me they're keeping you here overnight. Be back in the morning." With a cheery wave he grabbed his hat from the chair and strode from the room.

Cameron turned to Kate. "I have to call Jeanie…"

"You do." And she had to call Aimee. Before she read about this in the papers.

She shook her head at the realization that for the first time in her career—if she could call this experience part of her career—she had helped capture a perpetrator she'd never even laid eyes on.

Cameron too was shaking his head. "I can't believe it's over…"

"Believe it, Joe. It's over."

19

"About goddamn time you bothered to call," Carolina Walcott growled into her phone.

"Captain, a lot's happened—"

"Here I am on a Sunday morning," Walcott continued right over her, "sitting at my kitchen table looking at a wire services report sent to me by that pest, that goddamn *LA Times* beat reporter—"

"Corey Lanier," Kate said.

"Yes, her. Asking for comment on a piece that'll be in tomorrow's paper with the headline 'Off-duty LAPD Detectives Survive Arson in High Desert, Suspect Captured.'" Her voice acid with sarcasm, she went on, "Beyond the bare-assed fact that two of my detectives received quote, minor injuries, in an arson attempt that almost turned the two of you into crispy critters, what should I know here, Kate?"

Seated on a barstool, Miss Marple perched by her elbow on the kitchen counter, Kate was grinning at Walcott's diatribe, already suspecting that thanks to the *Times* reporter she might only have to fill in her story around the edges for sharp-as-a-tack Walcott who would punch holes straight through the gloss-over she'd given to the police officer in Yucca Valley. She ventured, "What you're reading is probably pretty much what happened, Captain. I found Joe, was with him, his brother turned up wanting to kill him."

"Yeah, right," Walcott snorted. Then she asked soberly, "You two being okay—I take it the report's got that part right?"

"Scrapes and bruises, minor burns, otherwise fine. Joe's dealing with damage from a break-in to his house here in LA compliments of that very same homicidal brother and he'll call you the second he can. I know he'll be in tomorrow regarding the Tamara Carter case."

"That's very good news," Walcott said quietly.

"It gets better. He's doing fine. Ready to get back on the job."

"Kate, I've worked with you too many years and you're too tight with Joe for me not to know I'll be getting squat about what actually happened. So, bottom line: is there anything, *anything* you now know about Joe Cameron that his captain should know before she puts her reputation and ass on the line recommending him for Homicide Special?"

Smiling, Kate shifted the receiver to her other ear, thinking that from now on, with his demons finally behind him, Joe Cameron would be driven only to be a better cop in his new assignment. "Not one single thing, Captain. He's a great choice, he'll be a credit to you. I give you my word."

Walcott cleared her throat. "Kate," she said, "the article mentioned you'd come there to be with Joe because your friend passed on. I'm so sorry."

"Thank you, Captain. A blessing, for her."

"But not for you. I asked for help during a very tough time for you, and I want you to know I'm grateful as hell you helped protect one of our own. I won't forget it. Anything you need, anytime…call me." Walcott clicked off.

Kate dropped the phone into its cradle, picked up a purring Miss Marple who tucked her little furry head under Kate's chin, and walked through her quiet condo simply to inhale and absorb the peace of her home.

Jean and Jason were gone. After the conversation last night in which Cameron had broken the news to his sister about the fiery destruction of the cabin and her car, the arrest of their brother and the damage Jack Cameron had perpetrated on her trailer in Victorville, Jean had rented a car this morning and she and Jason were on their way back to Victorville.

After Kate's phone call to Aimee, Aimee had called Jean at the condo, then stopped by last night to pick up a change of clothes for Kate since hers and Cameron's had been collected from the hospital as evidence. Aimee had also located her passport and other identifying materials she could lay her hands on since Kate's wallet had been destroyed in the fire, with everything gone including her driver's license and medical card.

Aimee had shocked Kate by walking into her hospital room at seven o'clock this morning, which meant she had left West LA before five a.m. Even though Kate had reassured her she was fine, that all her injuries were minor, Aimee's face had crumpled at her first glance at Kate's face and hands. She had quickly recovered: "Silly me, I thought leaving LAPD would make your life less dangerous."

Kate knew she wasn't referring just to the fire. "I'm doing my best," she told her. "With all that's happened, I didn't have a chance to tell you. I'm in therapy and this is my third day without a drink."

"No shit." The response came from Cameron in the bed next to her. Aimee's response was a nod; she'd heard this about the drinking before. Many times.

"There's something about being in the desert that seems to bring...I don't know, clarity I guess," Kate told her. "I feel different here. I'm even thinking I might get a place out here."

"No shit," Cameron offered again, and after Kate's single poisonous glance of warning he waved an apology and lapsed into silence. Again Aimee had merely nodded.

Cameron had gone back to LA with Dutch Hollander, and Aimee had brought Kate back with her in Aimee's roomy old Outback, the back of Kate's passenger seat lowered for her comfort. Fatigued from medication and a restless night filled with dreams of fire and blood that she only vaguely remembered,

Kate was determined not to take another pill for pain the Vicodin had not entirely vanquished—the stinging in her elbows and knees and throbbing in the burns on her hands, the ache from the wrenching she'd given her bad shoulder.

After her revelations to Aimee about the secrecy Cameron had maintained surrounding his family's tragic history and his brother, and her careful replies to questions verging on the accusatory about her activities of the past week, and after a few updates from Aimee about people Kate knew from Aimee's law office, there had been mostly silence between them over the two-plus hours' drive.

She had not felt up to talking about Maggie or the dispiriting topic of the Nightwood Bar. She had wanted to address Aimee's outburst at the cottage but did not have the wherewithal to go anywhere near that, not yet. Only yesterday morning it had been—a lifetime ago. She knew there was really nothing to be said about either the history that lay between them or any possible future. It had all been said before. Whether there would be a future with Aimee—before this smart, loving, beautiful woman opened herself to someone else and all possibility was lost—that outcome was mostly up to Kate. It always had been.

Now, returning to the kitchen, gently setting Miss Marple back on the counter, Kate sighed, sat on a barstool and braced herself and called her insurance company. She spent the next half hour wading her way through the complexities of a claim for the total loss of her car and arranging for a rental to be delivered to her before noon today.

The next call was to Calla Dearborn. Who called her back only moments after she had left a message asking for an appointment.

"How are you doing, Kate?"

"How am I doing," she repeated, standing up from the barstool to flex her shoulder. "Well, last night I lost my car and very nearly my life in an arson fire in the desert and I just got out of the hospital this morning."

The entire past week suddenly struck her as surreal, a massive absurdity, and she began to laugh. Dearborn chuckled briefly as if uncertain whether Kate was actually joking, then stopped as Kate's laughter, skirting the barest edge of all-out crying, ascended into near hysteria. Miss Marple leaped from the counter and fled down the hallway as Kate, snorting and gasping for breath, collapsed back onto the barstool, laughing and laughing till her aching sides joined the rest of her body's pains.

Calla Dearborn had uttered not a word during Kate's outburst, and silence now echoed over the phone as Kate finally subsided. "Are you still there?" Kate wheezed, wiping her eyes with the back of a hand.

Dearborn said in a calm, easy tone, "If what you told me is true, and I have every reason to believe it is, then in my profession we would call this 'inappropriate laughter.'"

Which set Kate off again into another paroxysm of hysteria.

"I'll tell you what, Kate," Dearborn said after Kate once more regained control. There was a smile in her voice, warmth. "You just get yourself here and we'll laugh about this together. Two o'clock?"

"Two o'clock," Kate said, and clicked off without looking to see what the time was now. It didn't matter. She would have a car by two o'clock and she would damn well drive without a license until she could get it replaced. What she most needed in this world was to see Calla Dearborn.

* * *

As Kate made her way down the path to the cottage/office the thought flashed into her that Aimee had stuck by her only because of Maggie's ordeal, and now that the ordeal was over—and given Aimee's distress in the hospital room and her reaction to Kate's usual reticence about what had really gone down between her and Cameron—Aimee dropping her off at the condo might have been the final time. Hollowed out by the thought, suddenly she could hardly put one foot in front of the other.

Calla Dearborn stood in the doorway watching Kate approach, her gaze progressing upward from Kate's plodding feet to her bruised face. "Come in," she said softly, then remained just inside the room as Kate entered.

She reached to Kate and placed her hands gently on her forearms. "I'm so sorry about all that's happened to you."

Kate lunged forward and found herself hugging her and being hugged in return, a full-bodied embrace that all but dissolved her in tears with its pure warmth and comfort.

Then she came to her senses and stepped away, mortified. "I'm so sorry, that was so uncalled for—"

"It wasn't. Not at all. I would have hugged you myself except we therapists can't take it on ourselves—"

"I understand. Professional ethics. I used to have a few." Kate smiled at her. "Feel free to hug me. Anytime."

Dearborn smiled back at her and walked toward her chair where a mug of coffee steamed on the end table next to it. "Get yourself some coffee and come sit down."

It took Kate two cups of coffee over the expanse of the next half hour to relate the events of the past two days, beginning with the nature of Maggie's death.

"It's a miracle I'm not under arrest," she confessed to Dearborn. "I *knew* Maggie was dying—it was just days—and even rationally knowing that, after being a cop for all those years, it took everything, absolutely everything I had in me not to physically attack Alice…"

"May I offer an explanation?" To Kate's nod, Dearborn continued, "What remained of Maggie's life was utterly precious to you. Alice didn't just take that away, she took what should have been a natural death of a dear friend and gave you a crime scene where this time you were the surviving victim."

Blinking in astonished recognition of this assessment, Kate sat in silence for a time absorbing it. Then, with more than a trace of appreciation, she met Dearborn's eyes and nodded. She continued with the events of the night of Maggie's death and the following morning at Aimee's cottage, then a full accounting of the why and how of the happenings in the desert.

Completing the last of a few brief notes, Dearborn sat back and shook her head. "You're very lucky to be alive, Kate. A life-changing week in every dimension. All the pressures you were under..."

Shifting back in her own chair, Kate realized she had lost awareness of her physical discomforts during her recitation. Unburdening herself of all she had had to withhold from so many people over the past days had brought lightness to both body and spirit. "What I wish I could understand," she said wryly, "is why I'm able tell you all this when every other person in my life always gets bits and pieces. Even Maggie. Close as we were, I tended to be...selective about some things with her too." She smiled. "Self-preservation."

"You can bring anything here, Kate, it's a place of safety. Do you feel safe here?"

"Safe," Kate repeated. "*Safe...*" Testing, almost tasting the word. "I don't think I've ever felt completely safe anywhere. Anything can happen anywhere, anytime—I should know. But...I guess here more than anywhere."

How would I even know if I was safe, she wondered. If I slept in this cottage, in the presence of this woman, would I sleep safe? Would I dream?

Dearborn let her sit with her thoughts for a time, then said, "Speaking of safe. You told me you shared none of the choices you made about Detective Cameron with anyone because you believed you had to be there for him no matter what. So tell me now: would he have died without you?"

Struck by the question, Kate sat with her head bowed, going over the events as they had unfolded in the desert. The key was whether Cameron, without their conversation on strategy and probabilities, would have figured out the same scenario for himself and gone out the cabin window before Jack climbed into that Toyota pickup...

"Joe was expecting something like a Molotov cocktail, so he'd have followed the same tactics we did," she finally concluded. "The answer is he'd still be alive."

Dearborn's face was stern, but she asked gently, "So you put your life on the line...for what?"

"Even before it all went down I realized being there was sheer stupidity—"

222 Katherine V. Forrest

"It was despair," Dearborn told her.

Kate nodded. "Some of it, yes it was, Calla. Despair. I didn't care whether I lived or died. By the time I got there I was two days clear of drinking. And I was forced to take a stone-cold sober look at what my choice to be there might cost the people I love."

Dearborn put her notebook on the end table and sat easily in her chair, hands folded in her lap, her gauzy pants and top in soft folds on her ample body. "What about the cost to you, Kate?"

"Yeah, well…" She shrugged impatiently.

Dearborn studied her for a few moments with something like frustration in her eyes. Then she said calmly, "Even so, you stayed. So there's more."

"Yes. Joe Cameron was my friend before—I thought. Till I found out how much I didn't know about him. About huge, really important parts of his life he felt he had to keep from me. Because it was a friendship without trust. Yesterday afternoon I decided both of us had to come through this. Last night what Joe and I found together was ultimate trust. And now I feel safe… safer with him. I know he'll always, always have my back. Like Maggie always did. He's closer now than a brother." *Closer than my brother, for sure.*

Her face softening, Dearborn conceded, "A great insight. Greater love hath no man…"

"I didn't want to die," Kate stated, "and I'm glad I didn't have to lay down my life for my friend. But without Maggie in my life, Joe means more to me than anybody else right now. Except Aimee."

"We need to talk about Aimee."

Kate nodded. "About my drinking too. But Calla," she said earnestly, "it's no use talking about any of it till I find some kind of answer to the big question. The last time I was here you said you had a few thoughts…" She shifted in the chair, and stared down at her lap thinking that any useful answer to her dilemma was as likely to be located in the mesh pattern of her black linen pants as it was in Calla Dearborn. "I have to figure out what the hell I do with the rest of my life."

Dearborn did not reply until Kate lifted her head and met her gaze. "Okay, let's go there. Especially since your trial by fire in the desert seems to have brought some major insight and clarity."

"Clarity," Kate repeated. "That's the word I used with Aimee this morning about what I felt out there."

"So let's explore how deep this clarity goes. Beginning with the practicalities of your life. What's your financial situation?"

"I can afford you," Kate joked.

"I would hope so," Dearborn returned, smiling. "I'm depending on you for my old age annuity." She asked, "At some point will you need to work again to afford therapy or anything else essential to your life?"

Kate shook her head. "I have police and military pensions. An inheritance that's going toward an operation for my nephew—"

It occurred to Kate that Aimee would be in her life at least until after Dylan's operation. Aimee loved Dylan too—and along with his mother they would most certainly see his surgery through to his full recovery...

She pulled her thoughts together. "—and I'm thinking I might get a small place near Joshua Tree. I've been lucky."

Dearborn shrugged. "Yes, compared to many people. But you've earned your independence with all your service— everything you've laid on the line for your country, for this city. Have you considered using your experience in police work for something allied to it?"

Kate waved that away with the flick of a hand and a heavy sense of disappointment that this was what Dearborn had in mind. "I have zero interest in being a private detective."

"Why not?"

"I have more than two decades of investigative experience at the highest echelon of police work. I should now look for cheating spouses or missing people or larcenous employees? I'd rather spend my days reading and drinking."

"Except for the drinking part I happen to agree with you. Think about this, Kate: after you finished your college degree, every single thing you've done in your entire life, not just the police, has been focused in one very specialized area."

"Since college…" Kate ticked off on her fingers, "…the Marine Corps, Vietnam, LAPD, Homicide…All to do with killing." She shrugged. "Okay, I've been in the death business."

"The death business." Dearborn's dimple emerged with her smile. "I couldn't have phrased it more perfectly myself."

"I'll put it on my business cards," Kate muttered.

Dearborn's laugh quickly dissolved into solemnity. "You've talked before about the death business," she said. "What it was that set your work as a homicide detective apart from all other areas of police work."

"The victims were murdered," Kate stated baldly, irritated by the direction Dearborn persisted on taking.

"And your goal was?"

"To bring justice," she said with more than a trace of sarcasm.

"To whom?"

"The family," she said immediately, "it's all they have left. Society too, theoretically."

"And did you?"

"Sometimes. Somewhat. Who knows?" She shrugged impatiently. "Where are you going with this?"

"To you. To what you've been doing with your life during the last months and weeks of Maggie's illness."

"Beyond visiting her twice a day?"

"Maggie, and that other woman…"

"Ida. Ida Appleby."

Dearborn steepled her fingers. "Let me propose to you that people in a hospice are allied to victims of a homicide. They're terminally ill, their fate is sealed, a *fait accompli*. Like homicide victims, they're surrounded by helpless, grief-stricken people whose anguish offers no help or comfort at all—"

"True," Kate interposed, remembering her own struggles with her visits to Maggie in contrast to her pleasure in visiting Ida, and Ida's remarks about being able to talk about her dying with hospice volunteers—including Kate—but not her own family.

Then she asked in disbelief, "Are you actually suggesting I become a hospice volunteer?"

"Why not?"

"For starters, how about all those dreams of mine? All that death and blood? How would visiting dying people in a hospice make things anything but worse?" She continued wrathfully, incredulously, "I should stuff even more death into the cupboard that's already giving me nightmares?"

"How about confronting what's in that cupboard not just in this office but in a place of reality?" Dearborn's voice rose, took on a commanding tone. "Where you look dying in the face? Where you actually get to engage with death instead of cleaning up after it? Where you get to do something real, something tangible and valuable with your life?"

She leaned forward and jabbed a finger at Kate. "You—you especially can make a difference. Our culture doesn't deal with the mortality we all face, we run from it. But you—you never have. You've lived in it. You claim no one understands being a homicide detective. Well, damn few understand being a hospice worker. Damn few want anything to do with something so hard as sitting with the dying. They can't even conceive of it. Looking into the faces of dying people is hard. It's demanding. It's heartbreaking. It's *meaningful*. It has *value*. It's as real as it gets."

Kate remained silent.

Dearborn finally said, "Kate. What are you thinking?"

"I'm thinking you're crazy."

"Not a good reputation to have in my business," Dearborn said. She looked at the clock. "Enough for today. Besides, you have a stop to make."

"I do?"

"You do. You need to see a dying old woman named Alice. And another one named Ida. Don't you think?"

"You're just full of unpredictable and interesting ideas." Kate smiled. "Some of them might be crazy enough to even make sense."

"When are you going to look at what Maggie wrote in the novel Alice gave you?"

Kate got to her feet. "I don't know, Calla. When I feel ready."

"A good answer. You're still taking your medication?"

"Not since yesterday." She held up a hand. "My pills are teeny tiny crispy critters in that cabin in the desert. I need to get a new prescription."

"Yes. Right now. I'll call Natalie. You have to be taking them," Dearborn said, walking her to the door.

"I know. Thank you." Kate stopped, turned to her. "I could use another hug. Till I see you again."

20

"What's…th'other guy look like?" Alice asked in a slurred voice, peering up at Kate.

Standing at the side of Alice's bed, it took Kate a moment to understand, then she touched her bruised face and smiled down at her. "Him? Hamburger."

"…bet." Alice was bleary-eyed, obviously medicated. She managed a weak smile. "From…desert? Joe?"

"It was. We arrested Joe's brother. You don't miss much, do you Alice?"

"I…heard. She…" Alice lifted a few fingers in a weak gesture to the other bed. "…told me."

Kate glanced again at the neatly made up bed near the window.

"New roommate soon," Alice said, frowning.

Kate nodded. "Tomorrow, yes. Marla told me."

"…miss her," Alice said, staring at the empty bed, her eyes filling.

"Me too," Kate said gently.

Alice took a deep breath, seemed to marshal herself. "Gonna arrest me?"

Kate nodded. "You bet. Next time I'll remember to bring my handcuffs."

"Gonna be a next time?" Alice's eyelids drooped. "Kinda tired today."

"I thought I'd drop in tomorrow."

Alice smiled and made an attempt to reach for her. Kate picked up and held a hand that felt like a hot dry collection of bones. Alice's eyes fluttered shut and the hand in hers firmed slightly then grew slack and Kate placed it back on the bed and stroked it. Watching the almost imperceptible rise and fall of Alice's chest, she hoped there would be a tomorrow.

Moments later, walking down the hallway, she stopped and took a few steps into Ida's room. Ida was asleep. But Mary bellowed, "Ida! Wake up! It's Kate!" She said sheepishly, "She made me promise to wake her if you came by."

"My goodness, it's you, Kate," Ida said groggily, then lifted her head from her pillow to peer at her more alertly. "Your face—are you okay? What in the world happened?"

Kate came toward the bed. "I'm fine. You should go back to sleep. I can come back tomorrow and tell you all about it. Today I mostly wanted to come by to thank Marla and all the staff."

"As long as you're here..." Ida smiled. "As you very well know, in this place there's no tomorrow."

A half hour later, Kate emerged from the hallway feeling that something of Maggie still seemed to imbue this place. Resistant to going home just yet, she sat in an armchair in the conversation area near the fireplace and pulled out the new cell phone she'd gone out and bought as soon as her rental car arrived. At ease in the tranquil surroundings of the hospice, she spent some time talking quietly with Dylan about his mother and father, his surgery, Maggie, and, now that she knew something of her experience in the desert would be in the press tomorrow, offered him a condensed and highly edited version of the events, answering his excited questions and chuckling at his description of her as "my kick-ass aunt." Hearing that her brother was in full retreat from any threat against her in favor of the far greater imperative of repairing his marriage, she felt satisfied that Dylan was in as good a place as he could be with his parents and upcoming surgery. After making a date for lunch with him during the week, she clicked off and returned a call from Cameron.

"Joe, how are you doing with...the mess there?"

"The bastard," he said. Then, "Little did Jack know I was thinking of changing my art collection anyway."

His attempt at a breezy tone was not close to successful and she answered him seriously. "That's actually a good idea, Joe. With all that's gone down, how about we talk about making everything a new chapter for us both?"

"Kate..." After a long pause he said, "I don't even know where to begin with all I want to say. How about you come over tonight for a Joe's special?"

That meant a barbecued pork rib dinner. "I'll be there."

As she buttoned the phone into a pocket of her cargo pants, Marla came bustling up to her as if she had been waiting for Kate to finish with her phone calls.

"Visiting with Ida again, Kate?" she inquired, taking the armchair beside Kate.

Kate nodded. "I hadn't intended to do more than say hello to Alice. I hope it's okay?"

"It's more than okay. But I thought perhaps I should tell you...if you felt any inclination to continue...beyond Alice, beyond Ida, I need you to know the state requires...there's special training—" She broke off awkwardly.

"So this former police officer has been breaking the law?" She smiled at Marla. "I'm glad to know it, glad you have actual guidelines."

"Very good ones. Stringent. With oversight," Marla said. "There's such great need in every hospice and the training covers what you do in every situation..." She was studying Kate's face. "I didn't know if you'd be interested, but I thought I'd let you know."

"I'm glad you did."

Kate got up from her armchair, smiled at Marla. "I'll be thinking about it."

21

Two Days Later

Kate closed the door to her condo, went over and shooed Miss Marple from the leather recliner. Miss Marple, watching Kate seat herself with a package in her lap, condescended to arrange herself on the carpet at her feet. Kate pulled open the top of the light bamboo box she had picked up that morning and lifted out the contents, oblong, in a red velvet pouch. Setting the box gently on the floor beside her, she loosened the silk tie at the neck of the pouch and slid it down.

"Maggie," she said as she reverently lifted the urn, "I hope you like burnished brass…it was the warmest color I could find."

She rotated the urn in her hands, gazing at its polished, perfect surface. "Engraving was included but I didn't do that, my friend, I figured you'd think it was bullshit."

Bracing the urn on a thigh, cradling it in one hand, she reached over to pick up *The Kiss That Counted* from the top of the bookshelf next to her chair, placed the novel in her lap. Then she lifted and positioned the urn in the center on the bookshelf.

"I hope you're okay with me keeping you here so I can talk to you, Maggie. I hope you're okay with my keeping you with me for…till …whenever."

She picked up the novel, held it in both hands. "Since Patton didn't get a chance, being the book is so special now, I thought I might read it to you." She smiled at the urn. "Only if what you have to say in it doesn't make me chuck it right off my balcony. Along with your ashes."

She opened the novel.

The writing was spidery, shaky, hard to decipher. Ink had left slash marks and bled through in several places as Maggie lost control of the rollerball pen. Kate turned a few pages to see writing spread over the title and acknowledgment pages, that Maggie had not taken on the added challenge of making sentences, had used the girth of the book as a writing pad. She turned back to the title page and the start of what Maggie had written.

> *good thing alice going too*
> *maybe serial killer, that one*
> *kidding*
> *good woman*
> *forgive her*
> *Katie start loving yourself*
> *believe*
> *you deserve love*
> *you do*
> *do that and you get aimee back*
> *she loves you*
> *stop the drink*
> *every drop = poison body soul*
> *no more stubborn crazy you*
> *I'll nag you*
> *one day at a time*
> *I'll love you for eternity*
> *from lesbian heaven*

And then, her own name in caps, each letter gone over several times with the rollerball, underlined.

KATE. The clearest, most boldly written word. Just over chapter one. So that the symbolism would be inescapable: the first chapter of this book a stand-in for the first chapter of the rest of her life.

She turned and placed the book next to the urn, clasped the round warm base of the urn in her caressing hands.

I have Dylan. I have Joe. I have Calla. I maybe...just maybe...have Aimee.

It was enough.

For more Spinsters Ink titles please visit:

www.BellaBooks.com

Bella Books and Distribution
P.O. Box 10543
Tallahassee, FL 32302

Phone: 800-729-4992